PRAISE FOR AMANDA LEE'S EMBROIDERY MYSTERIES

Thread End

"This great cozy has a lively cast. . . . The pace is fast and the puns are amusing."
—*RT Book Reviews* (4½ stars, top pick)

"Amanda Lee weaves an excellent cozy mystery that will keep the reader hooked from beginning to end."
—*Affaire de Coeur*

Cross-Stitch Before Dying

"There's never a dull moment . . . with . . . touches of humor and a hint of sensual romance."
—Once Upon a Romance

"Marcy's character is full of humor and intelligence, and she shines in this cozy." —Fresh Fiction

"Well paced and a real page-turner . . . a great cozy mystery." —MyShelf.com

Thread on Arrival

"Lee is clearly a story wizard." —Blogcritics

"A great series with enough suspense and smart sleuthing to hook readers every time."
—*RT Book Reviews*

"A fun, fast-paced mystery that will be hard to put down." —The Mystery Reader

continued . . .

"Entertaining. . . . Readers will enjoy spending time with the friendly folks of Tallulah Falls as well as Marcy's adorable Irish wolfhound." —*Publishers Weekly*

"Fun, full of suspense, and . . . a satisfying conclusion—readers can hardly ask for more!" —Fresh Fiction

The Long Stitch Good Night

"Lee's fourth Embroidery Mystery is well planned and executed. . . . Marcy's keen sleuthing and tenacious personality allow her to solve this solid mystery with smart thinking and style." —*RT Book Reviews*

"Smart and interesting, well patterned, and deftly sewn together." —Once Upon a Romance

Thread Reckoning

"Lee's latest Embroidery Mystery will hook readers with its charming setting and appealing characters. Plenty of spunk and attitude follow Marcy as she solves this well-crafted mystery in a close-knit town full of colorful characters." —*RT Book Reviews*

"A fun mystery with compelling characters." —Fresh Fiction

Stitch Me Deadly

"The writing is lively, and the pop culture references abundant . . . a smartly written cozy that neatly ties up all the loose ends surrounding the murder but leaves the reader wanting to know more about the amateur detective, her friends, her life, and her future." —Fresh Fiction

Also by Amanda Lee

WICKED STITCH

AN EMBROIDERY MYSTERY

AMANDA LEE

AN OBSIDIAN MYSTERY

OBSIDIAN
Published by the Penguin Group
Penguin Group (USA) LLC, 375 Hudson Street,
New York, New York 10014

USA | Canada | UK | Ireland | Australia | New Zealand | India | South Africa | China
penguin.com
A Penguin Random House Company

First published by Obsidian, an imprint of New American Library,
a division of Penguin Group (USA) LLC

First Printing, April 2015

Copyright © Penguin Group (USA) LLC, 2015

ISBN 978-0-451-46740-9

Printed in the United States of America
10 9 8 7 6 5 4 3 2 1

To Tim, Lianna, and Nicholas

Chapter One

I was sitting at the sewing machine in my office working on a Renaissance costume for my best friend, Sadie MacKenzie. My dog, Angus, an Irish wolfhound, was lying in the hall. The office was a bit cramped for him. Plus, he liked to be able to see what was happening in the main part of the embroidery shop I own ... which wasn't much that day.

The shop is called the Seven-Year Stitch, and in fact it was Sadie who had urged me to leave San Francisco and move to the Oregon coast to open the shop. Sadie and her husband, Blake, own MacKenzies' Mochas, a coffee shop just down the street from the Stitch.

It was mid-September, which meant that all the kids were back at school and there weren't as many vacationers visiting the coast. Also, everyone was busy preparing for the upcoming Renaissance Faire.

The festival was starting this weekend and would be going on for the next two weeks. The theme was *Macbeth*, so, of course, someone dressed up as William Shakespeare would be on hand. There would be a king and a queen; Macbeth and Lady Macbeth; Hecate, Queen of the Witches; and the three creepy soothsayers who foretold Duncan's doom would be there to tell Faire-goers their fortunes. There would be jousting, human chess games, minstrels, faeries, pirates, and all manner of merchants. The Faire was to culminate with Macbeth murdering the king and then being killed by Macduff.

Every merchant I knew—as well as many others—in Tallulah Falls and the outlying region was planning to take part in the Ren Faire. Julie, a woman who took embroidery classes from me, would be coming in Friday to cover for me so I could go get my booth set up. She and her teenage daughter, Amber, would be taking care of the store on Saturday, and then Julie herself would be in charge for the next two weeks while I sold supplies and embroidery pieces at the festival.

Sadie and Blake were taking turns manning a booth and running their shop. Todd Calloway, of the Brew Crew, was setting up a booth, and Captain Moe—he of the delicious burgers and shakes—would be making all our corsets too tight.

I was really looking forward to the event. My mom was a costume designer, so she'd sent patterns for the outfits I'd been making for Sadie and myself. Since Sadie and I would be simple merchants, our costumes weren't all that fancy. But they were still beautiful. I loved the feeling of going back in time.

I had both a red and a blue jacquard skirt, a black velvet corset vest, and two cream-colored off-the-shoulder peasant blouses. I also had a very simple square-necked green velvet floor-length gown with gold brocade trim. I figured I might be pushing the "merchant" envelope a little with that last dress, but I didn't want to wear the same thing every day.

Sadie's outfits leaned more toward tavern wench costumes. Like me, she had two peasant blouses and two skirts—one brown and one yellow. She also had a black vest, but hers had laces and tied at the bottom. Since Blake—who said he'd go as a pirate or not dressed up at all—would be alternating days with Sadie, she wanted only the two outfits.

I was finishing up her yellow skirt when the bells over the door jingled and Angus leapt to his feet.

"I'll be right there!" I called. I quickly finished sewing the seam I was working on, then walked out into the shop.

It was Sadie.

"Hi! You're just in time to try on your yellow skirt," I said. My smile faded as I noticed the scowl on Sadie's lovely face.

"What?" I asked. "What's wrong?"

"I'm so mad I could spit!" She ran both hands through her long dark hair and paced in front of the window. "I cannot believe the nerve of that woman!"

"Who? What's going on?" I went over and took

her by the shoulders. "Calm down and tell me about it."

"Nellie Davis was in the coffee shop just now," said Sadie.

"Oh, no."

Nellie Davis had been a thorn in my side ever since I'd moved to Tallulah Falls. Her sister had wanted to lease the space the Stitch was now in, but Sadie had snapped it up for me before anyone else could lay claim to it. Then, after I'd found the former tenant dead in my storeroom, Nellie had said the Seven-Year Stitch was bad for everyone else's business and had gone on to say all kinds of other mean things about me and my shop. I hated to think that Sadie's friendship with me had turned the shrewish Nellie against her as well.

"I'm sorry," I said. "What did she do to you?"

"It's not what *she* did . . . and she didn't do it to *me*." Sadie uttered a growl of frustration. "She said her sister, Clara, is leasing the now-vacant shop between Nellie's shop and yours."

"Great. Now I'll have *two* neighbors to hate on me and the Stitch."

I'd met Nellie's sister a couple of months before when she'd angrily accused me of spreading gossip about Nellie. I'd done no such thing, but Clara had refused to believe me.

"That's not the half of it," Sadie said. "Clara is planning on selling knitting, crochet, and quilting supplies!"

I gasped. "She can't do that! Can she? That puts her in direct competition with me!"

"I don't know if she's within her legal rights or not, but the very idea of it makes me so angry I can hardly stand it!"

"She and Nellie are trying to put me out of business, aren't they?" I asked softly.

"I don't care what they're trying to do. They will *not* put you out of business. The people of Tallulah Falls are loyal to you. Your customers won't stand for this."

I nodded, carefully keeping my eyes on the floor.

Sadie pulled me into a hug. "Are you all right?"

I nodded again, patted Sadie's back, and then disengaged from the hug. "So . . . you wanna try on that skirt?"

"I have to get back," she said. "I'll come check it out in a little while."

"Okay." I managed a smile as Sadie left.

I turned and glanced at Angus, who was lying with his head on his paws, looking up at me apprehensively. Something was upsetting me, so he was upset, too.

"Everything's fine," I told him.

But he wasn't easily fooled. As I sank onto the navy blue sofa facing away from the window, he came and placed his wiry gray head on my thigh. I stroked his fur and let my eyes wander around the shop.

I'd opened the Seven-Year Stitch a little less than a year ago, and I was proud of the progress I'd made. It was a beautiful space. To the right of the front door was the sit-and-stitch square. In addition to the sofa on which I was sitting, its twin faced me across a maple oval coffee table. Beneath the table was a cozy red and blue braided rug. The other two sides of the "square" were made up of red club chairs and matching ottomans.

The left side of the shop was filled with embroidery supplies: flosses, needles, pattern books, hoops, frames, and canvas. I also sold yarn, knitting needles, crochet hooks, and cotton batting for quilts, since the Stitch was—or, at least, had been—the only shop of its kind in Tallulah Falls.

On the walls were embroidery projects I'd completed—some in frames, some in hoops. I'd also made candlewick pillows and placed them on the sofas, and I'd embellished outfits for Jill, the mannequin who bears a striking resemblance to Marilyn Monroe and stands near the cash register.

Today Jill wore a Juliet-inspired empire-waist gown of light blue velvet with gold trim, a white lace inset at the bodice, and white lace-and-gold trim on the sleeves. She had a matching velvet headpiece wrapped with gold cord, and a sheer tulle veil spilled down her back.

I sighed. I was all for free enterprise, but Nellie's sister was going to be directly competing with the Seven-Year Stitch right next door!

I picked up my cell phone and called my attorney friend, Riley Kendall. Riley's mom, Camille, was her administrative assistant, and she answered the phone.

"Good morning, Ms. Patrick," I said. "This is Marcy Singer. Is Riley available?"

"No, Marcy, dear. She's in a meeting at the moment. May I have her return your call?"

"Please . . . Well, actually, you might be able to answer my question." I quickly told her about Clara's plans for the shop next door to mine and how I thought—hoped—there might be some noncompete clause that would force her to pursue some other retail avenue.

She paused, and I heard regret in her voice when she finally answered. "Noncompete clauses are made between companies and their employees or between corporations and their subsidiaries."

"So she's acting within her rights," I said flatly.

"I'm afraid so," said Ms. Patrick. "I'll still have Riley call you when she's free, though. She might be able to work around this some other way."

I thanked Ms. Patrick and ended the call. I'd appreciate hearing from Riley, but I seriously doubted there was anything I could do to keep Clara from setting up shop, rallying her troops, and trying to destroy my business.

I supposed I *could* take the high road and welcome Clara to the neighborhood when her shop opened. Maybe she would learn to like me and we could find a way to work together. And maybe— somehow, somewhere—pigs could fly.

Still, moping wasn't going to solve anything. I got up and went back to the office to finish Sadie's skirt.

Detective Ted Nash, my boyfriend extraordinaire, brought lunch at around one o'clock. Angus and I had spotted him walking up the street and could see that he was carrying a bag from MacKenzies' Mochas. Sadie and Blake made the best chicken salad croissants, and I had a feeling that was what Ted and I would be having for lunch.

Ted was gorgeous. A good foot and two inches taller than my towering height of five feet, he was broad and muscular and had thick dark hair that was wonderful to run your fingers through ... well, *my* fingers through. He had the most intensely beautiful blue eyes ever. He would have made my heart soar even if he'd been carrying a sack of snakes. But food from MacKenzies' Mochas was way better than snakes.

When he walked through the door, he was accosted by both Angus and me. Angus was sniffing at the bag.

I giggled. "Please tell me you brought the chicken salad."

"I did. Sadie texted me earlier and said she thought you might be in need of your favorite comfort food today." He held the bag out of Angus's reach and dropped a quick kiss on my lips.

I led the way into my office. "Water, soda, or juice?"

"I'll take water, please," he said. "You want to talk about it, or are we avoiding the subject?"

"We're avoiding the subject," I said firmly, as I took a diet soda and a bottle of water from the minifridge. I handed Ted the water and unscrewed the cap on my soda. I took a sip and sat down at the desk across from Ted. "I just think Nellie and her sister have a lot of nerve, that's all. I know they schemed this up together to try to run me out of Tallulah Falls. But they won't succeed. And that's all I have to say on the matter. You don't think they'll succeed, do you?"

"I know they won't." Ted took the croissants out of the bag and placed them on the desk. "Oh, Sadie sent brownies, too." He set the brownies beside the croissants.

"That was very thoughtful of her," I said. "At least I have good neighbors to offset the bad ones . . . the ones who *despise* me. And what have I ever done to Nellie Davis? Or her sister, for that matter?"

Ted carefully avoided my eyes and opened the box containing his croissant. "I don't know, babe."

"We are so not talking about this and letting it spoil our lunch," I said. "How has your day been?"

"Fairly uneventful so far," he said. "I'm going through a cold case from five years ago, since—thankfully—there's not an open case I'm working on at the moment."

"That *is* good. Is it a murder case?" I bit into my croissant.

Ted nodded. "Hopefully, I'll find some new evidence, and either we'll be able to convict the person who was our main suspect or we'll discover that it was someone else."

"It must be hard to try to uncover anything new in a five-year-old case," I said.

"It can be. But sometimes people are more willing to talk because they aren't as afraid of suffering any repercussions as they are right after a crime has been committed."

"That makes sense." I tore off a piece of my croissant for Angus. "If there's anything I can do to help, let me know." I knew there wasn't, but I wanted to be polite and offer. "And if you come in here and find me dead, that case won't have time to get cold. If they're not still standing over my corpse, just run next door, where Nellie and Clara will probably be dancing with joy—and the murder weapons."

"I'm really glad we decided not to talk about the situation with Nellie's sister," Ted said with a grin. "I think it would've really brought us down."

"I'm sorry," I said. "I'm trying so hard not to think about it . . . but I can't help but think about it!"

He chuckled. "I know, sweetheart. I'm just teasing you. Want me to go over and arrest Clara?"

"Yes. Do you have any grounds?"

He thought a moment. "No. I'm afraid *upsetting the woman I love* isn't a crime, although it certainly should be."

I smiled. "I love you, too. And I know everything will be okay. We've weathered worse storms than this, right?"

"Exactly. This is nothing my Inch-High Private Eye can't handle."

"So stop worrying about it already and tell me what we're doing tonight," I said.

He gave a big, dramatic sigh. "All right, I'll do

my best. As for tonight, let's make dinner together and then watch a movie."

"Sounds wonderful to me."

I resolved then and there not to give Clara's shop another thought. Unfortunately, I knew it would be like a New Year's resolution—I'd start out strong and then cave by the next day.

Chapter Two

On a drizzly day exactly one week later, when I took Angus for his midmorning walk, I knew I shouldn't have walked past Clara's and Nellie's shops, but it was a habit. I almost always took Angus up the street to the square. To be perfectly honest, everybody's dog peed near the base of the large wrought-iron clock. It was a sure bet that Angus would go there, sniff, pee, and be ready to return to the Stitch.

As we were walking back, I saw movers unloading boxes into Clara's shop. One of them stopped to speak to Angus and to tell me what a handsome dog I had.

I thanked him. "It looks like the proprietor will be setting up shop pretty soon," I said.

Clara, her meaty arms crossed at her ample bosom, appeared at the door. "That I will, Miss Nosy Pants."

The movers looked confused and uncomfortable.

"Well . . . good luck," I said. I was talking more to the movers than I was to Clara.

Angus and I sidestepped the movers and went on back to the Stitch.

We hadn't been back five minutes when Vera Langhorne stormed into the shop. Fists on her hips, she kept shaking her head and sending her professionally highlighted blond bob flying in all directions.

Angus didn't know what all the fuss was about, but he sought refuge in his bed beneath the counter.

"I cannot believe this! I can't believe it!" Vera ranted. "Just who in the world does that Clara think she *is*, setting up a shop called Knitted and Needled? I'd like to needle her right in her big old butt!"

I laughed. "Thank you, Vera. But I'm sure Tallulah Falls can accommodate both an embroidery shop and whatever needlecrafts Clara will be selling."

She huffed. "I could have Paul do some sort of exposé on Clara. She's mean as the devil. Surely she's hiding some deep dark secrets we could use to run her out of town."

Vera dated Paul Samms, a journalist for the *Tallulah Falls Examiner*.

"That would make us just as bad as she and Nellie are," I said to Vera. "I appreciate your concern; I really do. But we have more important things to think about. Tell me about your Ren Faire costume."

Vera's attitude quickly changed. "Oh, Marcy, it's incredible. Paul is going as a minstrel, and I'm going as a noble lady. My dress is gold brocade with a square neckline and rounded shoulder pad thingies with puffy sleeves. And I'm wearing a matching Tudor French hood. I mean, it's not a hood like you pull up over your head in winter, it's . . ." She struggled to describe the Renaissance headgear.

"I know exactly what you're talking about," I said. "My mom is a costumer, remember?"

"Of course." She rolled her eyes. "Sometimes I can be dense. Still, it's a lovely gown, and I just can't come up with all the words to describe it. You'll have to see it for yourself."

"I'm sure it's beautiful and that you'll look stunning in it." I smiled.

"I hope Paul thinks so." She giggled. "Wait until you see his costume."

"He's a minstrel, right?"

She nodded. "But he looks like a little pumpkin in it!"

I joined in her laughter.

"I can't imagine Paul as a pumpkin," I said. "He's too thin."

"He doesn't seem to be in that blousy surcoat with the huge white ruffled collar. He's wearing black tights and black felt shoes with it. Thank goodness he isn't wearing green tights and that he has nice legs."

"What instrument is he taking along?"

"A lute," she said. "And it's not just for show. He can play the darned thing. I hummed 'Greensleeves' all day yesterday after he left the house."

"I can hardly wait to see the two of you," I said. "You'll look wonderful."

She smiled. "I think it'll be loads of fun."

"I started to make Angus one of those huge ruffled collars. I don't think he'd appreciate it, though."

"I don't think he would, either." She clucked her tongue. "You can come out and see me now, Angus. I've calmed down."

He peeped furtively from behind the counter.

Vera laughed. "Come here, boy. Let me love your sweet head before I leave."

Angus trotted over and allowed Vera to hug his neck.

"You're such a good boy," she said. She pulled back and smoothed the hair out of his big brown eyes. "You're a good, good boy."

He rewarded her with a kiss on the nose.

"I forgot to ask. Did you need anything or did you just stop in to rant?" I asked.

"I was mad," she said. "That's not to say that I won't remember something I wanted as soon as I leave, but if I do I'll be back."

As Vera stood up to leave, an elderly woman entered the shop. I instinctively took hold of Angus before he could exuberantly greet the newcomer and accidentally knock her down.

"Hello," I said. "Welcome to the Seven-Year Stitch."

"What a big dog!" the woman exclaimed. "I've always loved big dogs. May I pet him?"

"Of course." I still held Angus. By the looks of

this tiny birdlike woman, a strong breeze would knock her off her feet. A one-hundred-fifty-pound dog could certainly do so.

She came over and patted Angus on the head.

"I'll talk with you later, Marcy!" Vera called on her way out the door.

"I've come to ask if you have any Point de Beauvais embroidery patterns or kits," the woman said.

"I don't have either," I said, "but I'll be happy to order something for you. Let's go into my office and see what's available from my distributors."

"Thank you."

I led Angus, and the woman followed us into my office.

"Oh, what a lovely skirt," she said upon seeing Sadie's skirt hanging near the ironing board.

"Thank you," I said. "I made it for a friend to wear at the Renaissance Festival. Are you going?"

"I am. That's why I'm so interested in Point de Beauvais," she said. "You see, this form of embroidery came to France via Italy in the late Middle Ages through China's trade routes."

I had little knowledge of Point de Beauvais needlework, but I was eager to help my customer find something. According to the Point de Beauvais Embroidery at Bourg-le-Roi Web site, Point de Beauvais is an intricate process all around. The pattern must be traced onto paper. The paper is then pricked with a needle along the tracing lines, and ink is added to the cloth through the holes. The thread is worked with a very fine crochet hook. The site noted that the best examples of Point de Beauvais resemble paintings.

I was able to find a pattern book, but it was written in French. From a discussion forum on a needlecraft magazine's Web site, we learned that Point de Beauvais was known as tambour embroidery in English. I found a pattern book that included tambour embroidery and another book on eighteenth-century embroidery techniques that mentioned tambour in the description, but there wasn't very much specific to this ancient technique.

The woman had me order both books, and I told her they'd be in by Monday. I ordered a few additional copies of the one on eighteenth-century embroidery techniques because I thought it might sell at the Ren Faire.

My customer—whose name was Ms. Fields— gave me her number so I could call her when her books arrived. I walked her to the door and held it open. She truly appeared so frail that I felt particularly protective of her. I thanked her for coming in as she started off down the street.

Clara, who'd apparently been standing in the doorway of her shop, darted out onto the sidewalk to intercept the poor dear.

"Didn't *she* have what you were looking for?" Clara asked. "Come on in here and I'll see if I can't help you out."

"Now, wait a second," I said, pulling my door closed so that Angus wouldn't run out into the street. "I ordered what Ms. Fields needed."

"That's all right," said Ms. Fields. "I might as well browse this shop while I'm in town."

I managed a stiff smile. "Of course. Good luck."

"Please excuse the mess," Clara said. "I've just started unpacking boxes. My shop is brand, spanking new, you see."

I went back into the Stitch.

With a growl of frustration, I retrieved the laptop from my office and carried it to the sit-and-stitch square. Maybe I should beef up my marketing. There might be a *new* shop in town, but shouldn't customers put their trust in an *experienced* shop?

I pulled up the Seven-Year Stitch Web page. The header featured a photo of Angus lying on the floor near the counter. The embroidery supplies and some of my projects were visible in the background. It was a good picture. I liked it. But was it dynamic enough to draw customers in?

Maybe I needed to have a contest or something using social media. That might work. I could do a giveaway in conjunction with the upcoming Renaissance Faire. But what?

I called Mom for inspiration.

"Hey, Mom," I said when she answered.

"That was the most lackluster *Hey, Mom* I've ever heard," she said. "What's wrong?"

"You know Nellie Davis?" I asked.

"That nasty little woman who owns the aromatherapy shop? What's the name of it again? Scentsless?"

"Close," I said. "It's Scentsibilities. Anyway, her

sister, Clara, has leased the shop next to the Seven-Year Stitch."

"Oh, great. So you'll have two harpies to deal with."

"That's not the half of it. Clara's shop is called Knitted and Needled, and she's going to be selling knitting, crochet, and quilting supplies."

"Well, more power to her," Mom said. "You aren't afraid of a little competition."

"Right. I'm not. It's just that Clara tried to steal one of my new customers away as soon as she left my shop!"

"Did you sell something to the customer?" she asked.

"I ordered two books for her about tambour embroidery," I said.

"Tambour . . . hmmm . . . I haven't thought about tambour embroidery in years. It's rather difficult to do, if I recall correctly."

"It looked a bit tricky to me. But what do you think about Clara?" I wanted my mom to rant and rave like Vera had. I wanted her to tell me not to let Clara bully me. I wanted her to make me chocolate chip cookies and let me eat them warm from the oven. I wanted her to hug me and say that everything would be all right.

"Oh, I *know* Clara is difficult . . . especially if she's anything like Nellie," she said.

"She's even *worse* than Nellie."

"My precious darling," Mom said soothingly. "Let it go. You can't control what others do—only what you do. Continue providing your customers the best products and service you can, and everything else will take care of itself."

"Do you really think so?" I asked.

"I know so. Do you realize how many costumers in Hollywood would love to have my job?" she asked. "Do you know how many costuming jobs that I'd have loved to have gone to someone else? And yet the world keeps turning. There's room for all of us if we're dedicated."

"You're right."

"I know. I'm your mother. I'm always right," she said. "How's the baby?"

I looked over at Angus, who was sleeping by the window. "He's fine. He says we need another care package soon. He's almost out of those bacon treats you make for him."

"Tell him I'll see what I can do," she said.

"I was thinking of running some sort of contest in conjunction with the Ren Faire in order to drum up business," I said. "What do you think?"

"It would be awfully hard for you to try to keep things running smoothly at the shop, manage a booth at the festival, and execute a contest," she said. "My advice is to not spread yourself too thin. Don't panic over Nellie's sister opening a shop. Just keep doing what you're doing, and see how it goes for the first few months."

"Okay. That sounds like a good plan."

"How are preparations for the festival coming along?" she asked.

"They're going really well. I'm finished with my

costumes, and I'm working on Sadie's last one today. She's been swamped the past few days, but she
needs to come by and try on her skirt so I can see
where to hem it," I said. "The blackwork class has
been really popular, so I've made flyers with free
blackwork patterns and I'll be giving those away."

"I think that's an excellent idea. It's a nice way
to reward your current customers and to intro-
duce yourself to potential new ones."

Later I was ringing up a woman's purchase of
several skeins of embroidery floss when Riley Kendall walked through the door. Riley has black hair,
blue eyes, and a mischievous smile. She was carrying her seven-month-old baby, Laura, who was
adorable in her pink sweater and matching hat.

As I completed the transaction, my customer
fawned over Laura. She was such a pretty baby.
Who could help but smile and coo at her?

When the woman left with her periwinkle
Seven-Year Stitch bag in hand, I stepped around
the counter and held out my arms. Laura reached
for me, and Riley handed her over.

Angus came to sit at my feet, looking up ador-
ingly at the little angel.

"I'm glad to see you're in such good spirits,"
Riley said. "After hearing about Clara's shop
opening, I was afraid I'd have to talk you down
from a ledge somewhere."

I laughed. "I was rather upset over the whole
thing, and then my mom made me see reason. She
reminded me that everybody has competition and

that all I can do is run my shop to the best of my ability and hope my customers appreciate that."

"Your mom is one smart lady," said Riley.

"Yes, she is."

"Still, don't be a doormat." Riley held up her index finger. "If Clara is trying to sell something that you know comes from your distributors, she might be in violation of their noncompete clauses. For instance, some companies assert in their contracts that retailers within a certain distance from each other cannot sell the same products. That's why only one store in the mall carries Crazy Kitty products."

"I'll keep an eye out," I promised. "Still, I'm not as concerned about Clara and her shop as I was this morning." I looked at Laura. "You know, she would make the most incredible faerie baby on the planet. Let's dress her up for the Faire!"

"I already have the outfit," Riley said with a grin.

Chapter Three

I was so glad it was Monday and that Angus and I were on our way home. I taught embroidery classes every Tuesday, Wednesday, and Thursday evening from six to eight o'clock. But I was thrilled not to be going back to the Stitch this evening. I needed to decompress, figure out how to truly deal with Clara being right next door, drink wine, and eat chocolate.

Mom had absolutely been right on the money when she'd said I couldn't let a little competition get to me. But it wasn't the competition that bothered me—it was the fact that Clara and her sister hated my guts and would love to see me run out of town on a rail.

I pulled the Jeep into the driveway of my two-story white home. I grabbed Angus's leash and snapped it onto his collar before allowing him to get out of the backseat. He stopped to pee en route to the door, probably to let any other dogs wandering around the neighborhood know he was home.

We went into the house, and I dropped my keys

onto a tray on the table in the foyer and hung the leash on a peg. Angus trotted on into the kitchen, knowing very well that it was dinnertime. I plodded after him, kissed him on top of the head, and then filled his bowl with kibble.

I went upstairs and filled the tub with hot water and fragrant bubble bath. I stripped, put my clothes in the hamper, and sank into the tub even before it finished filling. My skin quickly adjusted to the temperature of the water, and I let the flow wash over my toes. I turned off the faucet, lay back in the tub, and closed my eyes.

How I wished I could find a way to make peace with Clara and Nellie. I harbored no illusions that the three of us could ever become bosom buddies—going to lunch, bringing one another coffee, sharing gossip over the proverbial back fence. But surely we could coexist without trying to best or belittle each other on a regular basis. Couldn't we? I knew neither Clara nor Nellie would ever extend the olive branch to me, but maybe I could come up with a way to show them that I truly believed—and I did . . . for the most part—that Tallulah Falls was big enough for all three of us.

"Hey, babe!"

It was Ted calling to me from the bottom of the stairs.

"I'll be right down!"

"Take your time," he shouted. "I'll let Angus out and start dinner!"

He was absolutely the most wonderful man ever.

I finished my bath, slipped on a fluffy terry robe, and padded downstairs. Ted was at the blue granite counter dicing tomatoes on a wooden cutting board.

I eased up behind him and slid my arms around his waist.

"Mmmm . . . you smell great." He turned and gave me an appreciative grin. "And I adore this dress you're wearing." He used the belt of my robe to pull me even closer for a heart-thumping kiss.

"Could you maybe put the knife down?" I asked. "You're making me a little nervous with that thing."

He chuckled. "Of course. I forgot I was still holding it. See? You drive me to distraction."

"I'm glad," I said with a smile. "We could both use some distraction tonight."

"Agreed."

"But first . . . what're we having for dinner?"

I noticed he had a couple pots on the stove, and the aromas of oregano, garlic, basil, and rosemary were making me salivate. Or maybe it was Ted standing there with his dress shirt open at the throat and his sleeves rolled up to his elbows— and the way his pants emphasized his trim waist and tight butt—that was making me start to drool. Either way, it was a tantalizing combo—gorgeous man in my kitchen cooking a delicious meal. Heaven on earth.

"We're having baked Parmesan garlic chicken breasts and new potatoes with herbs," Ted said. "Sound good?"

"Sounds wonderful." We'd both been working on our cooking skills lately. Ted seemed to have more of a knack for some things than I did. He was really good with Italian dishes. "What can I do to help?"

"You can relax. You've had a rough day."

"And you probably have, too," I said. "Going through a five-year-old cold case file can't be easy. How about I whip up some dessert?"

"Way ahead of you, Inch-High." He nodded toward my large square table. In the middle of the table was a small box from MacKenzies' Mochas.

I cocked my head. "Let me guess. Two fudge brownies?"

"And a peanut butter cookie for Angus." He winked. "Gotta take care of my boy."

"Have I mentioned how incredible you are?" I asked.

"Not lately. But we can talk about it after dinner. . . . And remember, actions really do speak louder than words."

Ted and I had enjoyed a really stellar evening, and I was in particularly high spirits when Angus and I arrived at the Seven-Year Stitch Tuesday morning. My buoyancy was short-lived, however.

I'd been at work about half an hour and was busily restocking the embroidery floss bins when Nellie Davis paid me a visit. As always, her short gray hair was sticking out in all directions. Some women used wax on their short hair to give themselves an edgy, piece-y look—I'd done that myself on occasion—but there was no rhyme or reason to Nellie's coif. She looked as if she'd rolled out of bed late and hadn't had time to even run a comb through her hair before coming to work.

She wore her usual black-on-black ensemble, which made her seem even paler and thinner than she could possibly be. The only spot of color Nellie entertained was the red-rimmed glasses perched on her hawkish nose.

Recalling last night's bathtub resolution, I pasted on a smile and made a desperate attempt at a peace-generating greeting.

"Good morning, Nellie. Thank you for dropping in. Would you like a cup of coffee?"

She eyed me suspiciously. "No . . . er . . . no, thank you." She scratched her chin. "So what do you think of Clara's shop?"

"I haven't had an opportunity to stop in yet and welcome her to the neighborhood," I said. "Is everything all set up?"

"Almost." Nellie glanced around the shop and then snorted. "It's nice that people will have an alternative to *this place* for their sewing notions."

I refused to take the bait. "I believe it speaks well of needlecrafts and of people's continued interest in the art that Tallulah Falls will be able to adequately accommodate our two successful shops."

She sniffed. "I suppose we'll see about that."

"I suppose we will."

At that point, my dear friend Rajani "Reggie" Singh burst into the Stitch. Reggie, Tallulah Falls's librarian and wife of chief of police Manu Singh, also has short gray hair. Unlike Nellie's, however, Reggie's is always elegantly styled to fit her refined persona. This morning Reggie wore a mint green tunic over matching slacks.

Angus, who'd not acknowledged Nellie's presence, hurried over to greet Reggie.

She laughed as she rubbed the dog's head with both hands. "And a good morning to *you*, Angus! Hi, Marcy . . . Nellie."

"Reggie, it's so great to see you," I said.

"I'll go now so you can wait on your customer," Nellie told me. She opened her mouth as if there was something else she intended to say, but then she closed it again. With a curt nod, she left.

My body sagged with relief. "I was serious about how glad I am to see you."

"I know. I was actually on my way to MacKenzies' Mochas and saw Nellie come into your shop. I found a parking space as quickly as I could and came to rescue you."

"Thank you. You don't know how much I appreciate that. It's certainly not up to MacKenzies' Mochas' standards, but I'll be happy to get you a cup of coffee."

"That sounds nice," Reggie said. She went over and took a seat in one of the red club chairs.

I poured us each a cup of coffee and arranged the cups, spoons, packets of sweetener, and individual cream pitchers on a tray and took it out to the sit-and-stitch square. I put the tray on the coffee table and sat on the sofa facing the window.

"I heard about Clara moving in next door,"

Reggie said as she emptied a packet of sweetener into her coffee. "How's that going?"

"It shouldn't be such a big deal," I said. "And I even resolved last night to extend an olive branch to Clara and Nellie. But before I could come up with a way to do that, Nellie went on the offensive and came over here to run down my shop." I sighed. "I have no idea what I ever did to those women to make them despise me so."

"With some people, the only thing you have to do to make them dislike you is to be different from them."

I smiled. "Then, in that case, I'll take their dislike of me as a compliment."

Reggie sipped her coffee. "Just don't let them get to you. When they see that they can't bully you, they'll leave you alone."

"I hope so," I said.

After Reggie left, I took out my latest embroidery project. I'd ordered white poet's shirts in several sizes and was adding blackwork to the collars and cuffs. I would be selling the shirts at the Renaissance Faire. I'd already made several ruffs and cuffs to sell to Faire-goers, and I had finished quite a few shirts. I was even teaching an Elizabethan blackwork class on Tuesday nights, and given the interest in the upcoming Ren Faire, it was full.

I used a unique border on as many of the poet's shirts as possible. On this particular one, I was embroidering a pomegranate border. Traditionally, the pomegranate was the symbol of Spain, with a crowned pomegranate being the personal insignia of Catherine of Aragon. The pomegranate border would appeal to a buyer who wanted to appear to be of royal or noble birth . . . at least, if the buyer was familiar with Renaissance customs and traditions.

I outlined the pomegranate with thick black floss and then filled in the outline with a lighter-weight thread. I'd completed one pomegranate on the shirt's right cuff and was filling in the leaves connecting the pomegranate to the next one when Ms. Fields, the customer for whom I ordered the tambour embroidery and the eighteenth-century embroidery books, came into the shop.

"Hi, Ms. Fields," I said brightly, setting my embroidery aside. "Welcome back to the Seven-Year Stitch. What can I do for you today?"

She twisted her hands together. "I . . . I'm sorry to do this. . . ." She lowered her eyes. "But I need to cancel the order I placed with you yesterday."

I stood, wiped my hands on the sides of my jeans, and joined her at the counter. "That's all right. I can't cancel the order, since it's already gone through, but I'm sure I can resell the books."

She nodded. "I'm sorry."

"Just out of curiosity, what made you change your mind about the books?"

"The woman next door . . . she ordered them for me free of charge. She said it was a first-time-customer discount," said Ms. Fields.

"Oh." My initial surprise and jab of anger subsided enough to allow me to forgo taking my emotions out on my innocent customer—make that *ex*-customer. I even managed a smile. "How wonderful for you! I do hope you'll keep the Seven-Year Stitch in mind the next time you need embroidery supplies."

"Yes . . . yes, of course I will. In fact, I thought I'd get some skeins of floss while I'm here."

"Thank you," I said. "If you need help finding anything in particular, please let me know."

"I will." She hurried over to the embroidery floss bins and came back momentarily with a double fistful of skeins. "I'll take these, please."

I rang up her purchases and placed them in a periwinkle blue Seven-Year Stitch bag. "Thank you again for shopping with me. There's a flyer in the bag telling you about the embroidery classes taught on Tuesday, Wednesday, and Thursday nights. I and my students would love to have you drop in one evening. First class is always free."

"All right. Good-bye."

Ms. Fields took her bag and rushed out of the store. I noticed that she went in the opposite direction of Clara's shop. Poor Ms. Fields. I doubted she intended to get caught up in the middle of our retail war—a war that in my opinion didn't, or *shouldn't*, exist.

I went back to the sit-and-stitch square to resume my blackwork. But Angus suddenly began barking and nearly scared me out of my skin.

"What in the world . . . ?" I jumped up and ran over to the window to see what had him so excited.

There on the sidewalk was a large brown and white bunny. It was standing on its hind feet and was staring through the glass at Angus. Its little pink nose twitched as it moved its head back and forth. It seemed to be wondering how to get inside.

It was obviously someone's pet, and it didn't appear to be frightened of Angus. Worried that it might wander out into the street and get run over by a car, I stepped outside and carefully approached the bunny. To my surprise and delight, it hopped right over to me. I scooped it up and took it inside.

Angus immediately rushed to investigate. He'd been around cats a few times, but I didn't think he'd ever been near a rabbit. The dog was usually wonderful around new people and animals, but I thought I should handle the situation cautiously.

I sat on the tall stool behind the counter so I would be up high enough to get the bunny out of Angus's reach should things go badly. I recalled seeing a pet adoption notice once where an adorable Great Pyrenees puppy was asking, "Can you pass this test? Chickens are (a) to be guarded with your life or (b) tasty snacks. I couldn't pass the test, which is why I'm at the shelter looking for a new forever home." I'd already adopted Angus by that time, or I might've gone right to the shelter and gotten that sweet puppy. He couldn't help it if he hadn't understood the deal with the chickens.

I instructed Angus to sit. When he'd obeyed, I

lowered the bunny enough to allow the dog to give the much smaller creature a good snuffle. The rabbit stretched its neck out to sniff Angus's muzzle. I decided it was either brave or dumb. Angus licked his new buddy's head.

The bunny, whom I'd christened Harvey in my mind, leapt from my lap and onto the floor. It raced around the shop, with Angus loping after it. At first, I was concerned that Angus might hurt little Harvey, either on purpose or by accident. Then I had to laugh when Angus ran past me with the bunny in pursuit.

The pair took turns chasing each other until the bells over the front door indicated that someone had come in. I turned, smiling, to greet the newcomer. My smile disappeared when I saw Clara's face glowering at me.

"What are you doing to my little Clover?" she shrieked. "Clover! Clover, darling, come here!"

Clover, formerly known as Harvey, wisely ignored her and scurried under the counter to huddle with Angus in his bed.

Clara scowled at me. "Get my Clover away from that monstrous beast right this instant!"

"Angus isn't hurting your rabbit," I said. "In fact, they're having a blast playing together."

"What are you doing with her? How did you get her out of my shop without my seeing you?" She squinted, looking as if she half expected me to whip out a magic wand and conjure up a room full of helpless rabbits for Angus to devour.

"I saw the bunny on the sidewalk and rescued

it before it got hit by a car," I said. "I was hoping the owner would come looking for it."

"Oh." She pressed her lips together. "Thank you, then . . . I suppose. . . . But could you please give her to me now? I'd like to go."

I was happy to accommodate her—not because I wanted to deprive Angus of his new playmate but because I wanted nothing more than to get Clara out of the Seven-Year Stitch. I bent down and carefully picked up the bunny, which had snuggled between Angus's paws.

"Maybe you guys can play again sometime," I said as I cuddled Clover. *But don't count on it.* I walked around the counter and handed the bunny back to its owner. Without another word, Clara took Clover and left.

Chapter Four

Angus and I were both feeling a bit deflated on the drive home from work. He'd spent the rest of the afternoon lying by the window looking for his little cotton-tailed friend. I, of course, was bummed about the entire situation with Clara. I'd given myself at least a dozen pep talks throughout the day, but it was seriously hard to be optimistic when things kept going from bad to worse. I cheered up when I turned onto my street and saw Ted's car in my driveway.

I parked, got out of the Jeep, and snapped Angus's leash onto his collar. The dog pulled ahead of me as he hurried to the door in anticipation of seeing Ted.

Ted opened the door for us, and Angus thanked him with an exuberant hug. Ted laughed, removed the leash, and stepped aside so the excited dog could bound on into the house.

Ted gave me a quick "hello" kiss before closing the door to embrace me more thoroughly.

"It feels so good to have you in my arms," he

said, once we'd come up for air. "I hope you don't mind my being here when you got home."

"Of course I don't." I stood on my toes to brush an unruly strand of hair off his forehead. "Is anything wrong?"

"It's just this cold case. It's driving me up the wall. I had to get completely away from it for a while."

I smiled softly. "I understand completely." And I did. Ted's spare bedroom is a study, and on one wall he has dry-erase boards and corkboards detailing the cases he's currently working. Had he gone home, he'd have inevitably found himself in the study examining those boards.

"I ordered a pizza," Ted said. "It should be here soon."

"Great. I'll go ahead and feed Angus while we're waiting." I went into the kitchen and found Angus already standing there in anticipation, and I filled his bowl with kibble. As he dug in, I refilled his water dish.

Back in the living room, I found Ted stretched out on my white overstuffed sofa, staring into space. I snuggled next to him, and he wrapped his strong arms around me.

He kissed the top of my head. "I simply can't figure it out."

The case really did have him stumped.

"What can't you figure out?" I asked with mock innocence. "Why you love me so much?"

He chuckled. "No. That's an easy one."

"Talking about it—to the extent that you can— might help."

"It might. But I don't want to dwell on it and waste my time with you."

"You're already dwelling on it, sweetheart. Maybe the master detective Inch-High Private Eye can help you see the case in a new light."

"All right," he said. "Without naming names or giving you specifics, Master Detective, a man was murdered. Since he wasn't an ideal husband, his wife was the main suspect."

"But even if he'd been an exemplary husband, wouldn't you still look at his spouse first?" I asked. "I mean, he might be super nice, but she might not be."

"Of course, we always look at the person or persons closest to the victim first. The fact that he was an abusive philanderer simply gave the wife more motive. The main motive was a substantial insurance payout."

"How substantial?"

"Two million," he said. "The man owned a share in an accounting business. When he died, his partner became the sole proprietor. That's why the wife was so generously provided for in the in-surance policy."

"So the partner didn't have to buy out the man's share or anything?" I asked.

"Nope. Apparently, the two men went halves on everything, and their partnership agreement stated that upon the death of one, the other part-ner would inherit the business as a whole—revenue, expenses, capital, everything."

"You said the victim was a cheater and an

abuser," I said. "It sounds like maybe he cared more about his partner than he did his wife."

"Funny you should say that. I've been mulling over the same thing. The conclusion I drew was that the victim could never be sure if and when his wife might get tired of his behavior and leave him," Ted said. "I don't know if he and his wife had any sort of prenuptial agreement, but I'm guessing—based on the partnership agreement— that they did. The men had arranged their business in such a way that only the two of them could ever control the business."

"In other words, if the wife divorced the victim, she couldn't make him give her a share of the business or sell his share and split it with her." I burrowed against Ted's muscular chest. "What about the partner? Was he considered a suspect?"

"He was. But, like the wife, there was insufficient evidence against him to make an arrest."

"Any other suspects?" I asked.

"Only the victim's mistress at the time of his death . . . but she was dismissed fairly early on."

"Why was she discounted so quickly?"

"She had nothing to gain," he said. "Her only benefit from the relationship was gone as soon as he died. She had to start paying her own bills. There were no more expensive gifts."

"You don't think she loved the guy?"

"It's a little hard to believe after seeing the photographs of the two of them. He was old and paunchy; she looked like a model." He shrugged. "Maybe she *did* love him. Or maybe his death was a sad inconvenience that forced her to find another sugar daddy."

"Either way, I wouldn't be hasty in taking her off the suspect list," I said. "If she loved him, she might've been angry that he wouldn't leave his wife for her. If she was only using him, maybe he was ready to move on to someone else but she wasn't."

"Could be," Ted said. "But I don't think she's our killer."

"Who do you think *is* our killer?"

"I'm leaning toward the wife. She had the most to gain. She got two million dollars and stopped being humiliated and slapped around."

"When you put it like that, it makes thinking she might've gotten away with murder seem not so bad. But it is . . . I know it is," I quickly added. "Did they have children?"

"Yes, three daughters," Ted said. "Since his death, the wife has made wise investments and appears to be doing well."

"And the partner?"

"He seems to be doing great. He has tons of business, and he's—"

Ted was interrupted by the sound of the doorbell. Angus beat us to the door to greet the pizza delivery guy. I took the pizza while Ted paid the bill.

I put the pizza on the kitchen table, and then I put Angus outside.

"We'll save you some," I promised.

Then I washed my hands and got us plates and napkins.

Ted came up behind me, wrapped his arms around my waist, and kissed my neck.

"If you keep doing that, our pizza is going to get awfully cold before we eat it," I warned.

"I don't mind," he said. "But I know you have to get back to the Stitch soon."

"Did talking about the case help you any?"

"Yeah . . . some."

I knew he was lying, but I didn't call him on it.

"So how was your day?" he asked.

I put pizza on the plates, got us two bottles of water from the fridge, and we sat down to eat. While we ate, I filled him in on the episode with Clara and her bunny, Clover.

"She seems to be even more off her gourd than Nellie is," he said. "Did she think you came to her shop in stealth mode to steal her rabbit and give it to Angus?"

I giggled. "Apparently so. And, oddly, now I feel like doing just that! When Clara came after it, the poor thing tried to hide between Angus's paws!"

He laughed and then tried—and failed—to give me a serious look. "Darling, should we consider getting the boy a pet of his own?"

"No! It's all I can do to keep up with him!"

We both laughed.

"And, besides, who gets their dog a pet?" I asked.

"Who knows? Stranger things have happened, I guess." Ted shook his head. "But there's no fear of Angus being lonely."

"No, there's not. I'm leaving him home tonight, though. That blackwork class has a lot of students, and I think it's best not to bring him."

"Mind if I stay with him?" Ted asked. "We can watch the baseball game until you get back."

"That sounds wonderful," I said. "Two handsome guys waiting for me when I get home? Score!"

I knew I was leaving Angus in good hands as I drove back to the Seven-Year Stitch. He would have been fine had I left him home alone, but he was happy to be spending time with Ted. Before I left, Ted told me that he and Angus were planning on watching the Mariners play the Angels.

Interest in the Ren Faire had brought a lot of new students in for the blackwork class. That was really good, but it was hard to get to know everyone and to keep the class running smoothly when there were twenty-five students on the roster. My classes were typically ten and under. I probably should have set a cap on the number who could attend, but I didn't have the heart to turn anyone away. As it was, the sofas, the chairs, the ottomans, and the floor were filled with stitchers.

I unlocked the door and barely had time to restock the minifridge with bottled water before the students began arriving. Some of the regulars were present, of course—Vera, Julie, Amber, and Christine—as well as many people I'd never seen before I posted the class announcement at the library and the museum.

Once everyone was settled in, I handed out an artichoke border pattern.

"Artichokes were a recurring theme in Renaissance embroidery," I explained.

"Why?" teenaged Amber piped up. "I *hate* artichokes."

I smiled. "You remind me of an old joke. *It might choke Artie, but it ain't gonna choke me!*"

Amber laughed. "It's not gonna choke me, either. It *is* a pretty pattern, though."

"Since this pattern has both linear and diagonal elements, we'll break it down into runs to make sure it's clean, neat, and reversible," I said. "Be sure and keep your tension on the cloth even."

Rather than sitting and working on my own projects, I kept moving throughout the group during the blackwork class so I could offer my help wherever it was needed.

Suddenly, we were all startled by the sound of sirens blaring down the street. We looked out to see police cars and fire trucks roaring past.

"Wonder what's going on?" Vera asked, as she began digging through her purse. She brought out her phone. "I'll see if Paul knows."

As Vera was dialing Paul, my phone—which I had set to vibrate—buzzed in my pocket.

Ted.

I was right. He'd sent me a text saying, *Fire at a local business. Have to check it out. Leaving Angus with plenty of water and a rawhide treat. Be back ASAP. Love you.*

"Ted says a local business is on fire," I told the class. "I hope everyone's all right."

I was concerned about the fire for the rest of the night. On the way home, I looked to see if any nearby businesses looked damaged, but I didn't see anything out of the ordinary. The fire must've been on the outskirts of town.

When I arrived home, I was disappointed that Ted wasn't back. I was afraid that meant something even worse than a business fire had taken place. Had someone been working in the building and been unable to escape? Had the fire been the work of an arsonist?

I unlocked the door and walked into the house. Angus was standing in the foyer to greet me. I put my purse on the hall table and gave the dog a hug. He trotted into the living room to chew the rawhide Ted had given him.

I locked the door behind me and went into the kitchen. I was beginning to feel tired after the class, and the rain that had started that evening—along with the sirens and the dread—had chilled me. I wanted a cup of hot herbal tea.

I settled onto the sofa with my chamomile tea, my feet wrapped in a fleece throw, and had just reached for the television remote when my phone buzzed. I'd forgotten to take it off of silent mode. I looked at the screen and was relieved to see that it was Ted calling.

"Hi, sweetheart," I said. "Are you all right?"

"I'm fine," he replied. "And I smell like soot. So I came on home. I'm going to take a shower and hit the sack."

"Was everyone okay at the business that caught fire?"

"Yeah. There were no people inside, but virtually everything in the building was destroyed."

"I'm sorry," I said.

"You and me both, babe. Remember my telling you about the business partner who inherited upon the death of our cold case victim?"

"Yeah . . ."

"It was his building . . . his business." He sighed. "A whole lot of evidence in that case probably went up in smoke this evening."

"But surely he keeps backup files offsite somewhere," I said. "Wouldn't you think?"

"Maybe," said Ted. "But the man knew we'd reopened the investigation of his partner's murder. What better way to destroy evidence than with an *accidental* fire?"

"I'm sorry."

"Me, too. Hey, I know you won't say anything," he said, "but now you're going to know the name of one of the principals in this investigation."

"No one would be able to pry it out of me under threat of death," I said.

"I know." He laughed. "It's not that big a deal anyway. I mean, it was in all the papers during the initial investigation. I just don't want anyone to think I spoke out of turn."

"No one who knows you would ever think you

capable of doing anything to compromise an investigation."

"I'm glad you have such confidence in me."

"I love you," I said. "And I know you. You're a man of honor."

"You're laying it on thick, Inch-High. Maybe you should get some rest yourself."

I laughed. "I think you may be right."

Chapter Five

Just before I left for work the next morning, I got a call from Sadie telling me there was going to be a meeting of the Ren Faire merchants at MacKenzies' Mochas at lunchtime. I called Ted and told him I was planning to attend the meeting.

"Would you want to join me?" I asked, well aware of the hopeful note I couldn't keep out of my voice.

"I'd love to, babe, but I'm going over the details of the fire with the arson investigator at eleven thirty this morning. I was going to call you in a little while to tell you I might be running late."

"Oh . . . Well, that works out, then."

"Don't worry about this meeting," he said. "You'll have a lot of friends there."

"Plus two enemies," I said.

"You have way more friends than enemies. Look, I'll stop by after my conference to see how everything went, all right?"

"Oh, sweetheart, I'm only kidding." I laughed. "You don't really think I'm worried about two little old ladies, do you?"

"Good try," he said. "I *know* you are. You want everyone to like you, and it drives you up the wall when someone doesn't."

"True. But those two are a lost cause. I hope your meeting with the arson investigator is productive."

"That makes two of us, Inch-High. I love you, and I'll touch base with you soon."

After talking with Ted, Angus and I went to the Seven-Year Stitch. On the way, I reflected on what Ted had told me: I *would* have a lot of friends at the Ren Faire merchants' meeting. I was looking forward to seeing Captain Moe, Todd, and, of course, Sadie and Blake. And, surely, Clara and Nellie wouldn't choose such a public forum to air their complaints against me . . . would they? Of course not. This lunch would be fun.

Oh, how I ate those words with my Caesar salad a mere two hours later.

When I first walked in, my optimism was in full bloom. There were hugs from Todd and Captain Moe. One of Blake and Sadie's waitresses told me she'd heard about some of the things I was making for the Ren Faire and that she could hardly wait to visit my booth. One of my blackwork students was there, and she started talking with me about how much she was enjoying the class. Yep, it was all sunshine, flowers, and rainbows—a virtual Marcy Singer lovefest.

And then *they* walked in.

Had we been starring in an old B movie Western, I'd have been wearing a white hat, while the sisters would've been in black. Tumbleweeds would have blown across the coffee shop's polished hardwood floor between us.

Crazy Clara would've moved her piece of dirty yellow straw from one corner of her mouth to the other before telling me that Tallulah Falls wasn't big enough for the both of us.

Her cohort, Neurotic Nellie, would have spit on the floor as a sign of disgust and disrespect.

Then, since it was high noon, we'd have gone out into the street. Doves would have cooed and a child would've asked, "What's going on, Mama?" as we took ten paces in opposite directions, turned, and drew our guns.

I'd have been quicker on the draw, but Crazy Clara would have left nothing to chance. She was ruthless—she'd never fight fair.

Before I could fire off a round from my six-shooter, Neurotic Nellie would take me down with a shot to the back from behind a barrel in front of the saloon—in this case, the Brew Crew.

The townspeople would gather around and mourn my unjust passing. They'd turn on Crazy Clara and Neurotic Nellie, but those two hooligans would threaten the good folks of Tallulah Falls with gunfire and maybe even dynamite until they could make their escape.

My dying words would be, "Well . . . at least, they won't hurt y'all anymore."

No, actually, my last words would be, "Take care of Angus . . . and make sure Ted grieves for me and doesn't find another woman to take my place too soon."

Okay, that last part sounded selfish, so I deleted it from the script.

Of course, none of that happened. It was just part of the elaborate daydreams that are a product of growing up with a Hollywood costumer for a mom.

What *really* happened was that I merely stopped and stared at the two women when they walked into MacKenzies' Mochas—spurs a-jangling. All right . . . there were no spurs, except in my imagination. I hadn't quite kicked the Old West scenario out of my head yet.

"What're you looking at?" asked Neurotic Nellie . . . er, Nellie.

Determined to put my best boot forward, I drew myself up to my full five feet no inches, pasted on a broad smile, and said, "Hello, Nellie. Hello, Clara. Isn't this meeting going to be exciting?"

"I don't know what's so exciting about it," said Clara. "It's just a lunch where we all fight over who gets the best spots at the fair."

"I feel it's more than that," I said. "I think it's an opportunity for us to come together as a community and help each other succeed."

Captain Moe put his beefy arm around me and turned me away from the sisters. "Let's find us a seat, Tinkerbell."

I loved Captain Moe. He was a big guy with

white hair, a fluffy beard, and a fatherly disposition. And he made the best burgers and fries around.

I smiled up at him. "What will you be cooking up at the Ren Faire?"

"I'll be serving steaks on stakes, turkey legs, Scotch eggs, and barbecued ribs." He winked. "And I might be talked into making cheeseburgers for a certain wee merchant and her faithful hound."

I giggled. "I'm so looking forward to this. It's too bad Mom's on location in Arizona. She'd be in her element at a Renaissance festival."

"She would at that," he agreed. "And I believe you will be as well."

"I will . . . if I can see any peace while I'm there." My eyes strayed to Clara and Nellie.

"Pay them no mind. They can only bother you if you allow them to do so."

"Wise words," I said.

"But hard to put into practice." He grinned. "I know. I've been there. All of us have at one time or another. You'll emerge stronger because of this trial."

We sat down at a table in the designated part of the coffee shop, and Sadie called our meeting to order. She then introduced us to Nancy Walters, chairperson of the merchants' society.

Nancy was a small woman with a stiff helmet of brown hair. She wore sensible black shoes and a brown tweed suit. She stood on her chair in order to be heard and to command our attention.

"Good afternoon," she said. "I imagine many of you are surprised to learn that there is a chairperson and/or a merchants' society."

I know I was.

"I'm on the board of the Tallulah Falls Fairgrounds Committee," she continued. "As such, I was elected to oversee the merchants during the two-week festival. My job is to assign booths and tables to registered vendors. I have a map drawn up indicating where each of you has been placed. Sadie, dear, would you pass those out, please?"

"Of course." Sadie began passing out the maps.

"While the map isn't written in stone, I do have things the way I want them," Nancy said. "I'm not saying I won't budge on the arrangements, but it would have to be for a darn good reason."

I got my map and looked down at it. It was organized as I'd have expected. There was a food court where all the food vendors would be located: Captain Moe, the Brew Crew, MacKenzies' Mochas, and some I didn't recognize but would look forward to investigating, such as the Cheesecake Consortium, Festive Fudge, and Carol's Cake Creations.

I quickly spotted Ye Olde Seven-Year Stitch nestled right in between Nellie's booth, Scentsibilities, and Clara's Knitted and Needled. My heart sank. It was going to be a long two weeks.

"If anyone has any requests to change the arrangements, now is the time to speak up," said Nancy. "After today, no requests will be entertained."

Clara stood. "I'd like to request a change. I don't want Marcy Singer's booth beside mine."

"Why not?" Nancy asked.

"The woman has been an aggravation to my poor sister, Nellie, and her thriving business ever since she came here to Tallulah Falls," said Clara. "People have died in Marcy Singer's shop, and she's caused all manner of upset in the community. Neither Nellie nor I want anything to do with her."

"Request denied," Nancy said. "Perhaps you, your sister, and Ms. Singer will find common ground during those long hours working near each other at the festival."

Captain Moe patted my hand. I wanted to bury my face in his barrel chest and cry, but I didn't. I held it together . . . at least until I got back to the Stitch.

I was in the sit-and-stitch square working on my blackwork border when Todd came into the shop. Sadie and Blake had hoped Todd and I would be a love match when I'd first moved to Tallulah Falls. That hadn't worked out, but we'd become fast friends. And, like just about everybody else in town, he loved Angus.

He sat down on the sofa beside me and gave me a one-armed, brotherly hug. "How're you holding up?"

"I had a little cry when I got back here, but I'm all right now."

"Don't let those old crones get to you," he said.

I arched my brow.

"I know, I know. That's easier said than done." He grinned. "I don't have a problem with them. They think I'm adorable."

"You *are* adorable." And he was. He had curly brown hair, chocolate eyes, and a smile that could melt even the icy hearts of Nellie and Clara.

"You're pretty cute, too. I mean, you're no Todd Calloway, but—"

I playfully slapped his arm.

He laughed. "I'll keep you in apricot ale during the Ren Faire. Maybe that'll help you tolerate your neighbors."

"I just don't get it, Todd. What did I ever do to those women?"

"Who knows? You moved in, your shop is successful, you're young, you're beautiful, you have the love of a good man, and you have your whole life ahead of you." He shrugged. "There's plenty of reasons for two dried-up old prunes to hate you."

"Thank you so much." I giggled. "You say the sweetest things."

"I do, don't I? That's another reason the old broads like me," he said. "Pay attention. I'll let you use some of my lines."

"Gee, thanks."

I noticed something out of the corner of my eye and turned to look out the window. "Oh, no," I said.

Todd turned, too. "What is it?"

"It's Clover, Clara's rabbit. It got out the other

day, and I brought it inside. I didn't know it was hers."

"Bet that went over well," he said.

"Oh, you wouldn't *believe*." I sighed. "And now what? If I don't go out there and get the little thing, it could hop out into the road and get hit by a car."

"And if you *do* go out there and get it, you'll be accused of bunny-napping."

We watched as Clover came over to our window and stood up against the glass. Angus hurried over, bent down with his wagging tail stuck up in the air, and "woofed" at his friend.

"To heck with it," I said. "I'm going to get Clover." I got up off the sofa and went to open the front door. "Come on, Clover."

The bunny raced into the shop and happily reunited with Angus.

"Todd, do you mind holding down the fort while I go next door and tell Clara that Clover is here?" I asked.

"I can go," he said.

"No, that would make it seem like I'd stolen the bunny and you were coming to its rescue."

"I'll tell her you sent me."

"Thanks," I said. "But I'll do it myself. I'd simply take the rabbit back, but they enjoy playing together so much. . . ."

Todd grinned at Angus and Clover chasing each other back and forth around the sit-and-stitch square. "It's funny that a dog that big would have so much fun with such a little creature."

"True. Ted asked if we should get Angus his own pet." I laughed. "I don't think I'm *that* far gone yet."

"It might not be a bad idea," Todd said. "They are having a blast. Walk and talk slowly when you go next door."

"If I'm not back in ten minutes, send in a few Navy SEALs, please."

I took Todd's advice and walked slowly toward Knitted and Needled. The door was open slightly, so I saw how Clover had gotten out. I examined the doorframe and saw that the latch wasn't working properly.

"Hey! What're you doing there?" Clara called.

Thankfully, she didn't have any customers at the moment, and there wasn't anyone on the street.

"I'm examining your door," I said. "You need to have someone take a look at this latch. I don't think it's working properly."

"I believe it's fine, thank you very much."

"If it's fine, then how is Clover getting out so often?" I asked.

Her beady eyes widened. Then she began looking around the shop. "Clover! Clover! Where are you? You'd better get here right now!"

"She's at the Stitch," I said.

Clara gasped. "You left her alone with that mongrel?"

I clenched my fists. "First of all, Angus is not a mongrel. And, second, they are not alone. I left Todd Calloway in charge of the shop."

"That beer maker? He's no better than you are!"

So much for Todd being adorable . . . at least as far as Clara was concerned.

Clara stormed past me and out the door. Only then did I get an adequate look at her shop. She had a seating area to the right that was directly copied from my sit-and-stitch square—from the navy sofas to the braided rug on the floor beneath the coffee table. Her furnishings weren't exact replicas of mine, but they were close enough that there was no doubting her intentions. The other side of her shop was set up like the Seven-Year Stitch as well.

I'm well aware of the old saying that imitation is the sincerest form of flattery, but I was far from flattered. I was livid.

I whirled around and left the shop with every intention of confronting Clara at the Stitch. I burst through the door just in time to see her chasing the bunny around the red club chair. Todd was bent double laughing, and he wasn't doing a thing to help Clara. Angus apparently thought Clara had simply joined in his and Clover's game, and he was barking happily.

My anger died at the utter ridiculousness of the situation, and I joined in Todd's laughter.

That's when Ted came into the shop.

"Arrest them!" Clara shouted. "Arrest them both right now!"

"On what grounds?" Ted asked, his lips twitching to suppress a smile.

She plopped down on the chair and wailed, "I

don't know! I just want to get my rabbit and leave!"

I went over and calmly scooped up Clover. I kissed her soft head, whispered an apology to her, and then handed her over to her terrible owner.

"Thank you." With that, Clara left.

"Poor Clover," said Todd.

Chapter Six

The rest of the day had gone well. A few of the merchants who'd been at MacKenzies' Mochas came over to browse the shop, and they'd all bought something before they left. I felt like it was a show of support after the scene Clara had made at the coffee shop, and I was grateful. I was looking forward to supporting their businesses and getting to know them better at the upcoming festival.

My shipment of black embroidery floss came in, and after refilling my bins, I put the rest of it in the storeroom. The interest in blackwork had seriously depleted my supply, and I'd been afraid I would run out before the shipment came. So that was one crisis averted.

Ted had been working late, so I'd taken Angus home and fed him at five o'clock. I made myself a ham sandwich for dinner, and then Angus and I headed back to the shop for an advanced crewel class.

This class had only five students. They all loved

Angus, and the feeling was mutual. Overall, it was a more laid-back class than the blackwork class. I was able to chat with each of the students, give on-on-one assistance, and work on the butterfly pillow I was making during this class . . . and when I needed a more colorful project than blackwork.

When Angus and I got home after class, Ted pulled into the driveway behind me.

I got out of the Jeep and waited for him.

"Hi," I said. "This is a nice surprise."

"I'm glad," he said, walking toward me. "I didn't get to spend much time with you today, and I missed you." He pulled me into his arms and kissed me thoroughly.

Angus protested from inside the Jeep.

"May we continue this inside?" I asked.

"Absolutely."

I retrieved Angus's leash from the front seat, opened the back door, and snapped the leash onto his collar. Instead of rushing toward the house, he bounded over to Ted for a hug.

Once inside, Ted and I dropped onto the sofa to continue our make-out session. Soon, a wiry gray face pushed between us.

With a groan, I got up to let the dog out into the backyard to do whatever he needed to do before bedtime. When I returned to the living room, Ted was lying on the sofa grinning up at the ceiling.

"What's so funny?" I asked.

"I was thinking about Angus and Clover. It really is neat how they get along."

I lay down and snuggled against him. "It is. It's too bad Clara won't allow them to play together."

"Aw, maybe she'll come around," he said. "Eventually."

"You know, I'd been so looking forward to this Ren Faire, and now I'm dreading it."

"Because of Clara?"

I nodded. "And Nellie." I hadn't had the opportunity to tell him about the luncheon meeting during our brief afternoon visit, so I explained our placement assignments and the commotion Clara had made about it.

"I can't imagine Nancy Walters took that too well," Ted said. "From what I've seen of the grande dame, she doesn't appreciate anyone questioning her decisions without excellent reasons— say, you broke your foot, are on crutches for the next few weeks, and you need to be closer to the door. Not liking someone isn't going to cut it with her."

"No. It didn't. Ms. Walters told Clara that perhaps the two of us and Nellie would find common ground during our time together at the festival," I said.

"That sounds about right. In fact, Ms. Walters probably heard about the rivalry and put the three of you together on purpose, hoping it would force you into a truce at the very least."

"I'd be all for that, but I think Clara and Nellie would both die before granting me any concessions whatsoever." I was ready to move on from this depressing subject. "How did your day go?

Was your meeting with the arson investigator productive?"

"It was," said Ted. "It's apparent the fire was set on purpose rather than due to faulty wiring or anything like that. He just doesn't have enough evidence to prove the business owner is responsible for setting the fire."

"But he thinks that's the case?" I asked.

"Yeah, and so do I. I was practically convinced the widow had murdered her husband, but this entire incident places suspicion solely on the partner."

"What do you think the partner is so desperate to hide that he'd burn his business to the ground to do so?"

Ted shook his head. "I don't know. But I intend to find out."

On Thursday morning, Julie came in while I was helping a customer find a beginning needlepoint kit for his granddaughter. Julie was blond, thin, and of average height. She favored sweatshirts and jeans, and she was currently between jobs. I had hired her to watch the Seven-Year Stitch for me while I was manning my booth at the Ren Faire for the next two weeks.

Julie patted Angus and then browsed while I finished up with my customer. When he left, Julie asked me if I'd be taking Angus with me to the festival.

"I'd love to," I said, "but I found out yesterday that my booth is between Clara's and Nellie's, and

I don't know whether they'd appreciate my bringing him."

Julie grinned. "Then I'd take him or die!"

I laughed. "You know, I believe I will. It'd be nice to have one ally with me. And if the first day doesn't go well, I don't have to take him back."

"Why wouldn't it go well?" she asked.

"The main two reasons I can think of are his nose and the food court."

"I hadn't thought of that. That could be dicey." She moved over to a chair in the sit-and-stitch square. "Are you sure you don't mind Amber coming with me on Saturday?"

Julie's daughter was a fixture in many of my embroidery classes and was becoming quite an accomplished stitcher.

"Of course I don't! I think it'll be great for you to have her here."

"Well, she does love this place, and she's dying to help out," said Julie. "She'll feel like a kid in a candy store."

"I hope she won't be disappointed. It isn't the most glamorous job in the world." I smiled. "I do love it, though."

"Amber thinks you're the coolest adult in the world. She'll have a blast here Saturday. By the way, would you like to go ahead and start setting up at the fairgrounds today? If so, I'll be happy to watch the shop."

"I didn't think the vendors were allowed to set up their booths until tomorrow," I said.

"Technically, they aren't supposed to, but somebody got the festival's okay and now lots of the vendors are setting up early to get a head start on tomorrow."

"Well, that sounds like a good plan, but I have a class this evening. I'll just have to suck it up and get there first thing in the morning. Thanks for the offer, though."

Julie nodded.

There was something in that nod that told me she wasn't telling me everything.

"Julie, what is it?" I asked.

"It's just that I overheard Nellie Davis telling her sister at MacKenzies' Mochas a few minutes ago that they should go ahead and set up today," she said. "I don't want them getting the jump on you."

I smiled. "I appreciate your concern, Julie. But this is a good thing to me. Let them go on and prepare their booths today. Maybe then I'll have some peace and quiet while I work on mine in the morning."

"That's a good way to look at it. You're handling those two a lot better than I probably would."

"You'd handle them just fine," I said. "I'm sure you've rolled with more than your fair share of punches."

"True. But this layoff is one of the worst blows I've been dealt yet," she said. "Thank you for letting me work for you for the next two weeks."

"Thank *you* for helping me out," I said. "I only wish I could afford to keep you on full-time."

"You're doing plenty for me, Marcy. I really do appreciate this opportunity. I won't let you down."

"I know."

"I'd better run. See you in the morning." After patting Angus good-bye, she left.

So Nellie and Clara were setting up their booths today. Well, that was good in more ways than one. As I'd mentioned to Julie, I could work on my booth before they arrived tomorrow morning. And without seeing my booth as I stocked and decorated it, Clara wouldn't be able to copy everything I did. I was still dumbfounded that she'd taken the entire design concept from the Seven-Year Stitch and incorporated it into Knitted and Needled. Why on earth would she *do* that?

I sat down in the sit-and-stitch square to complete the blackwork border on the collar of a poet's shirt. I had several shirts and blouses ready to sell at the festival now, as well as ruffled collars and cuffs that could be worn with dresses and other Renaissance Faire costumes.

The thought suddenly struck me—what would I do if I was unable to sell them all? The answer came just as quickly—send them to Mom, of course. She'd be able to find homes for Renaissance couture in a heartbeat and a half.

I missed Mom and wondered how things were going on the set in Arizona. I'd taken my phone out of my pocket and was about to call her when the phone rang. It was Ted.

"Is this a tall, dark, handsome stranger?" I asked as I answered the call.

"No. You're the opposite of all those things," he said. "You're short, fair, gorgeous, and familiar. I'm a detective, remember? You can't fool me."

I laughed. "You're in a quirky mood."

"Loving a quirky gal does that to me sometimes."

"You're doing a lot of sweet-talking," I said. "What's up?"

"Ah, yes. I forgot that you're quite the detective yourself, Inch-High. I can't make it to dinner tonight. We're shorthanded at the station, so I volunteered to go to the fairgrounds with Officer Moore to oversee some of the festival preparations. He and I need to make sure that everything is up to code, see that no fights break out, that sort of thing."

"Since I have a class, there's one fight you won't have to worry about." I explained to Ted that Julie had overheard Nellie and Clara planning to set up their booths this evening, while I was waiting until tomorrow morning to do mine.

"Oh, joy. If I see the sisters of light, I'll be sure and pass along your tender regards."

I giggled. "Do that, won't you?"

"If it doesn't go too late, mayhap I will come to yon window and offer up a sonnet, fair maiden," he said.

"I'd rather thee come on inside and smother me with thy passionate kisses."

"Prithee . . . is that a word? *Prithee?*" he asked.

"Yes, I believe it is. I think it means *pray thee*. But thou veered off course, my love. What intendeth thou to say?"

"Only that thy boldness has stirred me and that I shall be there anon," he said. "Or, well, after work."

"I'll look forward to it. . . . Sorry, I can't think of any Old English to come back with. Oh, I've got it—huzzah!"

He laughed. "Right back at you, babe."

After talking with Ted, I went ahead and called Mom. The film set she was on was a western, and she answered the phone with "Howdy."

"Howdy?" I asked. "That sounds as strange coming from you as *prithee* did from Ted."

"Is he getting into the Ren Faire spirit, then?"

"Not really," I said. "He just called to tell me he's going to the fairgrounds this evening to oversee some of the setup to make sure it all goes smoothly."

"Will you be joining him there?" she asked.

"No. I have a class."

"You could go afterward," she said. "I know you said you wouldn't be setting up until in the morning, but swinging by to see Ted will give you a chance to get a real feel for the festival."

"Actually, Julie came by the Stitch earlier and told me that some of the merchants had been granted permission to go ahead and set up their booths this evening."

"Then why don't you go?"

I explained about Nellie and Clara going tonight and that I didn't want to be there at the same time.

"That's even better, then," said Mom. "You can

see Clara's booth tonight and then make doubly sure that your own booth is nothing like hers and that it's better in every way."

"That's not a bad idea. And it reminds me of something weird I learned yesterday." I described Clara's shop to Mom. "What is *up* with that, Mom? Why would she copy the design of my shop?"

"Well, darling, you *do* have a charming boutique . . . and I imagine that heifer has never had an original thought in her entire life." She huffed. "Imitation runs rampant in my business, so I know how frustrating it can be. But know this: everyone realizes the original is the best. *Always*. These days almost every designer has a wrap dress in his or her collection, but who did it first?"

"Diane von Furstenberg," I answered.

"Exactly," she said. "Now, be sure and go to the fairgrounds tonight and get a look at that old biddy's booth. Then go in tomorrow and blow everyone's socks off with yours! And be sure and send me a photo."

Chapter Seven

After my class was over, I took Mom's advice, and Angus and I headed to the Tallulah Falls fairgrounds. It wasn't that far out of town, and it would be fun to surprise Ted. Besides, I could hardly wait to get a look at the medieval village being set up.

The first thing I saw when I pulled into the fairgrounds was a large castle. I knew it was merely a facade, but it appeared so realistic that I could've almost been convinced that I was stepping into a Renaissance village.

Angus and I went through one of the gates where ticket holders would enter on Friday afternoon, and we could instantly see the bustling activity as people—both in and out of costume—transformed the fairgrounds into a Scottish village suitable for the two-week-long reenactment of *Macbeth*.

Over the course of the festival, Faire-goers would be treated to jousts, plays, music, and even fortune-telling by *Macbeth*'s three witches during the celebration of the visit of King Duncan and his queen. As they shopped, we—the merchants—were to gossip with customers about how Macbeth seemed to have a hungry eye or that we'd heard how Lady Macbeth wished to wear a crown someday. The other "characters" were also to tell the tale that would culminate in the performance of the play on the last day of the festival, which included Duncan's vanquishing Macbeth.

To perpetuate the superstition about the play being cursed, the Ren Faire hadn't included *Macbeth* on its flyers. The flyers had referred to it as *The Play About the Scottish King as told by Mr. William Shakespeare*. And, of course, Will himself would be on hand to make sure everyone knew exactly what king he meant. I wondered whether he would also tell Faire-goers *why* the play was said to be cursed.

Growing up with a mom who had Hollywood connections and lots of actors and directors as friends, I'd heard a lot about *Macbeth* and its superstitions. The play had supposedly been cursed by real witches of Shakespeare's day because he'd angered them by including actual spells in *the play which must not be named*. And lots of those actors and directors who'd spoken with me about it—namely, during the period in high school when I was studying the play—had stories about some disaster or another that had befallen cast or crew during productions of *Macbeth*.

I wondered if maybe I should spin around three times and spit just for good measure (one of the ways to dispel the curse), but I didn't want anyone to think I was crazy. I hoped they'd at least get to know me a little before calling my sanity into question.

As Angus and I got closer to the "village," the sights and sounds of the festival became more vivid. Horses wearing blankets that bore a royal crest were being led into a stable by pages. Angus lifted his nose and took in the smells of leather, hay, horse, and who-knew-what-else.

I was keeping an eye out for Ted, but I also didn't want to miss anything going on around me. I realized I'd forgotten my flyer and, with it, the map that directed me to the various areas.

I stopped an auburn-haired young woman who wore thick leather gloves to her elbows and had a falcon perched on her left wrist. As I spoke, I tightened my grip on Angus's leash so he couldn't get close enough to investigate the fierce-looking black-eyed bird. It might be tethered to its handler, but I imagined those talons could still inflict some damage.

"Excuse me," I said. "Do you know where the merchants' area is located?"

"Sure." She jerked her head backward. "It's that way, about fifty to seventy-five yards, in that red-brick building."

"Thanks."

She huffed, and I tore my attention from the bird to look at her. I wasn't sure how I'd offended this woman, but it was apparent that I had.

"I appreciate your help," I said. "I'm one of the merchants, and I forgot my flyer. I'm sorry to have bothered you."

"It's not that," she said. "It's the way you're looking at Herodias."

"Herodias?" I echoed. The only Herodias I'd ever heard of cost John the Baptist his head. Maybe that's why the bird looked so mean. Maybe it had gotten its name after beheading . . . Bunny the Baptist . . . or Mouse the Methodist . . . Chameleon the Catholic . . . Earthworm the Episcopalian. . . .

"The falcon," she said. "Her name is Herodias."

"Oh. I didn't intend to be rude," I said. "I've just never seen a falcon up close before. She is a little intimidating." A *little*? That was an understatement. "She's beautiful, though. Again, I'm sorry."

"No, I'm sorry." The falcon's handler blew out a breath. "I've been feeling defensive of her all afternoon. Many people around here—in particular, an old lady with a bunny rabbit—didn't seem to like Herodias—and she's a good girl." She looked at the bird. "Aren't you?"

Herodias's gaze never wavered.

I felt a stab of guilt. I, too, had judged Herodias on the basis of her looks alone . . . and the fact that her namesake was wicked.

"I'm sorry," I repeated. "Wait. The woman with the rabbit—was her name Clara?"

"Yeah. You know her?"

"I'm afraid so. If it's any consolation, she doesn't like Angus or me, either." I shrugged. "I don't know why she hates me, but she seems to think Angus will kill the bunny—even though the two of them love playing together."

"He's a pretty dog." She inclined her head. "Will you be bringing him with you to the Faire?"

"I'd intended to, but now that I'm seeing everything, I'm afraid it might be too much for him to handle, especially once the food vendors get cooking."

"That's true. Well, either way, good luck," she said. "And try to steer clear of the dragon lady."

So Clara hadn't even opened her booth yet but was already making friends and influencing people, I thought as I led Angus up to the merchants' area. I had to give her credit, though. I'd have been scared for little Clover, too, if I were Clara. Had that huge bird acted like it was going to fly off its handler's wrist, I'd have run screaming in the opposite direction myself. I knew it was wrong to judge a creature on the basis of its appearance, but that was one vicious-looking bird.

A juggler tossing bowling pins into the air passed us. I wondered briefly when bowling had been invented. Then I told myself that it didn't matter and that maybe the guy was just practicing. Who was I to be nitpicky?

I found the merchants' area and was surprised to see that it was practically deserted, especially given all the activity going on outside the building. Maybe most of the other merchants thought— as I had before Julie's visit to the Stitch—that we weren't supposed to set up our booths until the next day. A few of the booths had been decorated, but most were still bare.

I spotted the word *Scentsibilities* written in calligraphy on a huge sign in front of one of the booths. That must be Nellie's . . . which meant mine was the one to the right of hers and Clara's was the one to the right of mine.

I didn't see Nellie anywhere, so I went over to check out her booth. She had candles lined up on one side of her table. In the middle were pamphlets detailing the benefits of aromatherapy. And to the other side, she had rows of essential oils in small apothecary bottles. They were charming. I wanted some. They'd be so quaint on a small tray in the bathroom, and then I could add the oils to my bathwater. . . . I wouldn't give Nellie the satisfaction of buying from her myself, though. She might even refuse to sell to me. Maybe I could get someone else to buy them for me.

Nellie also had small round wooden tubs filled with soaps, massage oils, and incense. And a tall, narrow shelf in one corner contained herbal teas, lip balms, lotions, shower gels, and hand and foot creams. Her booth looked great. I resolved to compliment her on it when I saw her. If she didn't want to accept the compliment, so be it. I could still be nice.

I stepped over into my booth. It was a complete blank canvas, containing only three fabric-covered dividers and a long white table. I had bought a periwinkle tablecloth that matched my Seven-Year Stitch bags. It would be perfect to drape over the table. The dividers would hold a couple small pegboards on which I could display embroidery hoops, patterns, and the ruffled collars and cuffs I had made. I had an ornate wooden box in which I planned to arrange a variety of embroidery flosses, with several more skeins in a bin beneath the table. And since blackwork was such a popular Renaissance design, I had many skeins of black and various shades of gray floss to display in a separate box. I would bring a small rolling clothing rack on which to hang the poet's shirts.

I was excited. I knew exactly how to organize my booth. I only had to gather my materials when I got home this evening and bring them in tomorrow to get everything set up.

I heard some sort of scratching noise in the booth to my right. It was Clara's booth. That must be where Nellie and Clara were. Still, I hadn't heard any talking . . . only the scratching.

I peeped furtively around the divider. Clover was in a kennel with a litter box in one corner and a small bed in the other. Angus began pulling me toward the kennel.

"Angus, no!" I hissed, afraid that Clara would again accuse me of trying to feed her bunny to my dog.

He didn't pay any attention to me, and I was no match for a stubborn hundred-and-fifty-pound dog. We went into Clara's booth and over to the kennel.

Clover stood on her hind legs to greet Angus.

I looked around Clara's booth warily. It was nice, too, although not as well done as Nellie's. There were bins of yarn, knitting and crochet needles, premade scarves. . . .

I frowned. Something was off. Something about this booth just didn't look right. What was that brown wooden thing sticking up behind Clara's table?

I snapped Angus's leash to the kennel, knowing he would refuse to leave Clover to investigate the table with me. I hoped he wouldn't decide to take off, dragging Clover and the kennel with him, but I seriously doubted he'd do that.

When I walked farther into the booth and around the table, I saw that the wooden thing was the slats of an overturned rocking chair. I started to set the chair upright but noticed there was something lying in front of it.

I gasped. "Clara!"

Her back was to me, but I thought she must be unconscious. She wasn't moving and was unresponsive.

Maybe that was where Nellie was. Maybe she'd gone to get her sister some help.

What could I do? What *should* I do? If I moved her, I might hurt her worse. If I didn't move her, she might smother or something. I couldn't even see her face.

I called Ted.

"Hey, babe," he said. "I'm on my way."

"On your way where?" I asked.

"On my way to your house. Where are you?"

"I'm at the fairgrounds," I said. "You have to come back. Something has happened to Clara."

"What?"

"I don't know! She's here in her booth with her

back to me, and she isn't moving. What should I do?"

"First of all, stay calm," he said. "Yell her name. Right now."

"Clara!"

"Did she flinch or move at all?"

"No," I said.

"Can you tell whether she's breathing?"

I peered closer. "No, I can't tell. She's on her side with her back to me, and she's wearing a big scarf."

"I'm calling nine-one-one on another line," he said. "I'll be right back with you."

"What do I do in the meantime?" I asked.

"Nothing," he said. "Just stay where you are."

I waited for what seemed an eternity but was in reality only a few seconds.

"I'm back," Ted said. "Can you see what might've happened? Do you think she fell?"

"I don't think it was a fall. She's in a rocking chair which is turned over on its side." I tilted my head to look again at the chair. "It doesn't appear to be broken, but then I can only see one side."

"She might've passed out and turned the chair over when she fell, then," he said. "Do you smell any strange odors? Is there anyone else around?"

"No, and no."

"Where's Nellie?"

"I don't know," I said. "I'm thinking she might've gone to get help."

"If there's anyone else in the merchants' area, call them over to stay with you until I get there."

I looked out into the building. "Right now I'm the only one here."

"Sit tight. I'm about three minutes out."

"Three minutes driving, or three minutes getting here to the merchants' area?" I asked.

"Three minutes driving—five getting to you. Just sit tight."

"But shouldn't I be *doing* something? Should I nudge her? Roll her onto her back? Move the chair?"

"No," he said. "We don't know what happened to her, and until someone gets there to assess the situation, you could do more harm than good by moving her. The EMTs are almost as close as I am."

"All right," I said. "Should I at least check for a pulse?"

"Please, babe, just wait for me and the paramedics."

The paramedics must have been closer than Ted thought because they arrived before he got there. They came rushing into the booth with a stretcher, and several people followed them inside to see what was going on.

Angus started barking and pulling on the kennel, so I went and got him.

"It's all right," I said, shushing him and trying to get him to calm down.

He could tell I was upset, though, and he stood close to me, alert and wary of the men with the stretcher and the other people who were crowding around the booth trying to see what was going on.

Ted came in, shouted an introduction to the paramedics, and told the people around the booth to back away. He walked over to me, patted Angus's head, and put an arm around me. Angus visibly relaxed.

"What's the situation?" Ted asked the EMTs.

"Too early to tell," one said. He didn't look up from his task of helping his partner move the chair out from under Clara.

They rolled her over onto her back. The bright green scarf was wound tightly around her neck. The paramedics shared a look before unwrapping the scarf.

One took her pulse and then shook his head.

He motioned to Ted.

Ted gave me a reassuring squeeze and then went over and bent down beside the paramedic.

Please don't let her be dead. Please don't let her be dead. I know she's dead. Oh, no!

At that moment, Nellie came running up to the booth with a bag of take-out food in her hand.

"What happened? What's wrong with my sister?" She turned to me. "What did you do to her?"

Ted walked over and stood between Nellie and me. "We don't know what happened to your sister. Marcy came in, found that Clara had fallen over in her chair, and immediately called me. We'll tell you more as soon as we know more. Now please step back and let the paramedics do their job."

I felt sorry for Nellie. She was pale and trembling. I stepped over to her. I intended to put my arm around her shoulders and, hopefully, to be of some comfort.

"Get away from me," she said. "If something happened to her, it's your fault."

I bit back my words of defense and took Angus back to my booth to wait out of everyone's way.

I was leaning against the table and Angus was leaning heavily against me when I saw the paramedics wheeling Clara out of the building. A sheet completely covered her. She was dead.

Chapter Eight

I paced the living room as I waited for Ted to arrive. Angus was in the backyard. I thought it best that he run and play, since it was nice outdoors and I was a nervous wreck indoors. He's a sensitive guy. It upsets him when I'm anxious.

I kept wondering if there was something I could have done for Clara. Had she still been alive when I found her? Should I have knocked that chair away and rolled her over before calling Ted?

When Ted got there, I ran to the door to meet him. He swept me up into his arms.

"Everything's all right, babe. I've got you."

I buried my face against his chest. "Was there something I could have done? Could I have saved her, Ted?"

"No." He took my hands, kissed them both, and then led me to the sofa. He sat down and pulled me onto his lap. "There was absolutely nothing you could have done for Clara. She was most likely dead when you found her."

"But you don't *know* that," I said.

"No, but I've worked a lot of cases like this. My gut tells me she was dead."

"Cases like this?" If it was a *case*, that meant it was a homicide. "What was the cause of death?"

"The coroner hasn't examined her yet, but it looked to us—the paramedics and me—like a strangulation," he said.

"A strangulation? You mean, she was murdered?" I asked.

"I'm not saying *that* at this point. She was strangled with the scarf she'd been knitting." He frowned. "Having never knitted a scarf, I don't know if it's common practice to drape it around your neck as you work."

"I haven't knitted many scarves myself, but I've never—and haven't seen anyone else—wrap the scarves around their necks as they knit," I said. "Of course, Clara might have. She seemed to enjoy doing things in her own way . . . except when it came to decorating her shop." I shook my head. This wasn't the time to be thinking about Clara copying my decor.

Ted took out his notebook. "That's something I'll ask Nellie Davis about when we question her again tomorrow morning." He scribbled a note, then returned the notebook to his pocket. "If Clara did have a habit of wrapping her knitting around her neck as she worked, then the scarf could've become entangled in something and she might've accidentally strangled herself."

"How is Nellie?"

"She's distraught. We talked with her, but she

was verging on hysteria," he said. "We were able to get the name and number of one of Clara's sons from Nellie so we could notify next of kin. He said he'd drive over and stay with Nellie tonight."

"His mother just died, and he's calm enough to drive to Nellie's house?" I asked.

"Maybe someone was driving him." He shrugged. "Apparently, Clara has several children, counting stepchildren. They're all grown."

"So you're saying maybe this son wasn't particularly close to his mom."

He smiled and brushed back my hair. "The man I spoke with seemed like a very take-charge type of person. When I told him what had happened, he was quiet for a moment, and then he began rattling off things he needed to do: get in touch with the other family members, come stay with Nellie, have his wife make sure Clara had something nice for the burial. . . ."

"He sounds really . . . efficient."

"He is right now," he said. "While he has all these things to do, he doesn't have to process his grief. I've seen it before. People like him tend to take care of everyone else and then fall apart later."

"Oh. That's sad," I said.

"But someone has to do these things, and he knows it. He's probably the oldest child and has always been looked at as partially responsible for the others."

"I'd go berserk if someone called me out of the blue and told me something had happened to my

mother in Arizona." I couldn't bring myself to say
the words *told me my mother was dead*. "I don't
know what I would do."

"You'd have me to help you." He kissed me.
"Always."

Always. I liked the sound of that.

"Have you eaten?" I asked, suddenly aware
that it was nearly ten p.m.

"I'm fine," he said.

I studied his handsome face. "In your profes-
sional opinion, do you think Clara accidentally
strangled herself?"

He lowered his eyes. "No."

"You think she was murdered," I said.

"More than likely. Of course, that's only my
opinion. We're still waiting for the coroner to ex-
amine the body and determine cause of death."

"Where was Nellie when Clara was being strangled?" I asked.

"She said she'd gone for food."

"That's right. She was carrying a take-out bag
when she came into the building," I said.

"Nellie said she'd finished up with her booth
before Clara was done arranging hers," said Ted.
"She said she was hungry, but Clara wouldn't
leave. She went to get dinner for the both of them."

I frowned. "That's weird, don't you think? If
Clara had finished with her booth and was sitting
in a rocking chair working on a scarf, then either
Nellie went to Timbuktu for food or else Clara
was close enough to being finished that Nellie
could've waited on her."

"That's true. Maybe they'd had a falling-out, Nellie had left, and then later returned with the food as an apology," he said. "That's something else I'll need to speak with Ms. Davis about to-morrow."

"I wouldn't say it was out of the question for Nellie and Clara to have had an argument," I said. "I mean, I've never seen them fight, but, one, they're sisters, and two, Clara must've been in a pretty querulous mood to begin with. She hadn't made a good impression on the falcon lady."

"Do you have a suspect already, then, Inch-High?" Ted's lips twitched.

"You're making fun of me."

"I'm not," he assured me. "I appreciate your in-put . . . and your insights. Tell me about this falcon lady."

I told him how I'd stopped the falcon handler to ask her for directions to the merchants' area. "She acted kinda defensive about the bird—whose name was Herodias, by the way. Have you ever heard of a bird named Herodias?"

"I've never heard of anything named Hero-dias," he said. "Is she some sort of goddess of the hunt or something?"

"No, that would be Artemis or Diana or other names from other myths I'm unaware of," I said. "Herodias got her daughter, Salome, to ask the king for the head of John the Baptist on a platter as a reward for her dancing."

"Must've been some dance."

"I'm sorry. I didn't mean to veer off course," I

said. "Anyway, the lady falconer was upset with Clara. She told me that some *old lady with a bunny rabbit* didn't like Herodias. I correctly guessed that the old lady was Clara." I tilted my head. "I'm not saying this woman did Clara in, though. I'd say it would be hard to strangle someone while you had a falcon tethered to your wrist. Besides, why not have the bird do your dirty work for you? It looked like it could tear out your eyes in one swipe."

"Well, that was gruesome."

"I'm sorry. That was one scary bird." I nestled closer to him. "I'd never seen a giant bird like that up close and personal before."

"Says the woman with the giant dog."

I laughed. "That's entirely different."

"Besides the falcon handler, did you notice anyone else in particular when you arrived at the fairgrounds?" Ted asked.

"I saw a juggler," I said. "When was bowling invented?"

"Its origins date back to Alexander the Great," he said. "Why?"

"Really?"

"No, not really. How would I know when bowling was invented?"

"I just thought you might know. I need to look that up," I said. "The juggler was tossing around bowling pins. That's why I wondered if bowling was in vogue during the Renaissance period. Besides the juggler, I saw a couple of young men dressed as pages who were leading horses to the stable. And there were a couple of other people in the merchants' building when I got there, but I didn't pay any attention to them. By the time I'd heard Clover and gone to investigate the noise, they'd left."

Ted glanced at the clock. "It's getting late. I know you need to get to the fairgrounds early tomorrow morning to get your booth set up. Is there anything I can do?"

"Just pop your handsome face in sometime during the day to say hello if you're around."

"Oh, I'll be around," he said. "I imagine Manu and I will be there interviewing potential witnesses all day if Clara's death is ruled a homicide."

Since it was a sunny morning, I left Angus playing in the backyard. The fence was so high that I didn't have to worry about him jumping out, he had the swing he liked to lie on, and he had plenty of food, water, and toys to keep him occupied while I was at the Ren Faire.

I wore the green velvet square-neck gown with the gold brocade for my first day at the festival. I thought it would be more comfortable than my other Renaissance outfits when I was unpacking my supplies and setting up my booth.

Ted had helped me load everything into the Jeep last night, so all I had to do this morning was head to the fairgrounds. When I arrived, I was surprised to see that he was waiting for me at my booth to help me unload my supplies.

"Wow," I said. "What a wonderful man you are!"

"What can I say? I hate to see a damsel in distress." He smiled. "I couldn't stand the thought of you wrestling all this out of the Jeep on your own this morning . . . especially in your costume. You look gorgeous, by the way."

I smiled. "Thank you. Have you ever been kissed by a damsel in distress?"

"More times than I can count."

My jaw dropped.

Ted laughed. "I'm joking! Unless, of course, you count the times *you* were my damsel in distress."

"You'd better be joking," I said.

He pulled me to him. "Ever been kissed by a rogue?"

"More times than I can count!"

He laughed and kissed me. "And now you have been again." He lowered his head. "And again . . ." He kissed me. "And again."

I laughed and playfully pushed him away. "I've got to get my booth set up!"

"All right." He took the rolling clothes rack from the Jeep first. "Where do you want this thing?"

"If you can just get it to my booth, I can move it around later," I said. I took the suitcase containing my tablecloth, the ruffled collars and cuffs, and the poet's shirts out of the Jeep and trailed along behind Ted to the merchants' building.

We carried the items to my booth. I noticed that Clara's booth had been closed off with cinder blocks and rope.

Seeing the direction of my gaze, Ted explained

that they hadn't wanted to draw attention to Clara's death but had wanted to leave the crime scene—if it were deemed to be one—intact.

"The security guard has been instructed not to allow anyone in or out of that booth," he said.

I glanced around and saw a "knight" dressed in chain mail nod to Ted. Ted nodded back.

"So the knight is the security guard?" I asked.

Ted nodded. "That one is."

"I'm a little creeped out by having my booth next to the scene of a murder. Do you think Ms. Walters would consider moving me?"

"Nope," he said. "Besides, I doubt there are any other booths available. But no one would blame you if you chose to bow out of the Ren Faire."

I shook my head. "I'll be fine. What about Nellie's booth?"

The booth was currently unoccupied and there were white sheets covering Nellie's merchandise.

"The festival coordinators covered everything up for her last night," he said. "The guard will be keeping an eye on her booth, too. One of the people officiating the festival might come by and run the shop for Nellie."

"That would be nice," I said.

We put the suitcase and clothes rack in my booth. Ted went back to get the shelving units while I began setting up.

I opened the suitcase and removed the periwinkle tablecloth. I spread it out over the oblong table and placed my boxes of embroidery flosses on one end of the table. I had printed out some blackwork patterns to distribute for free, and I fanned those out at the other end of the table. I'd brought a few embroidered greeting cards, and I placed these on one corner with one card standing up so people would see them.

I hung the poet's shirts in order of size on the clothing rack. Beneath the table, I placed a bin of flosses and threads and additional copies of the patterns. I was waiting for Ted to bring the shelving units before I unpacked the collars, cuffs, kits, and other items I'd brought to display on those.

After a few minutes, I began to worry about Ted. He should've been back with the shelving units by now. Had something happened?

I was just about to call him when he walked back into the building. I could see that he was angry.

He strode into the booth. "Where do you want these?"

"I'll take care of them," I said. "What's wrong?"

He didn't answer. He just compressed his lips into a thin line. He wasn't just mad—he was furious!

I gingerly took one of the shelving units from him and hung it on the hooks on the opposite wall. I then retrieved the other one and placed it a short distance from the first.

Knowing Ted would talk about what was bothering him when he was ready, I arranged my merchandise on the shelves, then stood back to get the full effect.

"Ah . . . that looks good," I said. I went outside

the booth to see how it looked overall. For the most part, it was great . . . but it still lacked *something*. I needed some sort of decoration. I'd call Vera and see if she could run by the Stitch on her way to the festival and get one of my framed pieces to display here.

"I'm off the case," Ted said.

"What?" I hurried back over to him and placed my hands on his arms. "What are you talking about?"

"Clara's death has been ruled a homicide, and I'm off the case."

"Why?"

"I'm a suspect," he said. "Can you believe that? *I'm* a suspect."

My eyes widened. "That can't be right."

"It's *not* right, but Nellie told Manu she saw me arguing with Clara yesterday."

"Did you argue with Clara?" I asked.

"I wouldn't have called it arguing," he said. "I'd have called it discussing. I'd noticed her being belligerent with a few of the other merchants, and I asked her—nicely—if she would cut everyone here some slack."

"Of course, she thought you meant me."

"She did . . . and I *did* mean you, as well as all the other merchants and customers and everyone else involved with this Ren Faire."

"Why didn't you mention this before?" I asked.

He shrugged. "I forgot about it after everything that happened yesterday evening. And now even though Manu knows I'm innocent, he said he has to take me off the case because Nellie accused me of threatening Clara."

"But you didn't threaten her," I said. "Did you?"

"I didn't threaten her life," he said. "I only threatened to have her kicked off the fairgrounds."

I hugged him. "I'm sorry you won't get to work the case."

"Officially," he said under his breath.

Chapter Nine

Ted and I were putting the finishing touches on the booth at eleven that morning when the gates were opened to the public. People hadn't been lined up from the gates to the parking lot or anything, but there were many die-hard Renaissance Faire fans—some in full regalia—who came pouring onto the fairgrounds.

As those who entered the merchants' building slowly wound through the booths, I quietly asked Ted his opinion on why Nellie would want him off the case.

"She knows you're the best detective in the state . . . country . . . world!" I said. "What's her problem?"

"She doesn't trust me because I'm your boyfriend," he said.

I huffed. "So she cast you as a suspect? That's just ridiculous." I thought for a moment. "Wait a second . . . you don't think Nellie believes I might be responsible for—" I glanced around to make sure no one was listening. "For *what happened* . . . do you?"

"With Nellie, it's hard to say what's going on in that tangled-up paranoid mind of hers," he said. "That's why I need to get this case cleared up as soon as possible."

"We," I said. "*We* need to get it cleared up."

We both turned and smiled at the middle-aged pirate couple approaching the booth.

"Ahoy, mateys!" the man said heartily. "What be ye sellin' in this fine establishment?"

Playing along, I said, "We be sellin' embroidery notions, blackwork favored by the queen herself, and embellished shirts, Captain."

The woman went over to the clothing rack and picked out a shirt. "Oh, look, Harold! It's so pretty. I could wear it with my black skirt."

The man glowered at her. "Gladys!"

She blew out a breath. "What thinkest ye of this garment, milord?" She looked at me and rolled her eyes.

I stifled a giggle.

"Aye, it suits ye, wench," said Harold. "Give the lass a farthing and let's be on our way."

The woman—apparently named Gladys—paid me for the white shirt trimmed in blackwork, and I put it in a periwinkle Seven-Year Stitch bag along with a free pattern and a flyer with information about the store.

"Fare thee well, seafarers," I called after them.

Ted shook his head. "You're almost as bad as Harold."

"Don't start, Gladys. You'll kill the vibe."

He laughed. "Harold didn't want anything to

take him out of his world of make-believe, did he?"

I slid my arms around his waist. "Is that so bad? Have fun with it."

"I'll try." He kissed me.

"Is this the kissing booth?"

I blushed as I realized Manu had caught us.

Chief Manu Singh was only five feet seven inches tall, but he was solidly built, and his demeanor didn't tolerate any nonsense. If criminals were to make the mistake of not taking him seriously, they'd regret it quickly. Unlike his wife, Manu preferred Western dress. That day he wore jeans, boots, and a plaid shirt rolled up to the elbows.

"Aye, 'tis a kissing booth," Ted said. "For a chest of the king's gold, I'll plant one on thee."

Manu hooted with laughter. "I believe I'll pass, but thanks just the same." He turned serious. "I'm sorry I had to take you off that case, Ted."

"Hey, no problem. You gave me the day off, so . . . there's that."

"I know you'd much rather be working this investigation," Manu said. "And there's nowhere I'd rather you be. But after Ms. Davis made such a stink, I couldn't let her bring our integrity into question."

"I know," Ted assured him. "It's all right. Besides, I have this cold case to keep me occupied."

"Any progress on that?" Manu asked.

Ted lowered his voice, and I busied myself on the other side of the booth. I tried not to eavesdrop but couldn't help overhearing.

"Not much," Ted said. "The arson investigator and I are still trying to determine whether the businessman set the fire and, if so, what reason he had for doing so."

Manu nodded. He opened his mouth to say something else but thought better of it as a woman in a nun's habit came alongside him.

"Excuse me, fine sir," she said. "Don't mind me. I've been asked to man Ms. Davis's booth for a few hours since she's . . . um . . . under the weather."

I wondered if she'd been told not to mention Clara's death and the reason for Nellie's absence.

"Some of us volunteers will be taking shifts with this booth." She held out her hand, first giving Manu a brief handshake, then Ted, and then me. "I'm Mary Alice. *Sister* Mary Alice, if you will."

"Are you really a nun, then?" I asked.

"Heavens, no, child!" She chortled. "I'm only pretending to be a nun for the Faire. It was the easiest costume I could come up with. I'm a retired nurse . . . you know, in real life."

The rest of us introduced ourselves.

"One of you strong-looking men couldn't be persuaded to help an old lady fold these sheets up, could you?" she asked.

Of course, we all pitched in to help.

"I have to keep an eye on my booth right now," I said. "But I want to come back later and get some of those little bottles of essential oils. Aren't they darling?"

"They are," Mary Alice agreed.

"Go ahead and shop," Ted said. "I'll watch the booth."

He and Manu went back over to my little corner of this strange world, leaving me to shop Nellie's boutique.

First, I perused the bottles of essential oils and selected several to buy.

"Set these aside for me, please, while I look around at everything else," I said to Mary Alice. I went over to the sachets. "She has some really nice things in here. Do you know Nellie, or are you just a volunteer with the Ren Faire?"

"Both," said Mary Alice. "I've been acquainted with Nellie for years, but she's a rather hard person to know. Does that make sense?"

"Yes," I said. "I've worked down the street from her for almost a year now, and I couldn't really say that I *know* the woman."

"Some people are that way." She walked over to the soaps. "These look nice . . . and they smell wonderful. Do you shop at Scentsibilities often?"

"I don't. Nellie and I tend to give each other a wide berth." I selected a couple of candles.

"Here. Let me put those with your oils," said Mary Alice.

"How about Clara, Nellie's sister?" I asked. "Did you know her?"

"Yeah . . . about as well as I knew Nellie, I guess. That Clara . . ." She blew out a breath. "Well, she could be a pistol, couldn't she?"

"A pistol?"

"Sure, you know . . . a crackerjack, an odd duck, a . . ." She spread her hands.

"An ornery old cuss?" I asked.

Mary Alice smiled. "There you go."

"Were you here yesterday evening?"

"When Clara was . . . found, you mean?" she asked.

I nodded.

She lowered her voice. "We aren't supposed to speak of that, you know."

"I guess not . . . but I'm the one who discovered her," I said. "I just wondered if you'd seen anyone skulking about or arguing with Clara or anything like that."

"Skulking, no. But Clara argued with almost everyone she met," said Mary Alice. "She infuriated the bird lady."

"The one with the falcon?"

She nodded.

"Yes, I met her, and she mentioned it. Apparently, Clara thought the bird might take off with Clover."

"How a falcon tethered to her handler's arm could swoop down and attack a rabbit—especially one in a kennel—is beyond me, but what do I know? I'm only a nun." She winked.

"Do you know of anyone who'd want to harm Clara?"

"Only everyone, dear," she said. "But most of us don't act on our baser instincts, do we? I imagine it was some vagrant who was passing through, noticed that she was here alone, and attempted to rob her."

"But the police didn't mention that anything was missing," I pointed out.

"Maybe the robber was scared off." She patted my shoulder. "Don't fret about it, dear. I believe we're all perfectly safe. The fairgrounds will be teeming with people from here on out, we have plenty of security guards, and you have your own handsome fellow watching out for you."

"Yes, that's true." I paid for my purchases and went back to my booth.

Manu had left, and Ted was checking his phone.

"Do you need to go?" I asked.

He shook his head. "No. Just checking my e-mail while I was waiting for you. What'd you get?"

I showed him what I'd bought from Nellie's booth.

"Nice," he said. "It's a shame you have to wait until Nellie isn't around to shop for things you obviously enjoy."

"What's really a shame is that her sister had to die before I was able to shop from her," I said. "I really hate this whole . . . feud, for lack of a better word. I don't understand Nellie's animosity toward me, and I wish I could find a way to just resolve it."

He lowered his voice. "I heard you asking Sister Mary Alice about Clara. Good move."

I spoke quietly, too. "Thanks. I'd hoped maybe

she'd seen something. Did you hear her response?"

"Some of it," he said. "Not all."

"She thinks Clara was murdered by a vagrant or a robber," I said. "When I pointed out that the police didn't mention anything being taken, she said that maybe he was frightened away before he could steal anything."

"I don't buy it."

"Me, either. She did go out of her way to assure me that we were safe," I said.

"I heard. Of course, anyone *would* rather think someone they knew was killed by a stranger rather than someone who might be walking among us here at the Faire." He looked out at the people milling around in the building. "She didn't seem terribly broken up about Clara's death."

"No, she didn't," I said. "I'd hate to think that if I died—particularly died a violent death—none of my casual acquaintances would even gasp and say how terrible my last moments must have been."

"If you died, the flags would be flown at half-mast, and the whole world—nay, the *universe*—would mourn," he said.

"As long as you'd be heartbroken, I'm good," I teased.

"My heart would shatter into a billion trillion pieces," he said.

"And you'd never look at another woman again," I said.

"Never. I'd gouge out my eyes first."

I giggled. "You're silly . . . but I love you."

"And I love you," he said. "Why don't you go explore? I'm back on duty tomorrow. Take advantage of my being here to enjoy the festival a little bit."

"No. I don't want to leave you with the booth and go have fun at the Faire. Maybe later I can get Vera to come watch the booth for a while, and we can explore the Faire together."

"Maybe you can. But for now, go . . . shop . . . ask questions." He'd played the trump card. He wanted me to investigate.

I smiled. "I'll be back as soon as I can." I gave him a quick kiss. "I'll start with this building. The merchants here would be the most likely to have seen something."

I headed for the booth nearest the door on the other side, deciding to go to each one in order to ever so casually question everyone. I just had to keep my purse strings tied tight for the most part. I could easily spend a small fortune here.

In the first booth, I found an assortment of beautiful handmade jewelry. There were ornate pearl chokers with cabochons of sapphire, ruby, lapis lazuli, and emerald.

"Wow, are these real?" I asked.

The woman smiled. "No, they're costume, but they do look authentic, don't they?"

"Yes, they do. Do you have a card? My mom is Beverly Singer," I said. "She's a costume designer, and she—"

"Yes! I've heard of her!" She plucked a card off

her table and handed it to me. "Please tell her I thought her costumes in *Once a Queen* were breathtaking."

"I will. She'll be delighted that you're familiar with her work," I said.

"I'm really into costumes," she said. "I've done a few things for local theater companies, and it's such fun . . . but really hard work! Even in a small theater like that, you'll have people who'll call you out on any errors you might make in wardrobe."

I picked up one of the chokers offset with emeralds. "This is lovely."

"Take it," the woman said. "It would go marvelously with your gown. Did your mom design it?"

"She sent me the pattern," I said. "She's on location in Arizona right now, or else I'm sure she'd be here. She loves this sort of thing." I opened my purse.

"Oh, no! I mean it. Take the necklace. You can show it to your mom as a sample of my work."

"I will, but I'm paying for it. I'd feel terrible if I didn't pay you. How much do I owe you?" I asked.

The woman gave me a price I thought was too low, but I didn't push it. I would pass her information and a photo of the necklace on to Mom, and if Mom could use her work, she definitely would.

"By the way," I said, leaning in conspiratorially, "did you hear about that poor woman who got strangled with her scarf yesterday?"

"I did," she said. "She and her sister had a terrible argument while they were setting up their booths. I didn't catch what it was about, but several of us heard their raised voices, and it was obvious they were angry with each other." She tsked. "Her poor sister . . . she must feel terrible now. Wouldn't you? Fighting with someone you loved and then having them wind up dead? How awful!"

"That *is* awful."

As I strolled to the next booth, I wondered what Nellie and Clara had argued about. I didn't think Nellie was strong enough to have killed her much larger sister . . . but, still, she had been quick to throw suspicion onto Ted and get him kicked off the case. What was she hiding?

Chapter Ten

Before going outside the merchants' building, I went back to my booth and stored my purchases under the table.

"You made quite a haul," Ted said.

"I actually showed great restraint and didn't get half the things I wanted. And I *was* able to learn a few things about yesterday." I told him that while few of the merchants had anything nice to say about Clara, most of them had seen her arguing with someone yesterday. "One of the people she was arguing with was Nellie."

"And that never made it into Nellie's statement," he said. "Imagine." He took out his cell phone. "Granted she was shocked and upset last night, but I'm still going to call Manu and let him know so he'll be sure to bring that up when they question Nellie later today."

"Okay, sweetheart." I kissed his cheek. "I'm off to do more sleuthing."

He grinned. "Don't forget your purse."

I held up my arm and showed him that the

dainty drawstring purse was hanging from my wrist. "I'll be back as soon as I can. If you need me before then, call me."

"I will."

He was already talking with Manu when I left the merchants' building.

As I walked out into the sunshine, I was happy we had such beautiful weather for the opening day of the festival. The first person I encountered as I began strolling through the fairgrounds was the lady falconer and Herodias.

"Hello!" I said. "Good morning, Herodias."

The bird peered at me. I'm a dog person. I can tell what Angus is thinking . . . or at least I can *imagine* what he's thinking. I had no clue whether this falcon was happy, unaffected either way, or wanting to rip my eyes out.

Her handler, however, was friendly today.

"Hi, there," she said. "I'm sorry I didn't get your name yesterday."

"I'm Marcy Singer," I said. "I own the Seven-Year Stitch, and I have a booth set up in the merchants' building."

"Of course. Your shop is there on Main Street. I'm Amelia Banks."

"Nice to meet you, Amelia. Do you do needle-crafts?" I asked.

She shook her head. "No. I've never had enough patience for it. My mom does, though. I think she's been in your shop a time or two. It has a memorable name—I like that."

"Thank you. How's Herodias today? Does the crowd bother her, or does she just take it in stride?"

"She's pretty used to it by now," said Amelia. "We go to a lot of these types of festivals, and we go to schools and nature centers . . . things like that. Where's Angus?"

"I decided to leave him home this morning," I said. "I thought the food and all the commotion might be a bit much for him to handle. We have a high fence around our backyard, and since the weather was so pretty today, I let him stay out there. He has the back porch, a swing—which he loves to lie on—and plenty of food, water, and toys."

She laughed. "By the end of the day, I'll probably wish I'd gone to your house to stay with him."

"Me, too," I said. "Incidentally, did you happen to see anyone else arguing with the lady with the rabbit yesterday, or did you notice anyone hanging around the merchants' building who looked as if he or she didn't belong there?"

"Not that I recall. Why?"

"Haven't you heard? That woman was found strangled to death with the scarf she was knitting," I said.

Amelia gasped. "Here? That happened *here*?"

I nodded. "I'm the one who found her. I didn't realize she'd been murdered, though. I thought maybe she'd just had a heart attack and had fallen over or something, but I later heard it was murder. The woman manning the booth next to mine said she thought it might have been a vagrant, so you and Herodias be careful."

"We will. You, too." Amelia looked distracted as she started walking away. "Talk with you later!"

"See ya!"

Well, she hadn't appeared to know anything. But maybe if she picked up any information, she'd stop by the merchants' building and share it with me. People were going to think me a terrible gossip when this was over, but how else was I going to help Ted find out who'd killed Clara? So far, the only viable suspect we had was Nellie . . . and frankly, I didn't think she was all that viable.

I walked past archers who were shooting at their targets—away from the other Faire-goers, thank goodness. I spotted the juggler again. This time, he was tossing four balls of different sizes and colors. There was a large red one, a smaller blue one, a yellow one, and then the smallest, a green one.

"Hey, there! Hey, pretty one! Stop and talk with me!"

I turned, realizing the woman's lilting voice was directed at me. "Hello."

"Hello. I am Hecate, Queen of the Witches, goddess of magic and witchcraft."

She was a lovely older woman with red hair and green eyes. In fact, it struck me that she faintly resembled the actress Agnes Moorehead, who was famous for her role as Endora in the sitcom *Bewitched*.

"Beware," she told me. "That Macbeth has a

lean and hungry look about him. Wouldn't you agree?"

"I haven't met Macbeth yet, but I'll certainly take your word for it," I said. "Tales of his ambition precede him."

"That they do." She brought her hand around with a flourish and directed it toward a tent. "Won't you come in and have my sisters tell your fortune?"

Okay, with that enigmatic expression, she looked a *lot* like Agnes Moorehead playing Endora.

I hesitated, and she gave a throaty laugh.

"Come, darling. Don't you want to know what's in store for you?"

"I'm not sure," I said, with a nervous chuckle. "It depends on whether it's good or bad."

She arched a brow.

I suppose I *could* question the witches while I was having my fortune told.

"Okay," I said.

"Fabulous. Step right this way."

Hecate ushered me into the tent. "My sisters, we have a seeker."

Three tables were set up inside the tent, each draped with an ornate fabric. The "sisters" sat in chairs behind the tables. My mind might have been playing tricks on me, but they looked enough like the actresses Jessica Lange, Angela Bassett, and Kathy Bates that they could've been their stunt doubles.

"These are the three witches from *Macbeth* that

chanted *double, double, toil and trouble*?" I asked. "I didn't expect you guys to be so pretty."

The one that looked like Jessica Lange threw her head back and laughed. "I like this one, Hecate. I'm glad you brought her to us."

Hecate laughed, winked at her, and then left me alone with the witches.

"How does this work?" I asked, looking from one to the other.

"You start with me and pay Hecate on your way out," said the one who resembled Angela Bassett. "Come on over and let me see your hands."

I walked over to the table that was draped in black and gold velvet. There was a stool in front of the table, and I sat down.

"Place your hands on the table, please," she said. "As a woman, palmistry of your right hand reveals what you were born with. Your left hand shows what you've accumulated, your potential, what *could* be."

"All right." I stared down at my hands, eager to hear what she saw in them.

"You have water hands. You'd be successful in some artistic endeavor . . . fashion or beauty, perhaps," she said.

"I run an embroidery shop."

She smiled but continued looking at my hands. "Your emotions are more important to you than reason. You often go with your heart and not your head."

"Well, that's true . . . although I *do* think I'm a reasonable person."

"We have only five minutes," she said.

In a nice way, she was telling me to hush and listen to what she was saying.

"I see love in your life. You've been hurt in the past, but now you've found a love greater than the one you had before." She glanced up for confirmation.

I nodded.

"You are a lucky woman. This love . . . this passion . . . runs deep. You also have a life filled with adventure." Her brow furrowed. "Some good adventures . . . some not so good." She straightened. "Be careful, child. I think maybe you tend to meddle where you have no business sometimes. That can be dangerous."

My eyes widened. "It's—"

Faux Angela raised her hand. "Shhh. Tell us nothing yet. Go to my sisters and see what they have to say first."

"All right." This experience was starting to unnerve me and make me feel that my money could've been better spent on another ornate necklace or more essential oils.

"Come on and have a seat," said the woman who reminded me of Jessica Lange.

I went over to her table. It was draped in blue and silver velvet. These women liked their velvet.

Faux Jessica placed a deck of cards in front of me. "Shuffle those and then remove three from the deck. Put them facedown in front of me."

I did as she requested.

She watched my eyes as she turned the first

tarot card over. The picture on the front was of a woman in clerical garb.

"It's the High Priestess," she said. "This card signifies some mystery . . . and silence. The High Priestess is the guardian of secrets, so this card might mean that someone is trying desperately to keep something hidden."

She flipped over the second card. "Interesting."

There was a man on the card holding a wand.

"It's the Magician," she said. "He represents communication . . . and sometimes trickery. You should be careful who you trust."

The final card was the Ten of Swords. It showed a man lying on his stomach with ten swords in his back.

Well, that *can't be good.*

I tried to read the expression on faux Jessica's face, but it was unfathomable. I wouldn't want to play poker with this woman . . . especially given the fact that every time I have a good hand, I squeal with delight. Fortunately, I only play with Ted.

"The Ten of Swords is a card representing betrayal, overthinking, or mental defeat," said faux Jessica. "It's a sign of conflict. Given these three cards, I'd say . . . well . . ." She gave an elegant shrug. "If I were you, I'd watch my back."

I gulped. "Thanks."

"Oh, sweetie, don't let those two freak you out!" called the Kathy Bates look-alike. "Come on over here and let me find your Life Path number."

"After all this good news, I can hardly wait," I

said, making my way to faux Kathy's red-and-blue-velvet-draped table.

She laughed. "Now, really, was what they told you all that bad? You've learned you have a good man who loves you—but you already knew that—and that you've got some mystery and conflict in your life. Let me see what I can come up with."

She asked me my birth date and promptly told me that my Life Path number was seven.

"One of the things your Life Path number says about you is that you enjoy piecing together intellectual puzzles," said faux Kathy.

"Now tell us what's weighing on your mind, child," said faux Angela.

"It's the death of that woman in the merchants' building yesterday," I said. "I'm the one who found her. Isn't there any way you guys can tell me who killed her?"

Faux Jessica smiled. "I wish we could, but things are never that easy."

"I can tell you one thing," said faux Angela. "This was not a random act. That woman had many enemies."

"I don't want a murderer to go free," I said. "And I don't want people to blame me because I'm the one who found her body. I want to find the person responsible and bring him or her to justice."

"That's very noble," said faux Kathy. "But be careful, sweetie. Make sure your risks and potential rewards outweigh any negative consequences."

Faux Jessica nodded. "Be cautious and judicious." She tapped the Magician card. "Remember the trickster."

"Thank you," I said. "I will."

I paid Hecate as I left, and she smiled and gave my shoulder a reassuring pat. I didn't feel comforted in the least. I wanted to get back to Ted. I decided I'd get us some lunch and head back to my booth.

I walked to the food court and looked around at the various trucks, carts, and tents.

"Tinkerbell!"

I turned and smiled. "Captain Moe!"

I hurried over to his tent and hugged him fiercely.

After giving me a comforting hug, he held me slightly away from him and looked down at me. "Are you all right, Marcy?"

"I'm just on edge," I said.

As he led me over to a couple of folding chairs in a deserted corner of the tent, he called out instructions to his two staffers to take care of everything for a minute.

We sat down and he took my hands.

"You're trembling, Tink," he said. "Let me get you a drink."

"No. I'll be fine," I said. I told him about the encounter with Hecate and the three witches.

"It's their job to foretell gloomy fortunes," said Captain Moe. "It lends itself to the atmosphere building up to the play."

"I know," I said. "But I'm the one who found Clara dead . . . and then Nellie had Ted thrown off the case . . . and then these fortune-tellers basically told me to watch my back and that not everyone is who they claim to be."

"Which is advice they could've given to *anyone*, Marcy. Think about it. You're letting your emotions rule your head."

I took a deep breath. "You're right. But they told me I meddle in other people's business and that I should be careful who to trust."

"King Duncan trusted Macbeth. Remember?"

I nodded. "So you think it was just . . . an act?"

"Of course. If you'll notice the fine print on the sign outside their tent, it says 'For entertainment purposes only.'" He squeezed my hands. "You read more meaning into their interpretations because you have Clara's death on your mind. My suggestion is to steer clear of the witches. Maybe *they're* the ones you can't trust."

I smiled. "You're a wise man, Captain Moe."

"I'm just happy to see you smiling again."

"If you want to make me positively delighted, then put some burgers on that grill for Ted and me," I said.

Chapter Eleven

I went back to my booth and found Ted looking almost as frazzled as I felt. He'd obviously been running his hands through his hair. Seeing it that way made me want to do the same, but not necessarily out of frustration.

I placed the bag containing our food on the table. "Are you all right?" I carefully smoothed his hair back into place.

He smiled, but the smile didn't reach his eyes. "I'm great . . . maybe feeling a little like a fish out of water, but I'm trying to get the hang of things."

"You don't have to now. I'm back. And I think I've done all the exploring I care to do," I said. "Let me go get us a couple of drinks and—"

"I'll get those," he interrupted. "It'll be my pleasure. Is water okay?"

"Water will be great. Thank you," I said with a grin.

He walked away from the booth, and I moved the bag to the corner of the table until he returned. I wondered what kinds of aggravation he'd endured while in charge of the booth. The prices for everything were clearly marked, unlike the merchandise in some of the other booths I'd visited, so I couldn't imagine there'd be a dispute over cost . . . unless someone had wanted to haggle. I'd heard that some people liked to haggle the way they supposedly had at medieval marketplaces. Everything was still neatly arranged, just as it had been when I'd left.

Ted returned and set two bottles of water on the table. "Why are you looking so perplexed?" he asked.

"I'm simply wondering what made you so uncomfortable while I was gone," I said.

"Oh, it was nothing."

At my urging, he finally related the tale of two elderly, hard-of-hearing ladies who'd come by and asked Ted about every item in the booth. First, they wanted him to tell them what he knew about blackwork. The extent of Ted's knowledge was that it was embroidery done with black thread. They wanted to know if blackwork had been popular during the Renaissance era. Ted, figuring the blackwork class wouldn't be so popular and that I wouldn't have so much of it for sale in my booth had it *not* been, had told the ladies that indeed it had been outrageously popular.

"When they began questioning me about motifs, I asked them to please come back by in about half an hour when you'd be here," he said.

"How long ago was that?" I asked.

"About an hour ago."

I giggled. "You're wonderful . . . and I truly do appreciate your holding the fort for me."

"Now, what about you?" he asked. "I thought you'd come back here bursting with tales of all the fun you'd had. I figured you'd be spouting Old English to the point that I wouldn't be able to understand thee a whit."

"Yeah . . . well . . ." I opened the bag, took out the burgers, and handed Ted his. "These were made by Captain Moe, so that's a plus . . . maybe two or three pluses."

"So give me the minuses."

I told him about Hecate and the three witches of *Macbeth*. "I realize it was only for fun and that they're probably being spooky when predicting everyone's future, but that entire episode made me feel off-kilter. Especially the part where faux Jessica told me I should watch my back."

"I can understand that."

"I know it's ridiculous, but I'm on edge over finding Clara"—I lowered my voice—"and the fact that she was murdered." I unwrapped my burger before looking up at him. "Will Manu be interviewing me again?" He'd questioned me briefly before I'd left last night, and, of course, I'd already told Ted everything I knew.

"More than likely," Ted said. "He'll need to make sure you didn't forget anything when you gave him your statement last night . . . see if there's something else you might've remembered . . . that sort of thing."

"Right . . . because until the killer has been

found, as the person who found the body, I'm still a suspect."

"Not necessarily," he said. "Time of death should put you in the clear."

"Really? Or are you just telling me that to make me feel better?" I asked.

He bit into his burger and then held up his index finger to let me know he couldn't answer with his mouth full.

"Hmmm . . . well played, detective," I said. "When I talk with Manu, I should probably stick to the facts and not mention the gossip I heard while out exploring the festival, right?"

He swallowed. "Absolutely right. You should spill the gossip to me, and let's see what we can make of it."

"I didn't hear much," I said. "I asked around to see if anyone had seen anybody lurking near the merchants' building that looked like he or she didn't belong there or might be up to something, but no one noticed anything. The witch faux Angela did say this was no random act of violence . . . that Clara knew her killer. But then, that, too, could have been merely some drama to add to the witches' flair."

"I'm inclined to agree with her, though. I mean, it's an understandable observation," he said. "The killer strangled Clara and then left."

"Someone had to have seen *something*, Ted. A person can't just come into a crowded festival, kill a woman, and then leave without a trace."

"The festival wasn't so crowded last night. And

sometimes crowds are the easiest places in which to disappear."

We fell silent as some Faire-goers—not the two ladies who'd been by earlier with all the questions for Ted—came and bought some collars and cuffs from me. Once they left, we finished our burgers.

"We're too late for lunch, Paul," said Vera, as she and Paul approached our booth.

I wiped my mouth on a napkin. "You guys look adorable!"

"Thank you!" Vera twirled so I could further admire her gold brocade dress. The matching Tudor French hood had a white tulle veil that flowed out behind it.

"You're positively elegant," I told Vera. I turned to Paul. "And you . . ."

Vera hadn't been kidding about that blousy orange surcoat with the huge white ruffled collar. He also wore a floppy hat and carried a lute.

"You're quite the minstrel," I finished.

He swept the floppy hat off and bowed. "Thank you, m'lady!"

"Might you play us a tune?" Ted asked.

"Maybe later," said Paul. "I'm here mainly as a reporter rather than a troubadour." He lowered his voice. "Especially given the events of yesterday evening."

Vera jerked her thumb toward the booth beside mine. "What's with the old nun? Is she a friend of Nellie's?"

"She's a festival volunteer," I said. "Her story to me was that Nellie was under the weather. I'm guessing the fairgrounds committee is trying to keep the death hush-hush for fear that it will scare people away."

"If anything, it would do just the opposite," said Vera. "People can be gruesome. The festival would probably have a big bump in attendance from rubbernecks who wanted to see where someone died."

"That's true," Ted said. "What's your take on everything, Paul?"

"If it's the committee's hope to keep Clara's murder under wraps, they're out of luck," he said.

Ted jerked his head backward, indicating that Vera and Paul should come deeper into the booth so the four of us could talk with less fear of being overheard.

I stood and we went to the back corner of the side where Clara's booth was located. We knew no one would be shopping in there.

"Why do you say that?" Ted asked Paul.

"Of course you know the coroner is finishing up the autopsy today and that every reporter in Tallulah Falls County is going to want the details—including yours truly."

"Actually, I'm currently out of the loop on this one," said Ted. "Nellie Davis had me removed from the case."

Vera gasped. "That old shrew! Why would she do such a thing?" She narrowed her eyes. "Maybe she had something to do with her sister's death, and she knows that if you're on the case, you'll find it out."

"The lady in the jewelry booth told me she saw Nellie and Clara arguing yesterday," I said.

"I haven't been to her booth yet," said Vera. "I came directly to yours. Does she have some pretty pieces?"

"She does." I placed my hands on my collarbones to draw her attention to my choker. "I bought this from her. I'm going to send Mom her information."

"Ooh, that's lovely. And it matches your dress perfectly. Paul, we have to go there next."

"Of course, dear," said Paul. "Is there any way you can override Nellie and get back on the case, Ted?"

"Not as things stand right now," said Ted. "But I'm still unofficially looking into things. And I know you well enough to guess that you are, too."

Paul smiled. "Absolutely."

"What have you found out about Clara so far?" Ted asked.

"She was widowed about six months ago," said Paul. "She has two children and four stepchildren. I get the feeling that she and the stepchildren don't get along very well."

"Why is that?" I asked.

"Because she was Clara," said Vera. "You'd met the woman."

"True," said Paul. "But she and the stepchildren were at odds over the fact that Clara—who'd only been married to their father for two years—was appointed the administrator of his estate. She'd been fairly lenient in the disbursement of funds to her own children, but she wasn't as generous with her husband's brood."

"That figures," Vera said. "And the man wasn't even the father to Clara's children." She shook her head.

"How do you plan to write this up?" I asked Paul.

"Well, naturally, I won't mention her history with her stepchildren because I imagine Manu is looking into their alibis and things of that nature," he said. "And while I'll mention that she'd recently opened a shop in Tallulah Falls, I certainly won't comment on its similarity to your shop, Marcy. That sort of thing is fodder for a tabloid, not a respected newspaper, eh?"

We agreed that he was correct.

"I imagine the article will be brief. I'll state that she was a widow who'd recently started a business called Knitted and Needled in town, that she was the sister to Nellie Davis, owner of Scentsibilities, and that she is believed to have been murdered here in her booth at the Renaissance Faire."

" 'Believed to have been'?" I echoed.

"Of course. There's always the possibility she was murdered elsewhere and moved here, isn't there?" he asked.

"I suppose," I said.

Ted gave his head just the slightest of shakes, and I had to admit that when I found Clara, I thought perhaps she'd gotten that scarf hung up in the rocking chair and accidentally strangled herself. I didn't believe she'd been killed at another location.

"I'll have to wait and see what the coroner thinks about that," said Paul. "Vera, darling, would you like to go on to the jewelry booth now?" He looked at Ted and me. "We'll be back along shortly to let you know what we turn up."

They headed out, and Ted and I remained where we were.

"I *know* she was killed here," I said. "And I know that someone is bound to have seen something."

"I agree with you, Inch-High. But Paul is being thorough . . . and that's good."

"It is. You know what, though? I don't think he realizes I'm the one who found Clara's body."

"I don't think he does, either," said Ted. "Despite his not wanting to sound like a tabloid reporter, I'm afraid he'd jump on that tidbit if he knew of it. I mean, I trust Paul. I think he's a good guy and all . . . but the fact that Clara's rival is the one who found her body might be too juicy to ignore."

I went back to the table and got a drink of my water.

Nellie Davis walked past my booth and into her own. I was glad I'd put all my purchases—especially the ones I'd gotten from her booth—under the table.

I started to speak to her, but she didn't even glance in my direction. She stared straight ahead as she passed.

As unobtrusively as possible, I slid to the left, hoping to hear what Nellie might be saying to Sister Mary Alice.

Ted came up behind me and placed his hands on my waist. I started at his touch.

He suppressed his laughter as I glared at him.

I nodded in the direction of Nellie's booth.

"I know," he whispered. "I saw her."

"I want to know what they're saying," I said.

We were both quiet and straining our ears, but although we could hear sounds, we couldn't make out either woman's words.

"I could just happen to wander into the booth," I said.

Ted shook his head gently. "Wait to see whether Nellie leaves. Maybe you can speak with her yourself, or maybe you can go talk with Sister Mary Alice afterward."

"You're right. I don't want to be rude . . . I just want to know what's going on."

He placed his fingertip on my nose.

"I might be nosy," I said. "But we need to know what happened to Clara."

"Even if Nellie did it, I doubt she's confessing her sins to the nun . . . who isn't really a nun," Ted pointed out.

"I know. This is just frustrating."

At that moment, Nellie came out of the booth. Ted and I quickly began looking at some patterns.

She stopped, turned, and stepped inside my stall. When she spoke, her voice was low and ragged. "My sister's death will be avenged."

"I hope it will be," I said.

Nellie merely turned and left without another word.

"Still want to go over and speak with Sister Mary Alice?" asked Ted.

"No, I believe we're pretty clear on what Nellie's thinking. She's convinced that one of us killed her sister . . . and I'm fairly certain she thinks I'm the one."

Faux Jessica's voice came to mind: *Watch your back.*

Chapter Twelve

It was nearly closing time when Todd came by my booth with two cups of apricot ale. I wasn't a big beer drinker, but I liked Todd's craft-brewed ale.

"Where's Ted?" he asked. "I brought you guys some refreshment."

"Thank you," I said. "But he wanted to go by the police station before Manu left for the day, and he said he'd stop at the house and check on Angus."

"Well, then, I guess I'll have to drink his." Todd put both cups on the table and came around to sit on the vacant folding chair. "Have you done good business today?"

"Pretty good." I took a sip of the ale. "This hits the spot. Thanks. How about you? How's your business been?"

"Fair. I expect it to be better tomorrow and Sunday." He winked. "The rowdy revelers always come on the weekends."

"I hope they bring the sassy stitchers with them.

I'd hate to think you were having all the fun," I said. "By the way, have you visited the fortune-telling tent yet?"

"Yet? You say that as if you actually expect me to go." He took a drink of his ale.

"I'll take that as a no."

"And the very fact that you asked me the question lets me know that you've been there," he said. "So, how'd it go? Did they tell you you're going to fall in love with the craft brewer across the street, dump Marshall Dillon, and make sweet apricot ale with the other guy?"

"No, they did not. And it's a good thing because I don't want Deputy Dayton to shoot me." Todd had been dating Deputy Audrey Dayton, and I felt certain she wouldn't appreciate his joke.

He laughed. "So what *did* they tell you?"

"To watch my back," I said.

"That's fairly vague and common, right? Like a fortune cookie saying." He shrugged. "It's no big deal . . . is it?"

"I don't know. I've never got a fortune from a cookie telling me to watch my back. *Good things will come your way* maybe, but I've never been warned by a cookie."

He pushed my cup closer to me. "Drink up. It sounds like you need it. I can't believe you took that stuff seriously."

"Maybe I wouldn't have if I hadn't found Clara strangled to death in her booth last night," I said.

"Yeah . . . I heard about that. Are you doing okay?"

I took a small sip of the ale. I knew I'd be driving soon, and I didn't want to overdo it. "I'm all right . . . pretty much."

"Spill it."

"I don't know, Todd. I have to look like the main suspect to Manu. Clara opened her shop right beside mine selling the same types of things. . . . She even copied my decor!"

"But you were in your shop until late yesterday with your class," he said. "Heck, even I can vouch for that."

"Still, I found her. And Nellie has always hated me. She'll try every way in the world to convince Manu that I killed her sister," I said.

"Manu knows you," Todd said. "And Ted knows you even better than that."

"But Ted isn't on the case anymore. Nellie has accused him as a suspect, too."

"You're kidding!"

"I wish," I said. "This is such a nightmare." I bit my lower lip. "You know . . . she likes you."

"Nellie?"

I nodded. "You could stop by, see how she's doing . . ."

"You want me to fly under the radar and get you some intel. That *is* what you're saying, isn't it?" He finished off his ale.

"Would you?"

"For you, yes." He nodded at my cup. "Are you planning on finishing that?"

"No. I'll be driving soon."

"I have a higher tolerance level than you do,"

he said, finishing off my ale himself. "And I need all the courage I can get before going to visit Nellie Davis."

I hugged him. "Thank you, Todd."

He kissed my cheek, and his breath was fruity. "You owe me . . . big. I'll stop by and tell you what I learn, if anything."

Before going home, I went by the Seven-Year Stitch to see how Julie had done. I hoped she didn't think I was checking up on her. I suppose that *is* what I was doing, but I simply wanted to make sure everything went well and that there was nothing she needed from me before calling it a day.

"Hi!" I said when I walked into the shop.

"Oh my gosh, you look fantastic!" she said. "Spin around and let me get a three-sixty view of that dress."

I did as she asked.

"That's great, Marcy. You really look the part. Did you do well at the Faire today?"

"I did. I had a lot of fun . . . more than Ted did." I laughingly told her about the elderly women who'd stopped by while he was watching the booth for me.

"Did they ever come back?" she asked.

"No, they never did." I giggled. "Poor Ted . . . he'd run his hands through his hair to the point that it was standing straight up. I hope your time managing the Stitch was a much better experience."

"It was. Traffic was sporadic and of course there were a few lookie-loos who came in because they were passing by Clara's shop and wanted to know if I knew anything about her death." Julie shook her head. "I said I didn't know anything and asked them if they preferred cross-stitch or needlepoint."

"Oh, that was good," I said. "I'll have to remember that. I never know what to say when I'm put on the spot like that."

"When you have a teenager in your house, you learn to think on your feet." She smiled. "One odd thing, though. There was a young woman who came in looking for Clara. She said she'd heard about Knitted and Needled and came by but was surprised to see that it was closed. She wondered whether that was just for today."

"What did you tell her?" I asked.

"I didn't know if she was merely fishing for information or what, but she seemed genuine," said Julie. "I told her that I was just filling in here for the owner today but that if I wasn't mistaken, the proprietress of Knitted and Needled had suffered some sort of accident yesterday and I didn't know when she'd be back."

"Wow, you really are good at deflecting questions," I said.

She spread her hands. "Again, mother of a teenager—what can I say? I couldn't figure out if she was looking for the shop or for Clara, though, so I asked her if there was anything here I could help her with or have you order for her, but she said no."

"I wonder who she was."

"I have no idea, but I'll find a way to ask if she comes in again," she said. "I doubt she'll be back if she was truly looking for Clara instead of the shop."

"It couldn't have been a member of her family because they would all have been notified by now," I said.

"That's what I thought, too. She seemed troubled, but I didn't get the impression she was terribly upset. She could've been a distant relative who hadn't heard about Clara's death yet, I guess."

"Did you ask if she knew Nellie?" I asked.

Julie shook her head. "I figured it was best if I said very little, which is what I did."

"You're probably right. I try to stay out of the middle of these things . . . and yet, time and again, I find myself right there."

I was happy to see Ted's car in my driveway when I got home. I went inside, and he was stretched out on the sofa watching the local news.

I dropped a kiss on his lips before stretching out beside him. "Are they saying anything about Clara?"

He nodded. "Paul was right. Clara's murder is the big headline. The anchor reported that Clara had been found strangled to death last night in an apparent homicide in her booth at the Tallulah Falls Renaissance Faire. They asked for anyone with any knowledge of the incident or who might've seen something strange at the merchants' building to come forward."

"Do you think anyone will?" I asked.

"I hope so, but it isn't likely. Manu questioned people all day, and if anyone saw anything, they're not talking about it," he said. "By the way, I fed Angus and let him go back outside for a bit. Are you hungry? I thought maybe we could make dinner."

"I am hungry. What are you in the mood for?"

"I'm in the mood for lasagna, thick crusty bread, and a Caesar salad," he said.

"Works for me," I replied. "Do I have time to take a quick shower before we get started?"

"You go on and take your shower, and I'll work on dinner. How's that?"

I kissed him deeply. "You're wonderful."

"I know." He smiled.

I went upstairs, took off my dress, and hung it up. I'd drop it off at the dry cleaners on the way to the fairgrounds tomorrow morning.

The shower felt wonderful. The warm water seemed to wash my fatigue away and left me feeling refreshed.

I dressed in a pair of jeans and a T-shirt and went back downstairs. I went into the kitchen and was a little surprised to see Ted and Todd sitting at the kitchen table.

"You smell amazing!" Todd said. He looked at Ted. "You're a lucky man."

"I know," said Ted. "Now put your eyes . . . and your nose . . . back in your head."

Todd laughed.

"Did Todd tell you I asked him to go see Nellie?" I asked Ted.

Ted nodded. "And the result of that visit is playing in the backyard with Angus."

"What?" I hurried over to the door. Clover and Angus were lying near the door. Angus looked up at me, mouth wide and tail wagging.

I went back to the table. "How'd you end up with Clover?"

"Apparently, Nellie is allergic," said Todd. "Plus, she's grieving and doesn't have time to care for an animal." He spread his hands. "On top of that, she doesn't strike me as the caregiving type. So I told her I'd ask around and see if I could find Clover a good home. Next thing I know, she's packed up all its stuff and is handing it to me."

"So now you're the proud owner of a bunny," I said. "Congratulations! Bring her by to see Angus whenever you want. They really do like each other."

"Well . . . you see . . . I was . . . sorta thinking . . . you know . . . *you* might want to keep Clover," he said. "I told you that you'd owe me big time for my going to see Nellie."

"Aw, come on, Calloway," said Ted. "It would be a great mascot—the Brew Crew Bunny."

Todd's eyes were pleading with me. "I have no idea how to take care of a rabbit."

"Neither do I," I said.

"It can't be that much different from taking care of Angus, can it?" Todd asked.

"They're two different *species*," I said.

"We can talk about Clover in a minute," said Ted. "Tell us what of value—if anything—you managed to glean from Nellie."

"When I went in, I took her a pie from MacKenzies' Mochas and told her how sorry I was about Clara," said Todd. "Then I asked what happened. She said she didn't know . . . that she'd gone out to get them something to eat and that when she got back—" He glanced at me.

"Go on," I said. "I can take it. What would surprise me would be if she'd said anything *nice* about me—like the fact that I was trying to help."

He swallowed and looked down at the floor. "She said that nasty Marcy Singer was there, of course, looming over the body and that she just knew the woman had killed her sister."

"See? That wasn't so bad," I said. "I already knew she'd try to pin the blame for Clara's death on me." I shook my head. "I really did try to help Clara. I just didn't know how. I didn't know whether she'd had a stroke or a heart attack and had fallen over in her chair or what. I was afraid to attempt to move her, so I called Ted."

"And I immediately called nine-one-one," Ted said. "You did everything you could possibly do, babe."

"Did she say anything about Ted?" I asked. "She told Manu that she saw him arguing with Clara, and that's why Manu took him off the case."

Todd looked at Ted. "Were you arguing with her?"

"I wouldn't call it *arguing*," said Ted. "I went by her booth, complimented her on her knitting—even though I was really comparing her to Madame Defarge, the evil knitter from *A Tale of Two Cities*, in my mind—and I encouraged her to have fun at the festival, to be gracious even to the customers who would try her patience . . . and I said I hoped she and Marcy got to know each other better during their time at the festival."

"I bet *that* went over well," I said.

"Yeah." Ted nodded. "That's when she started yelling at me and telling me that Marcy had been a detriment to this town ever since she arrived, that Nellie was a saint, yadda, yadda, yadda. So, basically, I didn't argue. Clara did."

"That was it? Manu took you off the case because of that?" I asked.

"No, Manu took me off the case because Nellie made a stink over it," he said. "She cited conflict of interest and a bunch of other junk. It really doesn't bother me. I just want to get to the bottom of this so everybody can move on."

"Me, too," I said with a sigh.

"For what it's worth, I did ask her if she honestly thought you'd hurt her sister," Todd said.

"What did she say?" I asked.

He looked at the floor again. "She said, *I'd hate to think so . . . but you've got to admit, a lot of people have come to harm since that girl has been in Tallulah Falls*." He raised his eyes. "Not that these people wouldn't have wound up hurt anyway."

"Yeah, well, a few months ago she actually entertained the thought that an exorcist should come in and . . . I don't know . . . do whatever exorcists do . . . to the Seven-Year Stitch," I said. "I think she's a nut, but I agree with Ted. The sooner we find Clara's killer, the better."

"She didn't let on to you that Clara had any other enemies?" Ted asked. "She didn't say anything about Clara being upset or arguing with anyone else?"

"Not to me," Todd said. "I'm sorry. I'll keep my ear to the ground, and if I hear anything, I'll let you guys know."

"Thanks," I said.

"About Clover . . ." Todd cleared his throat. "You guys don't know anyone who might want him . . . or her . . . do you?"

Ted smiled. "I believe I do."

Chapter Thirteen

Ted and I had invited Todd to stay for dinner, but after Ted said he knew of someone who might be willing to take Clover off his hands, he made a beeline for the Brew Crew. Not even the smell of a scrumptious pan of lasagna baking in the oven could tempt him to hang around.

With our tummies full and our moods uplifted—and me with a bunny on my lap while Ted drove the Jeep—Ted, Angus, Clover, and I headed off to see the wizard. Okay, she wasn't the wizard, but she might as well be given the fact that she was the *great and powerful* Veronica . . . Ted's mom. The first time I met the woman, she basically put a federal agent in time-out. I could hardly believe *she* was the person Ted thought would want Clover.

"Are you sure about this?" I asked Ted for the umpteenth time.

"I'm *positive*. I can't guarantee that Mother will take him . . . her?"

"I have no idea," I said. "I've been calling the

bunny a her because Clara did. I guess she'd know."

"Anyway, I can't promise you anything, but I think Mother is our best bet," he said.

"For a pet."

Ted laughed. "My mother doesn't cook, if that's what you're getting at. The condo staff takes care of all her meals."

When Ted had first told me that his mom lived in an "upscale condo," I didn't dream it was up-scale enough to have a *staff*. And then he took me to this upscale condo, and the place looked like a resort hotel. It even had a doorman. His name was Bill. I quickly learned that the emphasis was on ease at this facility. Residents had chefs, maids, hairstylists, manicurists, and a nursing staff at their disposal. Of course, they were free to utilize these services or not, but the perks were part of the complete package. Mama Nash was living large! I thought everybody should be so lucky!

"Do they allow pets at your mom's condo?" I asked.

"Yes, if they're small and house-trained." He glanced over at me. "Don't worry."

"I can't help it! You didn't even call ahead to let her know we're coming."

"Trust me," he said. "It's better that way."

"But what if she isn't there?"

"Stop worrying."

I cupped my hands over Clover's long ears, though it appeared the little creature was asleep and not listening anyway. "You know, springing a bouquet on someone is one thing . . . but a bunny is something else entirely."

"Of course it is. Bunnies have a much longer shelf life than flowers."

"I certainly hope so."

And then we were pulling into the drive.

Parking.

Getting out of the Jeep.

We were probably looking as goofy as could be. Ted was leading Angus, and I was carrying Clover. And we were heading into the lobby to call Veronica to let her know we were there.

Bill, the doorman, was probably calling security.

Or maybe not.

He stepped out onto the sidewalk to greet us. "Well, what a fine crew of furry beasties you have with you this evening! Please allow me to call your mother for you, Mr. Nash. It appears everyone's hands are full."

"Thank you, Bill," said Ted. "If you don't mind, ask her to meet us in the garden."

"Will do," said Bill.

"Oh, and the furry beasties are a surprise," I said quickly before Bill could go back inside.

Bill smiled, nodded, and went to make the call.

Ted strode toward a walkway that led from the front of the facility to the back. Round stepping-stones took us to a garden that was even more breathtaking than I could have imagined. White Adirondack chairs, benches, and swings flanked on each side by trellises provided plenty of seat-

ing for the residents. Flower beds were separated
from the well-manicured lawn by landscaping
timbers and contained torch lilies, blue-violet hy-
drangeas, and chrysanthemums in yellow, white,
pink, and orange. Lovely evergreen shrubs with
clusters of white flowers, weeping Japanese ma-
ples, and heather added more color and beauty.

"Clover would love it here," I said, my voice
hushed with reverence. "*I* love it here."

Ted smiled, put his hand at the small of my
back, and led me over to a bench. Angus, of course,
wanted to sniff all these wonderful things, most of
which he'd never seen. Ted took him for a stroll
around the garden while I sat on the bench with
Clover. I was afraid to put the bunny down. What
if she ran off into the shrubbery and wouldn't
come back?

We had been waiting only a couple of minutes
when Veronica emerged. She wore jeans, a light-
weight red sweater, and tan peep-toe wedge san-
dals. Her light gray hair was cut in an angular bob
that framed her face, especially offsetting those
brilliant blue eyes that were so much like Ted's.

"Hello," she said, walking over to the bench toward Clover and me. "What have we here?"

"Hi, Mother," said Ted. He and Angus joined
us.

"Good evening, Veronica," I said.

She sat beside me. "Have you added a bunny to
your brood?"

"Not exactly," I said. "Clover here belonged to
a woman who . . . passed away."

"We're trying to find the poor little thing a home," Ted said. "We hoped you might know of someone who's looking for a pet."

"May I?" She held out her hands, and I gave her the bunny. She cradled the brown and white rabbit on her shoulder, carefully supporting its feet with one hand.

"Is Clover house-trained?" she asked.

"Yes," I said. "There was a litter box included among her belongings."

"That's good." She held the bunny out from her and looked into her face. "Are you a good girl?"

Clover twitched her little pink nose. I, personally, took that as a yes.

"And you say that Clover's owner died?" Veronica asked, returning the bunny to her shoulder.

"Actually, she was murdered," said Ted.

"Given your line of work, I didn't think she'd gone peacefully," said Veronica. "I worry about you." She silently petted Clover for a moment before continuing. "Who was she?"

Ted gave her a quick rundown of the entire situation, including the fact that Nellie Davis had pushed Manu into taking Ted off the case.

"That's silly," Veronica said. "It seems to me this woman is trying to use a personal vendetta to pass blame for her sister's death." She gazed up at the darkening sky. "You say this Nellie was seen arguing with her sister before she left for food?"

"I'm not sure anyone officially made that statement, but we understand that to be the case," said Ted.

Veronica frowned at her son. "I wouldn't be surprised if she didn't kill the sister herself, leave to deflect blame, and then decide she had a wonderful scapegoat when Marcy found the body."

"At this point everyone's a suspect," Ted said.

I was sure that both his mother and I had known that line was coming.

"Including, so it seems, the two of you." Veronica bent and set Clover on the grass.

"Aren't you afraid she'll run off?" I asked.

"If she does, you and Ted will catch her." She smiled.

Angus immediately went to his new buddy and licked the bunny's head. He then lay down, and Clover nestled between his large paws.

"They're sweet together," said Veronica. "Are you sure you don't want to keep her?"

"I really can't," I said. "I know nothing about rabbits."

"They aren't hard to care for. Ted and Tiffany had a couple at one point in their childhood." She shrugged one shoulder. "I suppose many children do at some time or another."

"She'd be good company for you, Mother," said Ted.

She rolled her eyes at him. "You knew I wouldn't be able to resist. That's why you brought her here."

He grinned. "Would I do something like that?"

"Yes. You would." Her face softened. "I suppose you brought her things with you?"

"Of course. They're in the Jeep. Want me to go get them?" he asked.

"Please." She huffed in mock exasperation. "Have Bill help you."

Ted handed me Angus's leash before trotting off to unload the Jeep.

"I was surprised when Ted told me he thought you'd want her," I said.

Veronica arched a brow. "I don't strike you as the warm and fuzzy type?"

Well, no, she didn't, but I couldn't admit that. Instead, I said, "I just didn't think you'd want the responsibility of caring for a pet. It can be hard sometimes."

"I know it can. Ted and his sister had lots of pets growing up, and it always fell to me to care for them," she said. "I haven't had a pet in years. I think it will be a nice change of pace."

"I'm glad. She seems awfully sweet."

"Yes, she does," said Veronica. "About that other matter . . . If I were you, I'd simply enjoy the Renaissance festival without being flanked on either side by two sisters who despise me . . . God rest the one woman's soul."

"Clara," I said.

"Whatever. She seems to have been a horrible person, she's gone, and there's nothing you can do about that. Life is for the living . . . so enjoy the Faire." Veronica steepled her fingers. "If the sister returns to manage her booth—though I doubt she will because that would be wretchedly crass—then simply ignore her. Certainly don't engage in any sort of conversation with her. She'll only hurl accusations and insults."

"Okay," I said. "Although I keep thinking that if I could talk with her, I could find out more about who Clara saw that day, what was going on in her life, who might want to kill her."

"That's not your duty," said Veronica. "That obligation rests solely on the shoulders of Manu Singh . . . especially since his head detective is off the case."

Ted returned to the garden. "Bill and I got everything into your condo. I figured you'd want to take a look at it and arrange it however you'd like."

"Of course. Thank you, darling."

"It looked as if I was interrupting a serious conversation," Ted said.

"We were talking about Nellie," I said. "Your mom doesn't feel I should try to communicate with her."

"It's obvious the woman resents Marcy and wouldn't believe that she truly wanted to help her find her sister's killer . . . if indeed she didn't strangle Clara herself," said Veronica. "Trying to talk with this Nellie would be like trying to hug a skunk—painful, beneficial to no one, and with lingering consequences. I'd leave it alone."

"That's a valid point," said Ted. "Manu has already been interviewing her, anyway. He's an excellent interrogator, and he'll find out whatever she knows."

"I know," I said. "You're both exactly right. I'll avoid Nellie like the plague . . . or a skunk."

"Good." Veronica turned to Ted. "As for you, I

believe you should leave this case entirely up to Chief Singh."

"Mother, I'm the best detective on the force."

"I know that," she said. "But you are not on this case, and it would be counterproductive to pursue it. I'm sure you have other cases."

"I do, but—"

"I'm only expressing an opinion," said Veronica. "This Nellie sounds like a beast to me. Both of you would do well to steer clear of her since she's trying to implicate you in her sister's death. Remember your Miranda rights—anything you say can and will be used against you. She will surely twist everything around to make you appear guilty."

"She has a point," I said to Ted.

"Besides, if Nellie didn't kill her sister, then whoever did might have designs on murdering her next," said Veronica. "Until you find the motive, you can't narrow down your field of suspects. And if Nellie winds up dead, neither of you wants to be the one finding her body."

"Were you ever a detective yourself?" I asked Veronica.

She laughed. "No. I simply read a lot . . . and I try to keep informed about my son's line of work."

"We should get going," Ted said. "Marcy has an early start tomorrow morning."

"Thank you for taking Clover," I said. "If it doesn't work out, please let us know and we'll find her another home."

"All right." Veronica stood. "Come, Clover."

The bunny got up and hopped over to Veronica's feet. She bent and picked it up.

"Good night." She looked down at Angus. "Don't worry. I'll bring your friend to visit you soon."

Ted was quiet on the drive back home.

"You're thinking about what your mom said, aren't you?" I asked.

He nodded. "She's right, you know. You should absolutely stay away from Nellie. You won't get any useful information from her; and if someone has a grudge against both sisters, you could be putting yourself in danger."

"And you?"

"I won't approach Nellie, either," he said. "Manu is getting all the information we need from her. But I won't stop investigating this case on my own until Clara's killer has been caught."

Chapter Fourteen

On Saturday morning, I arrived at the Ren Faire looking more like a merchant and less like a noblewoman. I wore my red jacquard skirt, a cream-colored, off-the-shoulder peasant blouse—that I had resisted the urge to embellish with black-work, mind you—and a black corset vest.

Ted was working from home, and he'd taken Angus along with him. He said they'd stop by and see me later.

I got to the fairgrounds before the gates opened, but people were already lining up. I anticipated a busy day as the good folks of Tallulah Falls were eager to make an adventure of stepping back in time.

The horses were being prepared for the jousting tournaments as I made my way to the merchants' building. As I sidestepped them, a man wearing a black hat, a cape, and a gold Plague Doctor Venetian mask blocked my path.

He held up a carved staff. "Where might ye be going, lass?"

The man looked creepy, especially since I couldn't see his face, and something about him made me uncomfortable. "I'm on my way to the merchants' building, good doctor. I must hurry to my stall before the gates open or else my partner will give me a thrashing."

Okay, that last part was a lie . . . and I felt bad about telling it. But for some reason, I wanted the man to think someone was waiting for me and would come looking for me if I didn't arrive at my booth soon.

"I warn ye to be careful among those merchants," he said. "There might be a viper in your midst."

I hesitated. Did he know something about Clara's murder?

"Why do you say that?" I asked.

"One of you suffered a dreadful fate on the eve of the Faire. Keep a weather eye out, my friend. The evildoers might not be finished yet."

I swallowed hard. "What's your name, good doctor?"

"I'm known only as the Crow," he said.

Then he walked away, leaving me confused and bewildered.

I hurried on to the merchants' building. I'd left the booth tidy yesterday, and today everything was still in order. However, the encounter with the Crow had made me nervous, and so I bustled around the booth straightening everything again.

A woman dressed as a washerwoman in a white muslin dress with a blue checked gingham overdress and matching muffin cap stopped by my booth.

"A merry morning to ye, fellow laborer!" she called out cheerily.

"Good morning!" I went closer to facilitate chatting with her. I was eager for some conversation that would clear my mind of my experience with the Crow. "How are you today?"

"I am happy to say nothing is awry . . . at least, as of yet. My name is Jan, and I will be thy neighbor for the day, as Mistress Nellie is still in mourning."

"It's nice to meet you, Jan. I'm Marcy. How is Nellie . . . er, Mistress Nellie, by the way?"

"Ah, she grieves as any good sister would," said Jan.

"Of course. Were you here on Thursday?"

She shook her head. "Nay, I was not . . . and glad of it I am."

Gee, she was really taking her part to heart.

"I was," I said. "In fact, I found Clara."

"Oh, you poor dear. What a shock that must have been!"

"Yes, it was." I frowned. "Have you met a man wearing a Venetian Renaissance costume with a gold, long-nosed mask who calls himself the Crow?"

"Nay, I have not. Did he behave in an untoward manner?"

"No," I said. "He was just . . . creepy. He told me to beware because the evildoers might not be finished yet."

She chortled. "Oh, my dear, you must not take him seriously. We are all to extend warnings about Macbeth and his treacherous wife and to encourage our customers to visit with Hecate and her sisters." She lowered her voice. "It's all part of the fun."

"Oh . . ." I forced a laugh. "Of course. I guess Clara's death has just put me on edge."

"Certainly, it has. But now we must put aside our worries, for the show must go on," she said. "I will be in thy neighboring stall should you need me."

"Thank you, Jan . . . and likewise."

I didn't care what Washerwoman Jan thought. There was something about the Crow that was downright ominous, and he *hadn't* been warning me about Macbeth.

I was delighted when, soon after the gates opened, Riley, her husband, Keith, and their beautiful baby daughter, Laura, came to visit me. Riley was dressed as a noble lady in a rose empire-waist gown, Keith was dressed as a knight, and Laura was a baby faerie.

"You guys look fantastic!" I said, rising from my chair and going to hug Riley and to take the baby from her. Laura had inherited her parents' dark hair and olive skin tone and her mother's blue eyes. She was so precious in her green leotard, lavender tutu, and green and purple wings that I could hardly stand it. I kissed the baby's cheek, and she cooed and giggled.

"Oh, I love her so," I said to Riley. "Please let me have her. You two can make another."

Riley laughed. "You'd regret that request at about"—she looked at Keith—"what? Two thirty in the morning?"

"Two forty-five," he said. "You could set your watch by it."

"Here, let me take a photo of the best-looking family at the Faire." I handed Laura back to Keith, and the threesome posed while I snapped a picture with my camera.

"Thank you," I said. "I might even pass it along to Paul Samms, if you don't mind, so he can put it in the newspaper."

"Well, I'd be flattered," said Riley. "Anytime I have the opportunity to gush over Laura, I take it."

"I don't blame you a bit," I said.

"It is getting to be kinda rough having her at the office all the time, though," Riley said. "Mom is considering retiring as my administrative assistant in order to babysit Laura full-time. But I don't know how I'd ever replace her at the office."

"Maybe she could still handle some of the administrative tasks in the evenings or part-time, and you could hire someone to staff the office during the day," I said. "In fact, I know someone who was recently laid off . . . and I think you know her, too. Wasn't Julie in that last stitching class you took?"

"Yes, I believe she was. She has a daughter named Amber, right?"

"She does," I said. "When you and your mom reach a decision, if you're interested in having Julie apply, please let me know."

"All right," said Riley. "I'll talk with Mom this evening."

"We'd better find your uncle," Keith told Riley. "He'll tar and feather us if he doesn't get to see *his baby* before he gets too busy."

I laughed. "Give him a hug from me and tell him I hope to see him later." Riley's uncle was Captain Moe. Captain Moe was Riley's dad's brother, not Camille's.

I was a little sad to see the Kendalls go. I'd have liked to spend more time with Laura myself. The thought of having to get up with her at two forty-five notwithstanding, I really do think I'd like to have a baby sometime. I believe I'd be a good mother. And I know Mom would be delighted. She'd be making the child fancy clothes before she even knew whether it was going to be a girl or a boy.

Maybe one of these days . . .

I had a steady stream of customers from the time the gates opened until Ted and Angus strolled into the merchants' building at around noon. I was selling a blackwork-embellished shirt to an older woman who declared Angus to be a "noble beast indeed" when he strode up to her.

"I fancy myself something of a scholar of canines," she said. "The Great Irish Hound, as the breed was previously known, was prominent in Irish history going back to the fifth century. The dogs were allowed to be owned only by royalty and nobility at that time. And here is a cautionary tale to warn you always to trust your hound, sir."

She spoke to Ted, as he and Angus were together, and she obviously didn't realize Angus belonged to me.

"Llewellyn, prince of Wales, was given the noble Irish wolfhound named Gelert by then Prince John of England. Although Llewellyn had many hounds, Gelert became his favorite. One morning Gelert greeted Llewellyn covered in blood. Llewellyn rushed to his infant son's room and, to his horror, found the baby missing from its overturned cradle. He thought Gelert had killed the child."

I gasped. Earlier this morning I'd been playfully entertaining the thought of having a baby, and now this lady was telling a story of a missing infant and an Irish wolfhound covered in blood? Not that I believed for one instant that Angus was capable of hurting a child, but this was a strange coincidence.

"Llewellyn drew his sword and killed Gelert," the woman continued. "Poor Gelert howled in pain as he died, and it's said that his howl was followed by the cry of an infant. The prince searched and found his child unharmed beneath a pile of bedding from the cradle. Near the baby was a dead wolf."

"Gelert had saved the baby from the wolf!" I cried.

"Indeed," she said. "Some say the story of Gelert is merely a myth. Maybe so, but either way, the moral is the wise advice to heed the counsel of your dog. He is a loyal friend." She took her periwinkle bag and waved good-bye to us.

I stepped out from behind the table and hugged Angus. "I knew you wouldn't hurt our baby."

Ted's eyes widened. "Did you say *our baby*?"

I laughed. "Just got caught up in the story."

He smiled. "Whew! Not that I don't want children someday . . . just . . ."

"Not yet," I said.

"Right."

"Have you two had a good day?" I asked.

"Fair," Ted said. "No pun intended. We actually learned, thanks to a call from Manu, that the man whose business burned earlier this week has gone missing."

"That certainly lends credence to the belief that he torched his own building, doesn't it?"

"I'm not sure." Ted came around the table and sat down beside me. Angus lay between us. "Either the man did set the fire himself, he's dead, or he's afraid of the person who burned his office."

"So you think the person who killed his partner five years ago might have set the fire?" I asked.

Ted nodded. "I think it's a strong possibility."

"But, then again, wasn't the partner a suspect in the murder?" I asked.

"Yes. There's just something I can't put my finger on . . . a gut feeling that tells me the man is running scared."

"If anyone can find him, you can," I said.

"Thanks. So how's your day been so far?"

"It got off to a weird start, but since then, it's been great." I told him about my meeting with the Crow.

"I wouldn't worry about it, Inch-High, unless the man starts seeking you out or something," said Ted. "You're going to run into a *lot* of eccentrics at a festival like this."

"I guess, but—" My thought would have to wait because William Shakespeare had just come up to our booth.

"Good day, Mr. Shakespeare," I said. "Welcome to the Seven-Year Stitch booth."

Will placed a hand upon his chest. "You've heard of me? Why, I'm flattered! Unless, of course, your account of me came from that wretched critic Greene, who described me as an upstart crow."

"You . . . you were called the *Crow*?" I asked.

"Only by Robert Greene, that I'm aware," he answered. "That's not how you know me, then?"

I smiled. "Not at all, sir. I've heard of your plays."

I glanced at Ted, and he winked at me. Obviously, William Shakespeare was also the Crow. Washerwoman Jan had been right—he'd been drumming up excitement for the play!

"What is your favorite to date?" Will asked.

"I have to say *The Merchant of Venice*. I love them all, but that one struck a particular chord," I said. "What about you, Ted?"

"I'm torn between *Julius Caesar* and *Othello*," Ted said. "Although a patron who came by the shop earlier spoke about wise people trusting their dogs ... I think even wiser people would trust their spouses."

Will held up an index finger. "Ah, but some love not wisely but too well. And some spouses are not trustworthy. I'd have to agree with your patron about trusting your dog. He'll always be faithful." He bowed, making a flourish with his right hand. "Fare thee well, new friends. I hope to see you again soon." He reached into a leather pouch hanging from his waist and produced two business cards. He put them on the table in front of Ted and me.

ARTURO FELDMAN
PROFESSOR OF ENGLISH AND DRAMA
TALLULAH FALLS COMMUNITY COLLEGE

His contact information followed.

"Should you need to get a message to me, these wee parchments show the way," said Will. "Be on the lookout for a wicked woman with the surname Macbeth. She has a lean and hungry look about her."

"We sure will," I said.

Will moved on to visit with Jan the washerwoman.

"He was the Crow, wasn't he?" I asked.

"More than likely," said Ted. "Do you want to take a break while I'm here?"

"I would like to stretch my legs, maybe go check on Sadie and Blake and get us some lunch if you don't mind," I said.

"Lunch? I don't mind that in the least. Please do bring a couple bottles of water for Angus. I stopped at the pet shop and bought him a collapsible bowl."

I leaned over and kissed him deeply. "You are the most wonderful man in the world."

He grinned. "Prithee don't forget it."

"I won't!"

Chapter Fifteen

The aromas of steak on a stake and burgers on the grill drew me to Captain Moe's tent first. I was planning to buy lunch from MacKenzies' Mochas today, but it wouldn't hurt to stop and smell the beef, would it? Besides, I wanted to see what Captain Moe thought of Laura in her faerie costume.

When he saw me, he waved and mouthed that he'd be with me in just a minute. He then flipped the burgers he had grilling, and came over to talk with me.

"I can see that you're busier than a cat covered in peanut butter, so I won't keep you long," I said.

"I always have time for you, Tink," he said, with a warm smile.

"I just wanted to make sure you saw Laura in her faerie costume."

"I did!" He laughed and shook his head. "She's a charmer. I swear, she looks more like me every time I see her."

"Now that you mention it . . ." I laughed. "By

the way, how serious is Camille about retiring and babysitting Laura?"

"Very. This is her first grandchild, you know. She doesn't want to miss an instant of that sweet baby's life."

"I can imagine. And I know Riley doesn't want to, either. I'm so sorry it's getting more difficult to keep Laura at the office."

"Well, as wee ones grow, they get louder and harder to keep entertained. But if Camille does retire to babysit Laura in her home, then she can bring the baby in on days when Riley has no meetings or court appearances."

"That's true." I smiled. "I'd better go, and you'd better flip those burgers. I don't want to leave Ted manning the booth too long! Some of those stitchers and their questions leave him completely baffled."

"I can well imagine," said Captain Moe. "Come back and visit anytime, Tinkerbell!"

As I left Captain Moe's tent, I spotted the juggler. This time, he was tossing around what I hoped were plastic battle-axes. He tilted his head in greeting and just kept on juggling. I smiled, waved, and continued to move toward Blake and Sadie's tent.

I tried to ignore the fortune-tellers' tent as I walked past, but Hecate called to me.

"Hello, seeker! Will you be watching the jousts today?" she asked.

"'Fraid not," I said, slowing but not stopping to talk. "I have customers to attend to."

"Be sure and come back around," she called after me. "I feel we still have much to tell you."

I hadn't walked two yards when a young knight stepped into my path.

"Where is the fire, m'lady?" he asked.

"I have to hurry and get lunch to take back to my booth in the merchants' building," I said. "Please excuse me."

"But won't you first give me your favor to take into battle?" he asked. "I'm in the jousting tournament this afternoon."

"Well, good luck, but I have no favor . . . no scarf, no handkerchief . . . nothing."

"Ah, you're in luck!" A woman with one of her front teeth blacked out muscled in front of the knight. "I happen to sell ladies' favors—hair ribbons, scarves, handkerchiefs—starting at a mere dollar. Won't you please buy a favor for the lad to take into the joust? He might never return, you know."

"Yeah, okay." I opened my purse and gave the woman a dollar.

The knight grabbed my hand and bowed on one knee. "Thank you, kind lady. Know that Sir Reginald carries your favor into battle with honor."

"Thanks," I said. "And good luck. Now I must be on my way."

I finally made it to the MacKenzies' Mochas tent.

"Is everything okay?" Sadie asked. "You look wild-eyed."

"You wouldn't believe the obstacles I had to

overcome to get here," I said. "Hecate the Queen of the Witches tried to get me to have my fortune told *again*; I passed a juggler throwing battle-axes around; and then I was delayed by a knight begging favors."

Sadie's brown eyes widened. "He what?"

I shook my head. "Not *those* kinds of favors."

"How do you know what kind of favors I'm thinking of?"

"By the look on your face," I said. "He was asking for a handkerchief to take into battle."

She frowned. "To what? Serve as a bandage? A handkerchief wouldn't do much good."

I smiled. "No. It was a chivalry thing. Knights took their ladies' favors into battle to honor them with their fight or something. It was supposed to be romantic. Of course, that was then and this is now. When I told Sir Reginald that I didn't have a favor, a shopkeeper stepped out and offered to sell me one."

"You're kidding! I hope you told her to bugger off! They sound like extortionists."

"I gave her a dollar for the cheapest thing she had," I said. "I figured it was quicker to give them a dollar than to debate it. I probably got off easier than some people."

"Probably," she said. "But I'd have told them both to bugger off."

I laughed. "Where did you get that expression?"

"One of my customers said it to another yesterday." She grinned. "I liked it and have incorporated it into my vocabulary."

"I can see that."

"What can I get you?" she asked. "Or did you just come by to say hi?"

"I came for chicken salad croissants," I said. "Two . . . and five bottles of water."

"Five?" She raised her brows. "Are you getting dehydrated in that little building or what?"

"Ted got Angus a collapsible water bowl today on the way here," I said. "So I'm taking the extra water to Angus. Isn't that the sweetest thing—that Ted would care so much about Angus?"

"Yes, it is. But then again, who doesn't love Angus?"

"I don't think Ted's mom is all that wild about him," I said. "But I believe he's growing on her."

Sadie got the chicken salad out of a large cooler and put some on two croissants. I love Sadie's chicken salad—in addition to all the usual ingredients, it has pecans and white seedless grapes.

After she bagged up my order, I paid her and told her I'd talk with her later.

"If anyone bothers you, tell them to bugger off!" she called.

I smiled and shook my head. I hoped she didn't learn any more colorful phrases.

When I returned to the booth with the bag, Ted quickly stood and took it from me.

"This is heavy," he said. "I should've gone and got the water myself. I'm sorry."

"I'm quite capable of carrying a heavy bag. I work out with weights, remember?"

"Oh, that's right." He gave an exaggerated nod. "I do recall seeing those glittery purple two-pound dumbbells in your office."

"And I work out with them every other day . . . or so," I said. "Where's Angus's bowl?"

Angus had leapt to his feet the instant I arrived, but it wasn't water he was interested in. He could smell those croissants. He held his nose aloft and sniffed.

"We'll save you a bite," I promised him. "Now sit down and have a drink of water."

Ted set up the bowl and poured one bottle of the water into it. Angus lapped it greedily. He was thirstier than I'd realized. I was glad I'd gotten the extra bottles.

I took the croissants from the bag and put them on the table. I had a bottle of hand sanitizer in my purse, and I insisted that we both use it before we began eating.

"After all, we've both been handling money today—I mean, I hope you have, too. Did you have sales while I was gone?" I asked.

"Yes, I had sales," he said. "I also had a phone call."

"Should I be worried?" I asked. "It wasn't your mom asking us to come get Clover, was it?"

"No. It was Manu. He and Reggie would like for us to come to dinner this evening. Do you want to go?"

"Sure," I said. "That'll be great . . . unless you

don't want to go. Then I'm too tired or something."

"Thank you for your thoughtfulness." He poured the sanitizer into his palm and rubbed his hands together. "I think what this dinner is really about, though, is Clara's murder case. I got the impression Manu wanted to talk with me about it."

"And he can't at work because you're not on the case," I said.

"Exactly. So, yeah, I'd like to go."

"Then that's settled. We'll go." I sanitized my hands and opened the small box containing my croissant. "This is delicious. I didn't realize how hungry I was."

Angus inched closer to me, and I pinched off a piece of the croissant for him.

"What time are we supposed to be there?" I asked Ted.

"I don't know. I told them I'd have to talk with you before accepting. I'll call Manu back after we eat." He, too, took a bite and then gave Angus a bite. "I'd like to take in that jousting competition later this afternoon."

"By all means," I said. "Be sure to root for Sir Reginald. He's taking my favor into battle."

"Oh, is he, now?"

"He is. I think the favor is a hankie . . . or it could be a ribbon. It's whatever I could get for a dollar." I explained about the encounter.

"I'll certainly keep my eye out for my competition," he said.

"My darling, you have no competition . . . least of all, Sir Reginald of Tallulah High."

"How about Sir Loin of Beef?" he asked. "Or Sir Osis of Liver? Or Sir Cough of Gus?"

I smothered my laughter because my mouth was full. When I could finally swallow, I said, "All right, I know the first two were vintage Bugs Bunny. But where did you come up with Sir Cough of Gus?"

"Off the top of my head, babe. Sarcophagus? Get it?"

I closed my eyes. "I'm afraid so."

When I opened my eyes, he was staring up at the ceiling in thought.

"Sir Real of Ism? Nah, that doesn't make sense. Sir—"

"It's okay," I interrupted. "I get what you're saying, and no *Sir* could ever take your place."

"I know," he said offhandedly. "Now I'm just trying to come up with cool knight names."

"How about Sir Pepperoni of Pizza?"

He frowned. "Now that's just crazy talk. You've been out in the sun too long."

I huffed and slapped his shoulder.

Angus woofed.

"I can come up with good names, can't I, Sir Angus O'Ruff?"

He woofed again.

"See?" I asked Ted.

"Yes, I see. You might not be in the same league as Chuck Jones, but you're pretty good."

"How do you even know Chuck Jones wrote

the Bugs Bunny cartoon where Bugs went to Camelot?" I asked.

"I don't," Ted said. "But he wrote a bunch of them. How do you know he *didn't* write that one?"

"Touché." I smiled. "Be sure and cheer for Sir Reginald at the joust. I'm anxious to see how my honor fares in this tournament."

When Ted returned from the tournament, he gleefully told me that Sir Reginald's jousting attempt was nothing more than a "dream within a dream," as our pal Will might say.

He took a dramatic stance, feet shoulder width apart, hands out in front of him. "Picture it. Sir Reginald rides onto the field on a magnificent white horse. It holds its head high majestically as Sir Reginald looks around and waves to the spectators. After all, many of them bought him favors to carry into the joust." He gave me a pointed look.

I laughed. I felt I was enjoying Ted's rendition more than I would have appreciated the joust itself.

"Sir Giles, the competitor, rides out on an equally handsome bay. He pays little attention to the onlookers because he appears to be concentrating on the match," Ted continued. "King Duncan gives the signal for the joust to begin. A trumpeter sounds a couple toots, and off they go! Sir Reginald's noble steed races toward the center of the field. Sir Reginald slides off the back of his horse!"

"Oh, no!" I tried not to laugh as I said it, but Ted was laughing really hard—it must have been a funny sight. "Was he hurt?"

"I imagine his ego was bruised," Ted said, wiping the tears from his eyes. "And, unless he padded his pants with all those dollar favors, I'd say his butt was, too!"

At that, I did laugh. Poor Sir Reginald. Maybe my dollar had gone to a good cause after all. Soon I was wiping tears from my eyes, too.

"I'm definitely going to have to freshen my makeup after this," I said. "Will you help me cover everything up so we can go on home?"

"Sure. Are you planning to go by the Stitch?"

"No. I don't want Julie to think I'm checking up on her. I'm sure she's doing a great job." At that, my phone emitted the first few bars of the theme song from the television show *Law & Order*. Riley.

"Hold that thought," I told Ted before answering the call.

"Hey, Marcy," Riley said. "I talked with Mom, and she thinks it's a great idea that she keep working part-time while we hire someone full-time in the office. Give Julie a call and see if she's interested, would you?"

"I'll do it right away," I promised.

After ending the call, I turned to Ted. "On second thought, I need to run by the shop and talk with Julie about working for Riley."

"Okay. I'll take Angus home and feed him so that'll be one less thing you'll have to do when you get there."

"Thank you," I said. "But let's all leave here together, all right?"

"Sure, babe."

I know it was crazy, but there *could* potentially still be a killer in our midst. I didn't want to take any chances.

Chapter Sixteen

When I went into the shop, Julie was dusting the shelves, and Amber was sitting on the sofa facing the window playing a game on her phone.

Amber jumped up when she saw me come in. "Marcy! Hi! Cool outfit! You look great!"

I smiled. I'd forgotten how exciting everything was when you were a teenager.

"Thank you, Amber. To tell you the truth, though, I envy you your jeans and T-shirt right now." I put my thumb through the armhole of the vest and held it out slightly. "This thing got so hot today!"

"I can imagine," said Julie. "Did you do well?"

"I did. Business was fairly steady all day." I then entertained them both with the story of Sir Reginald and how my "honor" bit the dust when the knight came out from under his horse. "Ted said he hoped my *favor* and any others Sir Reginald had managed to obtain had been used to pad his breeches!"

We all had a good laugh about that, Amber especially.

When Amber stopped laughing, she asked, "Where's Angus?"

"He spent much of the afternoon at the festival with Ted and me, and then Ted took him on home," I said. "The poor baby is exhausted."

"Angus or Ted?" Julie asked.

I laughed. "I was talking about Angus, but I'd say they both are. The reason I stopped by is to ask if you'd be interested in working for Riley Kendall."

Julie's eyes widened. "I'd love it. What would I be doing?"

"Riley—she's the pretty lawyer that comes to some of the classes, right?" Amber asked, flipping her long, honey-colored hair back.

"Yes," I answered.

Julie gave her daughter a sharp look to warn her not to interrupt.

"Camille, Riley's mom, is her administrative assistant," I explained. "They've been keeping the baby at the office, but as Laura grows, it's getting harder and harder for the women to get any work done. Camille is going to leave—or at least only work part-time—so she can keep Laura at home."

"So she's looking for a secretary?" Julie asked.

"From what I gather, Camille is like a receptionist, secretary, and paralegal all rolled into one," I said.

"Goodness . . . do you think I could do that?" Julie raised her hand to her mouth.

"Don't you dare bite your nails, Mom," said Amber. "And why couldn't you do it? You did practically everything at that stupid bank, and they didn't even appreciate you for it."

I smiled as Julie lowered her hand. It was cute to see the mom and the daughter switch places. "I'm with Amber. I know you can do it. Why don't you give Riley a call at her office first thing Monday morning?" I wrote Riley's office number on a small slip of paper and handed it to Julie.

"Okay," she said with a smile.

"Yay! We have something to celebrate this evening!" cried Amber.

"Don't be too hasty. I don't have the job yet," said Julie.

"But you have an interview. That's good enough for me. Can we get pizza on the way home?"

"We can get pizza." Julie shook her head at me. "Like, I *need* pizza."

"Of course you do. We all need pizza every now and then. And you're celebrating." I winked at Amber. "If the two of you see a disheveled knight walking along the road with dirty pants . . . speed up!"

They both laughed.

"Yeah," said Amber. "I wouldn't want him charging us a dollar for the privilege of giving him a ride."

"Before I go, did anything odd happen today?" I asked Julie, slightly inclining my head in the direction of Clara's shop.

"Fewer gawkers than yesterday, so that was good. I hope all that will end soon," said Julie. "One of the customers mentioned that Clara's funeral service is being held Tuesday morning."

"I wonder if Nellie plans on taking over her booth after her sister's funeral," I said. "For the past two days, festival volunteers have been overseeing it."

"Well, I don't mean to be hateful, but I imagine the longer Nellie stays away, the better for you," Julie said. "She's unjustly mistreated you ever since you've been here, and I'm afraid she'd be horrible to you if she had to occupy a space next to you all day."

"Actually, I don't see the person in her booth throughout the day other than to say hello and good-bye," I said. "I did talk with somebody calling herself Sister Mary Alice yesterday when I shopped in Nellie's booth."

"You actually *shopped* at her booth?" Amber asked. "You bought stuff from somebody who treats you like dirt? Girl, you need a backbone implant as much as Mom does!"

"Amber!" Julie's eyes and mouth both opened wide.

I laughed. "That's all right, Julie. She's right. I've tried my best to make Nellie like me these past few months because I absolutely *hate* it when someone doesn't. But the reason I bought some things from her booth was because, one, she had some really great stuff, and, two, I felt bad because

Clara had died, and I wanted to help somehow. I know I can't take food or send flowers, so I bought a few things."

"That wasn't a lack of backbone," Julie said, with a firm look at her daughter. "That was compassion and caring."

"And class," said Amber.

"Thanks, guys," I said. "I have to run, though. Ted and I are having dinner with Reggie and Manu this evening, and I need to go home and get changed."

"Have fun," said Julie. "And thank you so much for letting me know about Riley."

"She's looking forward to talking with you," I said.

When I got out to the Jeep, I called Riley and left her a voice mail telling her that Julie was interested in the job and that I'd told her to call the office first thing Monday morning.

The Singh home had been decorated with an eclectic blend of Indian and coastal decor. It sounds strange, but it was beautiful. The living room walls were painted a soft cream, and the floor was a dark hardwood. Covering most of the floor was an Indian rug containing shades of brown, blue, beige, and copper. A light blue sofa matched the color in the rug and was flanked by rattan rockers with blue-and-copper-striped cushions. An elaborate painting replicating the ceiling of the Taj Mahal hung on the wall directly across from the door.

Since we hadn't had time to stop anywhere to

get a hostess gift, I'd brought Reggie one of the bottles of essential oils I'd bought from Nellie's booth at the festival. I'd taken the small apothecary bottle of sandalwood oil, wrapped it in white tissue paper, and tied it with a green ribbon. I gave the bottle to Reggie as we walked in.

"I'm so glad you could come," she said. "Manu just put steaks on the grill. They're thick, so we'll have plenty of time to talk."

Manu joined us in the living room. "Hey, folks! Marcy, you look lovely. I half expected you to be wearing a Renaissance Faire costume."

"No," I said with a laugh. "I was happy to change out of that thing."

Reggie opened the gift and uncorked the apothecary bottle. "Oh, this smells amazing." She held it out to Manu.

He sniffed, cautiously at first, and then more willingly. "That does smell good."

"Don't sound so surprised," said his wife. "Do you think Marcy has bad taste?"

"Well, she *is* involved with Ted," he said.

"Ow!" Ted put his hand over his heart as if he'd been shot. "That was brutal."

"You know he's only joking," Reggie said. "He's in a mood this evening." She eyed her husband. "You haven't been in the wine already, have you?"

"No, I have not. You women are always suspicious," he said. "Speaking of wine, may I get you two something to drink? Wine, tea, water, soda?"

"I'd love some water," I said.

"I don't need anything right now," Ted said.

Reggie said she'd get the water, and Manu invited Ted out onto the patio to help with the steaks.

I went on into the living room and sat on one of the rattan rockers. When Reggie brought in our glasses of water, she handed me mine and sat on the sofa, curling her legs up under her.

"I suppose you already know that *helping with the steaks* was code for *talk about the murder of Nellie Davis's sister*," she said.

"I figured. Any leads?"

"Not that I'm aware of." She pushed her wire-rimmed glasses back up on her nose. "Manu has interviewed so many people. He's really missing having Ted on this case."

"Ted's missing being on the case," I said. "I think it's crazy that Nellie had him kicked off for merely talking with Clara."

"So do I. But apparently everyone who's ever talked with Clara is a suspect in her murder . . . at least, it seems that way. Manu is getting home late every night exhausted from talking with Clara's siblings, children, stepchildren, neighbors. . . ." She sighed. "Thursday night it was the people from the festival. Yesterday he spent the day talking with festival folks and the evening talking with others who knew Clara."

"What's Nellie saying?" I asked. "I know you don't know much of the inside information, but one of the merchants told me she saw Nellie and Clara arguing before Nellie left for food."

"Nellie denied arguing with her sister that day," said Reggie. "I only know that because Manu was aggravated about it. He said that more than one person had reported the two of them arguing but that Nellie denied it. If she won't be honest with him about that—even if she'd said, 'We weren't arguing; that's just how we talked with each other'—then he can't trust anything she says."

"Does Manu feel that Nellie is a suspect, then?" I asked.

"As both our men are fond of saying . . ."

"Everyone's a suspect." We said it in unison and then laughed.

"I don't think he really believes Nellie killed Clara, though," Reggie said. "I'm sorry you're the one who found Clara, by the way. Are you doing all right?"

"I keep wondering if there was something more I could have done, but everyone assures me there wasn't. Apparently, she was dead when I got there," I said. "And there are so many people in costume at the festival. Even on Thursday, people were in costume, and the Faire didn't even officially start until Friday. It would have been so easy for someone to slip in, kill Clara, and then discard their costume and escape."

"Manu hasn't said anything about finding any discarded costumes . . . but, of course, the killer could have ditched the costume off-site."

"That would've been the smarter thing to do."

I instantly thought of the Crow. "Let's talk about something more pleasant. How are things going at the library?"

"Traffic has been a bit slow since the Ren Faire started," she said. "Before that, patrons were checking out books on the Renaissance, the history of the English monarchy, pirates, and popular Renaissance festivals like crazy."

"I know what you mean. I can hardly keep black floss in stock due to the popularity of blackwork during the period."

"Maybe you and the Ren Faire will bring about a revival of blackwork in Tallulah Falls." She smiled. "I prefer my *chikankari*, but blackwork is beautiful, too."

Manu called that the steaks were ready, and Reggie and I went into the dining room.

On the way home, I leaned back in my seat and took Ted's hand. "That was fun."

"It was," he said. "I enjoyed it."

"Are you gonna tell me what you and Manu talked about out on the patio?"

He chuckled. "You gonna tell me what you and Reggie talked about in the living room?"

"I'll bet they're the same," I said. "Clara's murder."

"Ding, ding, ding! Give the lady a prize."

"I love prizes. What did I win?"

"How about an all-expense-paid trip to Merry Olde Tallulah Falls?" he asked.

I groaned. "Again?"

"So you're not enjoying the Ren Faire?"

"I am. . . . I would have enjoyed it more had Clara not been killed and if I wasn't looking for murder suspects around every corner." I sighed. "Reggie talked as if Manu doesn't have any really solid leads."

"He doesn't," Ted said. "He confirmed what Paul told us about Clara being lenient with her dead husband's funds with her own children but stingy with his. That certainly didn't endear her to her stepchildren."

"Now that Clara's dead, do the stepchildren inherit everything?" I asked.

"More than likely."

"And Manu's leaning toward one of them as the murderer?"

Ted inclined his head. "You know I can't go into specifics, but the stepchildren have alibis, and Clara had more enemies than you can imagine."

"Oh, I can imagine it, all right," I said. "I'd never met a more abrasive person in my life . . . with the possible exception of Nellie. I wish Manu could put you back on the case."

"So do I, Inch-High. But, *unofficially*, I'm doing what I can."

"Well, unofficially, so am I."

Chapter Seventeen

On Sunday morning, I wore my blue jacquard skirt, off-white peasant blouse, and black corset vest. The worst thing about these costumes was that I had to wear flats. I couldn't even wear wedge espadrilles with a slight platform. I had to try to look authentic.

As I walked from the parking lot to the merchants' building, a woman fell into step beside me. I glanced over and saw that it was the witch that reminded me of Kathy Bates, the numerologist.

"Good morning," I said. "How are you?"

"I'm fine, sweetie. How are you?"

"I'm doing well. Are you having fun at the festival?"

"Ah, it's a job, I suppose." She gave a rueful little smile. "I hope we didn't scare you overmuch when we told your fortune the other day."

"I'll admit it *did* make me nervous," I said. "So it was all make-believe?"

"Now, I didn't say that," she said, her smile

quickly fading. "We discussed . . . your situation . . . after you left."

I stopped walking, and so did she. We stepped over out of the way of the rest of the pedestrian traffic.

"What do you mean, you discussed my situation?" I asked.

"You're involving yourself in something that doesn't concern you," said faux Kathy. "You're asking questions, trying to help the police do their job, hoping someone saw the killer. We feel that if you don't back off, you're going to anger the murderer . . . and that he might retaliate against you."

"Why do you say that?"

She shrugged. "I'm just telling you what we saw . . . what we felt. We didn't intend to scare you, but I do believe that you should be warned. Leave the sleuthing to the detectives. Try to stay off this person's radar."

"Do you *know* something?" I asked.

"I don't *know* anything, sweetie. It's what I *feel*." She patted my shoulder. "Stay safe. I must get to the tent before the rest of the crew thinks I've gotten lost." She started walking away but turned back toward me. "Seriously . . . stay safe."

I let out a deep breath and got back onto the path to the gate. Now I didn't even have to pay to be frightened by Hecate and the three witches. Could there be something to what faux Kathy had said? Of course, I suppose it could just be common sense. Anyone who finds a dead body might want to lie low so the killer wouldn't think she saw something . . . but this felt like more than that. Whenever I came into contact with the fortune-tellers, they were warning me to be careful. They were starting to make me paranoid.

I strode into the merchants' building and over to my booth. I stopped. A wail rose in my throat, but I didn't make a sound. I covered my mouth with both hands. I felt rooted to the floor and couldn't move.

This can't be real. This can't be real.

"Good—" Sister Mary Alice's greeting died when she noticed the expression on my face. "Child, what's the matter?" She turned to look at my booth and gasped.

It had been trashed. The poet's shirts that I'd painstakingly embellished with blackwork had been cut into strips and crumpled onto the floor. Likewise, the collars and ruffs had been ruined. The bins of thread had been tossed, the shelves thrown on the floor, and the clothing rack overturned near the pile of demolished shirts.

Sister Mary Alice put her arm around me. "Oh, dear . . . I'm so terribly sorry. Is there anything I can do?"

"Is mine the only one?" My voice came out broken and higher-pitched than usual.

"I don't know. I'll go see." Sister Mary Alice took off. She seemed to be happy to make her escape from the awkward situation.

I turned and surveyed the expansive room. No one else was looking at his or her booth in horror. I must be the only one.

I went into the booth, pulled out a folding chair, and called Ted.

"Hey, babe! What's up?"

"Somebody destroyed my booth," I said.

"Sit tight and don't touch anything," he said. "I'll grab a crime scene tech and be right there."

"Thanks."

"Are you all right?" he asked.

"Physically, yes."

"I'm on my way," he said.

Within minutes, Ted, Manu, two crime scene technicians, and a uniformed officer were standing in front of my booth.

"Are you sure you're okay?" Ted asked.

"Yeah. While the crime scene guys do their thing, I'm going over to the shop and get a few things to replenish what I lost here," I said.

"We'll take photos," Manu said. "You can turn all this in on your insurance."

"Thanks," I told him.

"Do you need me to drive you?" Ted asked.

"No," I said. "I'd rather you stay here and find out who did this to me."

I didn't cry when I'd first discovered my destroyed booth. Nor did I cry as I drove the Jeep to the Seven-Year Stitch. Maybe I was in shock.

I parked in the alley and went in through the back door. I didn't want anyone to see my vehicle here and think the shop was open for business. Of course, it wasn't likely I'd be selling anything at the Ren Faire today.

I went to the counter and got a large Seven-Year Stitch bag.

"Hi, Jill. Yes, I know it's unusual for me to be here on a Sunday, but I had to come by and get some things to restock my booth." Sometimes the mannequin and I had imaginary conversations. It was probably therapeutic . . . or something.

Business is going that well? Woot!

"No, I'm afraid business is *not* going that well. Someone wrecked my booth, Jill! And I don't mean they just knocked my shelves down and turned my table over. They *shredded* those shirts I'd embellished with blackwork—cut them to bits! They destroyed the cuffs and collars, too!"

I sank onto the stool in front of the cash register and dropped my head into my hands. "I worked so hard! How could anyone be so cruel?"

At the gentle touch of a hand on my shoulder, I screamed and hopped off the stool. Personifying one's mannequin did have its drawbacks.

"I'm sorry!" cried Sadie. "It's only me!"

There were tears coursing down her cheeks, and that made my own tears flow even faster. We hugged and sobbed until we were all cried out.

I got some tissues, and we both wiped our eyes.

"I'll have to redo my makeup before I go back to the festival," I said.

"I'll have to touch mine up, too," said Sadie. "I'd hate to go back to MacKenzies' Mochas looking like a punk rocker."

"How did you know I was here? Did you see me drive up?"

She shook her head. "Blake called me. He heard about your booth getting ruined, left the manager who's there with him today in charge, and went to see about you. Ted told him you'd come here to get some things to restock your booth."

"I held it together until I got here and started thinking about all the hours I spent in the sit-and-stitch square making those shirts, collars, and cuffs. Those are things that can't be replaced . . . possible income from the festival that I've just lost."

"Your ability to hold it together explains Ted letting you drive here on your own." She gave me a rueful smile. "I remember back in college you could always keep your emotions in check until you were alone. I admired your strength."

"Ha! I admired *your* strength. It seemed like nothing ever got to you, and everything upset me. I might not have let it show all the time, but it did."

"Do Ted and Manu have any idea who did this?" Sadie asked.

"I don't know. My first thought, naturally, was Nellie. But could she really be that mean and vindictive?"

"I hope not." Sadie looked around the shop. "So, what do we need to put in that bag you've been holding on to since before I got here?"

Once Sadie and I gathered floss, pattern kits, canvas, hoops, frames, and pattern books into two bags, I returned to the Ren Faire and she returned to the coffeehouse. At one point, I'd almost thrown up my hands and said, "What's the use?" But Sadie reminded me that I was not going to be defeated by the slug who thought he or she could run me off from the Faire.

As I carried my bags up the hill, Ted rushed to meet me. He must've been keeping watch on the hilltop.

"How are you?" he asked, taking the bags from my hands. "I should've gone with you to the shop. I'm sorry I was so insensitive, but I was just so focused on finding out who did this."

I was glad I'd repaired my makeup and didn't look too much the worse for wear. "I'm fine. My guess is that you've been talking with Blake."

He nodded. "You seemed fine. I should've realized you were just holding it together until you got by yourself."

"Well, he sent Sadie to check on me, and we had a good cry," I said. "Yes, I'm terribly hurt about all the things I'd made to sell. Those can't be replaced. But I'll survive."

"I'm so sorry."

"Stop. You'll make me feel sorry for myself again, and I'm not going to do that." I smiled. "I won't be driven away from this festival. I'll still promote the Stitch, my classes, and my services, and this will all work out fine."

"I love you," he said.

"The ultimate balm to my soul," I said.

"Well, there might be other balms waiting for you at your booth."

I didn't understand what he meant until I arrived. Blake, Todd, Sister Mary Alice, and other merchants I hadn't even met were there. They'd thrown away everything that had been destroyed and tidied up the rest. The booth looked pretty bare, but it was neat. Somehow, the periwinkle tablecloth had managed to survive the destroyer's rage, and it was draping the table. I saw that some of the other merchants had even brought presents and lined them up neatly on the table.

Tears pricked my eyes. "Oh, my goodness! Thank you! I don't know what to say."

"You just did, dear," said Sister Mary Alice. "We were happy to help. This could've happened to any of our booths."

I gestured to the boxes and bags adorning the table. "What's all this?"

"Just something to let you know we care," said a soft-spoken woman with chestnut-colored hair and kind eyes. "I'm Cathy from the Noble Pig Vineyard and Winery in McMinnville. I brought you some streusel-topped pumpkin chocolate chip muffins and a bottle of our Pinot Gris."

"Thank you," I said.

"Cathy and her husband, Henry, and I go way back," said Todd. "I carry Noble Pig wines at the Brew Crew."

"It's very nice to meet you," I told Cathy. "And I certainly appreciate your generosity."

"You're welcome," said Cathy. "I wish there was more I could do."

"Again, thank you, everybody," I said. "You've been great."

I felt rather embarrassed by the gifts. But I really did value the other merchants' kindness.

The small crowd quickly disbursed, leaving me alone with Ted, Todd, and Blake—my three musketeers.

"Thanks, guys, for cleaning up the booth," I told them. "It would have broken my heart to have had to scoop up those scraps of shirts and cuffs and throw them away."

"We had plenty of help," said Todd.

"We couldn't salvage much," said Blake, "but there was one shirt the scumbag missed."

My eyes widened, and I gasped. "Really?"

"Really," he said. "I folded it as best as I could and put it on the table. It needs to be washed, but it's fine."

"That's wonderful!" I cried. I went over to the table, found the shirt, and hugged it to my chest.

"We're sorry there wasn't more to save," Ted said.

"I just want you to catch whoever did this," I said.

"Before we cleaned up, we took several pictures for your insurance reports," he said. "I know it won't compensate you for all the hard work you've put in, but at least it's something."

"I need to get back to my tent," Blake said. "My manager probably thinks I've deserted him."

"Me, too," said Todd.

"I really do appreciate you guys," I said.

"We know." Todd winked.

"Were any of the hangers usable?" I asked Ted as Blake and Todd walked away.

"A few were," he said.

"Good. I'm going to hang this one shirt up for display, and if anyone wants a blackwork-embellished shirt, they can order it." I lifted my chin and smiled. "I will not be defeated."

"That's my girl," he said. "Manu has instructed the force that one additional on-duty officer will be assigned to this building at all times during the remainder of the Faire. I mean, we've had people here all along and so has the festival, but this incident on top of Clara's murder emphasizes the importance for more security."

I knew what Ted wasn't saying. They were afraid that whoever had killed Clara hadn't moved on from the Faire. They were worried that her murder wasn't an isolated incident.

"I'll say. What do you and Manu think? Was I targeted because I'm the one who found Clara's body?" I asked. "Or do you think it's something else?" I hesitated. "Do you think it was Nellie?"

"Frankly, no," Ted said. "She may have the spitefulness to do this, but I think she lacks the courage. She'd be too afraid of getting caught."

"That's true. I hadn't thought of that."

"Still, Manu has gone to her house to talk with her about it. We're not ruling anyone out." He gazed warily around the merchants' building. "Somebody had to have seen something."

"And, yet, like with Clara's murder, nobody's talking?" I asked.

"Nobody's talking."

Chapter Eighteen

On Monday morning, even though I was wearing my green noblewoman gown, I went to the Seven-Year Stitch rather than the Ren Faire so that Julie could go to her interview with Riley. Julie had felt terribly worried that she was leaving me in the lurch, but I'd told her I'd be happy to open the shop and that she could come in after her interview and tell me all about it.

I was happy to help Julie, but the truth of the matter was I wasn't looking forward to returning to the Ren Faire. After what I'd found yesterday, I couldn't imagine that whatever awaited me today could be worse. And yet dread gnawed at my stomach.

One of the deputies processing the crime scene had found scratches on the lock at the rear entrance of the merchants' building, indicating that the lock had been picked. From that, the police consensus was the vandal had entered the building between the time the festival closed Saturday and the time it reopened on Sunday. That, of course,

explained how no one had seen anything or anyone suspicious. It also confirmed that the vandal's
attack had been leveled directly at me. No one
else's booth had been disturbed, and no one had
reported any missing merchandise.

Manu had assigned me a "security detail." My
security detail was currently sitting in his patrol
car across the street.

Naturally, Ted felt that I should have a team of
mixed-martial-arts fighters protecting me, but
since the Tallulah Falls Police Department didn't
even have a SWAT team on the payroll, the MMAs
were out of the question. Ted had been joking
when he mentioned the highly trained group—I
think—but he was checking in with me often
enough to make sure I was safe but not so much
that I completely freaked out because he and the
department thought my life was in danger.

I was tidying up the shop—dusting shelves and
restocking bins—when Vera and Paul came in.
Vera hurried over and crushed me to her in a
nearly suffocating hug.

"Oh, my poor darling, we just heard! Who is
the flea on a rat's butt responsible for demolishing
your booth? I want first crack at 'im!"

I gently extricated myself from her embrace before the deputy across the street barged into the
Stitch thinking Vera was trying to smother me.

"Let's sit down, and I'll tell you all about it," I
said. "Would either of you like some coffee?"

They both declined the offer, and we sat down
in the sit-and-stitch square.

"There isn't much to tell about what happened to my booth," I said. "Almost all my handmade items were destroyed, and everything else was broken or trampled on."

"Do the police know who did it?" Paul asked.

"Was it Nellie Davis?" Vera demanded.

"I don't believe it was Nellie," I said. "While she doesn't have a verifiable alibi—she said she was home alone—I can't imagine her going out in the middle of the night or the wee hours of the morning, climbing the fence at the fairgrounds, and picking the lock to the back door of the merchants' building."

"No, I can't see her doing that, either," said Vera. "But who else has it in for you?"

"The police seem to think that the person who killed Clara is trying to get me to leave the Faire," I said. "Maybe this person believes that I know or saw something. I certainly wish I had. I wouldn't be in this predicament right now if that were the case."

"They think your life is in danger?" Vera asked.

I nodded toward the window. She and Paul both turned to look out at the patrol car on the other side of the street.

"It's just a precaution," I said.

"I, for one, am glad they aren't taking any chances," Paul said. "You never know who could be out there. Take Marcus West, for example."

"He's the one whose building burned last week, isn't he?" Vera asked.

"Right. His building burned, along with all his files, and he hasn't been seen since," said Paul.

I didn't want to mention that Ted was investigating the cold case involving the murder of this man's partner, but I did want to know whatever information Paul could give me. "I heard something about Mr. West's business partner dying a few years ago."

"That's right. His name was Joe Palmer." Paul leaned forward, putting his forearms on his knees. "Joe was murdered, and it was never determined whether his killer was his wife, his business partner, or someone else. The wife, Lacey, got a heck of an insurance payout, but the partner inherited a very lucrative business. As for why someone else would've murdered him, the police were unable to find a motive."

"So now that Marcus West has gone missing, you think he's the one who killed his partner?" I asked.

"It looks that way. You see, officers had started asking questions again," said Paul. "I have to wonder if West didn't just get scared, burn any evidence that tied him to Palmer's murder, and skedaddle."

"On the other hand, West could've been killed," said Vera. "You said he'd gone missing. You didn't say it appeared he'd gone on the lam."

Paul straightened and patted Vera's knee. "Listen to my gal here. Does she have a knack for investigative journalism or what?" He chuckled. "West *could* be dead. His bank accounts haven't been touched in the days leading up to or after the fire, and his credit cards haven't been used."

"If Mr. West is dead, then suspicion falls back onto the wife or the unknown suspect," I said.

"Or the unknown *subject*—the *unsub*—as they say on *Criminal Minds*," Vera pointed out.

"Right. So what's your opinion?" I asked Paul. "Who do you think killed Joe Palmer?"

"At this point, I'm leaning toward Marcus West," he said. "If West is innocent—of the murder as well as of setting his business on fire—then where is he?"

"Unless they find Mr. West's body somewhere," Vera added. "And then, I suppose it's anybody's guess."

"There is that," Paul agreed. "I think I'll take you up on that coffee after all, Marcy."

I got up to get the coffee. "Vera, will you have some, too?"

"No, I'm still fine," she said.

As I returned with Paul's coffee, creamer, and sugar, Julie walked through the door. She was beaming. I handed Paul the cup, placed the sugar and creamer packets on the coffee table, and went to give Julie a hug.

"I take it by that smile that everything went well?" I asked.

"I got the job!"

"That's fantastic! When do you start?"

"I'm still going to be able to fill in for you here during the Ren Faire," Julie said. "But after working here, I'll go by Riley's office for some training each day."

"If you need to go ahead and start working, I can

work here during the day, reschedule my classes, and work at the festival in the evenings," I said.

"You can't do that," she said. "Everybody loves that blackwork class . . . and I'm sure they love your other classes, too. Riley said this would be an excellent transitional time for all of us."

"I couldn't help but overhear," Vera said. "You're going to work for Riley Kendall?"

"I am," Julie said. "And while I was there, I even got to meet a client. As a matter of fact, it was the young woman who was here looking for Clara that day."

"Well, that's great," I said. Naturally, I was dying to know what someone who'd been looking for Clara was doing in a law office, but I wouldn't have tempted Julie to break Riley's confidence.

Vera, however, had no such qualms. "When did someone come here looking for Clara? And what was she doing in Riley's office today?"

"She came in here on Saturday," Julie said. "She apparently hadn't realized that Clara had died. And I suppose there are any number of reasons she'd have been in Riley's office."

"That's true," I said. "I go by there as often as I can just to visit. I know you're going to fit in well there."

"Thank you," Julie said.

"What did this girl look like?" Vera asked.

"I'd say she was in her mid- to late twenties, blond hair, average height." Julie shrugged. "Pretty, but not remarkably so . . . your average girl next door, I suppose."

"She could be one of Clara's step-granddaughters," Paul said. "If that's the case, I imagine she retained Riley with regard to Clara's husband's estate."

"That would make sense," I said. "I imagine with Clara gone, there are going to be a lot of people fighting over his money."

I noticed Julie's eyes had widened. She was likely thinking she was going to lose her job before she even got to start it.

"But, again, we don't even know if that's who the girl was or why she was in Riley's office," I said. "Julie is going to make a wonderful administrative assistant. She didn't tell us a thing."

"No, you absolutely did not, Julie," said Paul. "Good show."

"We should be going," Vera said. "Marcy, I'll try to look you up later at the festival."

"Okay. I'll be looking forward to it."

"Good luck with your new job," Paul said to Julie.

"Yes, dear, we wish you well," said Vera. "I'll have to send you a plant once you're settled in."

"Thank you," said Julie.

After Paul and Vera had headed off down the street, Julie turned to me.

"Thank you for helping me with those two," she said. "When Vera started asking questions about the girl who was in here, I didn't know what to say."

"I think you did very well," I said. "They were good practice for you. Be sure and practice *I'm not at liberty to say* and *you'll have to speak with Ms. Kendall about that.* And if the person is brave enough to ask something of Riley that isn't any of their business, then they can simply suffer the consequences."

Julie laughed. "I'd only met Riley in one of your classes, and she was very sweet and laid-back there, but I can see that she takes her job and her clients seriously and that she could get her dander up in a hurry."

"I do hope you'll enjoy working with her," I said. I'd have hated to bring the two of them together only to have it not be a good match.

"I'm sure I will." Julie glanced at the clock. "Do you need to head to the festival?"

"Yeah, I guess I'd better."

She frowned. "Aren't you enjoying it?"

"Not as much as I'd hoped." I told her about the condition of my booth when I'd arrived yesterday morning.

She gasped. "I'm so sorry! Are you okay?"

"Sadie and I had an impromptu pity party-slash-memorial for the wreckage when I came here to get supplies to replenish the booth yesterday. I'm okay now. Sure, it still hurts, and it makes me furious when I think about it, but there's nothing I can do but move forward."

I didn't mention the security detail, but I wondered if someone should keep an eye on Julie and the Seven-Year Stitch while I was gone. If the person who killed Clara hadn't seen me but had only heard that the owner of the Seven-Year Stitch found his victim, then he might not know what I look like and he might think Julie was me. I'd call Ted and get his opinion as soon as I got in the Jeep.

I zoned back in to Julie telling me how sorry she was and how people could be so horrible.

I agreed but then said, "But we're not focusing on bad things today. Only good. You have a new job! Have you told Amber yet?"

"No. I'm going to call her as soon as she gets home from school."

"I'm really happy for you," I said, making another mental note—this time to have the bakery make a congratulatory cake and send it over to Julie.

I gave Julie a quick hug. "I guess I'd better go. Hopefully, I won't have any bad surprises when I get to the Ren Faire."

"I hope not, too."

"Hey, at least *some* good came of it," I said. "The other merchants were really supportive, and some even brought gifts!"

"That was nice," she said. "I'm glad they were there for you."

"Me, too. And don't look so worried. Manu really beefed up security after that."

"He hadn't done that after you found Clara dead?" she asked.

"He had, but he assigned even more officers to the Ren Faire. I'm sure they'll be thrilled when the whole thing is over. They're having to work double shifts now."

"They'll be fine for a few days," she said. "Besides, double shifts mean overtime pay. I was always happy for overtime at the bank . . . as long as it wasn't a full-time thing."

When I went out to the Jeep, I first called the bakery and ordered the cake for Julie. Then I called Ted and expressed my concerns for Julie's safety.

"I believe she'll be fine," he said. "It's broad daylight, with people walking up and down the sidewalk in front of that huge window all day long. Still, I'll make sure extra patrols are made. Did you warn her to call nine-one-one if she notices anything suspicious?"

"No. I didn't want to scare her," I said. "Do you think I should warn her?"

"Everything will most likely be okay," he said. "You were probably right not to mention it. If she's looking for something suspicious, she'll see something spooky everywhere she looks. By the way, how did her talk with Riley go?"

"She got the job!"

"That's great news," he said.

I laughingly told him about her telling Vera, Paul, and me that she'd already met her first client and that it was the young woman who'd come by the Seven-Year Stitch on Saturday looking for Clara.

"Vera immediately started grilling poor Julie. Who was this young woman? Why had she been asking about Clara? Why was she in Riley's office? But Julie did exceptionally well. She didn't give anything away."

"That's good," Ted murmured. "Although now I'm wondering . . . who *was* this young woman? Why had she been in the Stitch asking about Clara, and what was she doing in Riley's office?"

I laughed.

"Actually, I'm serious," he said. "Maybe I should go by Riley's office and—"

"No! You can't! She'll know Julie said something, and it might cost her this job. Please, Ted."

"Okay. I'm not on that case, anyway, remember? Besides, Manu is talking with everyone in Clara's immediate and extended family."

"Thank you," I said. "We'll find whoever is behind this whole mess."

"I know, Inch-High. I have faith in you."

Chapter Nineteen

I parked the Jeep, locked it, and headed up the hill to the gates of the fairgrounds. I wished I'd brought Angus with me, but I knew he'd be much happier in the backyard today.

I showed my merchant badge to the ticket master, and he waved me on through. The Ren Faire was in full swing, especially for a Monday. There were people everywhere.

I suddenly felt the presence of someone beside me. I glanced warily to my right. It was the Crow, his creepy gold mask bent close to my face, his cloak covering his hair and body.

I tried to hurry away from him, but his strides were longer than mine and he easily kept up.

"Leave me alone," I said. "Leave me alone, or I'll scream."

"Please don't," he said. "I have to warn you."

"Warn me about what?"

"I told you before that there was a viper in your midst," he said. "I know that the evil one's work is not yet done. You must get away from this place."

"Are you the one who destroyed my booth?" I demanded.

"Not I."

"But you know who did!"

He inclined his head. "I'm sure I do."

"Then, for goodness' sake, go to the police and tell them what you know! Or at least let me call Ted Nash, so you can talk with him." I took out my cell phone. "You can talk to him right now and remain anonymous."

"He wouldn't believe me," said the Crow. "I must remain in the shadows for now to protect myself from the very menace that's stalking you. Go. Be safe."

"There are a whole bunch of guards hanging around the merchants' building now, and I have every intention of staying," I said. "If you know something, the police will protect you. Trust them . . . *please*."

"The merchants' building might be safe now, but you never know where the viper will strike next." He started walking away.

"Wait!" I called.

I started after him, but a juggler stepped into my path. He was carrying unlit torches, and he held a lighted candle out to me.

"Not right now. I'm in a hurry," I said, trying to see past him to wherever the Crow had gone.

The juggler acted as if he couldn't hear me. He held the candle out again.

I took the candle.

He held out one of the unlit torches. I realized he needed me to light it for him.

I lit the torch and handed the candle back to him. He blew out the small candle flame and then used the lit torch to kindle the others. He smiled and nodded at me before starting to juggle the flaming torches.

"That's wonderful! Thank you!" I said, hurrying away.

As I did so, it dawned on me that the guy did *not* need to be juggling fire in the midst of all these people! He might set the whole Faire aflame! As soon as I found the Crow again, I'd report the juggler to . . . to someone. Maybe Sister Mary Alice was manning Nellie's booth. I could see the stern nun taking the juggler by the ear and making him blow out the torches.

Try as I might, I couldn't find the Crow. He'd lost himself in the crowd, and I had no idea where he'd gone.

Also, as luck would have it, Nellie's booth was being manned not by Sister Mary Alice but by Washerwoman Jan.

"Jan, there's a guy out there juggling flaming torches," I said breathlessly, having raced to Nellie's booth.

"Oh, where? That sounds exciting!"

"He isn't on one of the stages. He's out walking among the crowd."

"I wish I could go see him," she said, eyes sparkling.

"Don't you think that could be dangerous?" I asked. "Since you're on the fairgrounds committee, isn't there someone you could call to ensure that everyone at the Ren Faire is safe from this guy? I mean, what if he drops one of those torches?" I didn't mention that I'd lit the first one for him. *What was I thinking when I did that? Nothing, that's what. I had my mind focused on the Crow.*

She looked down at the floor for a moment, and then looked up brightly. "I know! I'll call and have someone watch the booth for me, and I'll go see to it myself. Thanks for telling me."

"You're welcome." I went over to my own booth. Happily, it was just as I'd left it yesterday afternoon.

I straightened the one blackwork-embellished shirt I had left. It was a little wrinkled and a tad soiled. I think some people who hadn't been to my booth before the . . . incident . . . might have thought that was simply part of the Ren Faire look. I was taking orders based on the shirt, and I'd received a few yesterday. I'd also had several people interested in that particular shirt. I'd told them to come back on the last day of the Faire and that I'd sell it to the first one to ask for it.

I heard a deep, sexy voice behind me say, "Ah, there is my fair Marcella."

I turned, laughing. "Don't you dare call me that." I threw myself into Ted's arms.

"Well, *Marcy* doesn't sound very Renaissance-y." He swept me off my feet in a fierce hug.

"Neither does Ted . . . *Theodore*."

"Yowch! You wound me . . . Marcy." He bent his head for a kiss before setting me back on my feet. "It looks like everything is in order today."

"It is," I said. "Well, as far as the booth goes."

"What's not in order?" he asked.

I lowered my voice and explained to him about the fire juggler.

"Oh, I saw him on the way in and had him extinguish those torches immediately."

I smiled. "Thank you. I'd have felt so guilty if something bad had happened."

He asked the question with one lift of his right eyebrow.

"I lit the first torch," I admitted.

Ted's blue eyes widened. "You what?"

"Okay, in my defense, I was really, really distracted." I went on to tell him about my encounter with the Crow.

"I've had enough of this guy," Ted said. "He knows something, and I'm going to find out what." He took out his cell phone, called Manu, and asked him to alert all officers at the festival to be looking for a man in a black cloak wearing a gold carnival mask with a long, beaky nose.

"If they catch him, let me know. I want to question him." He thanked Manu and ended the call.

"Are you afraid of this guy?" he asked me.

"Yes and no," I said. "I mean, I'm leery of him, but he told me he was hiding out. Do you think the same person who killed Clara might be after him?"

"Either that, or *he's* the person who killed

Clara," Ted said. "If he has nothing to hide, why wouldn't he talk with me like you suggested?"

"I don't know except that he said you wouldn't believe him." I shrugged. "I hope your guys do find him and can question him. Just maybe give him the benefit of the doubt."

He rolled his eyes. "You give *everybody* the benefit of the doubt."

"And you think everybody is a suspect." I grinned. "That's why we're so great together . . . opposites attract."

"Is that it? I thought it was because you were wonderful and I appreciate that fact."

"Well, there is *that*." I kissed him again.

"I stopped in to see Julie before I came here," he said. "I told her that since someone had vandalized your booth here at the festival, we were concerned that someone might try to vandalize the Seven-Year Stitch as well. I said everything would probably be fine but to keep an eye out for anything suspicious."

"Oh, that was really good," I said. "You warned her without putting her in a panic."

He nodded. "She was fired up about the booth. She said if she saw anyone even *thinking* about vandalizing the Stitch, she'd punch him in the nose."

I giggled. "Did she talk with you about her job?"

"Not much. I had to hurry. I can tell she's thrilled about it, though."

"Do you want me to go get us some lunch?" I asked.

"No, I've already taken care of it," he said. "It should be here any minute."

"You ordered in?" I asked.

He smiled. "In a way." He nodded toward the door of the merchants' building. "Ah, here it comes now."

I squealed with delight to see Captain Moe coming toward the booth with two boxes that smelled heavenly. I gave Ted a hug.

"What are you hugging *him* for, Tink? I'm the one with the burgers."

I went around to the front of the table. Captain Moe set the boxes on the table and gave me a bear hug.

"I heard about what happened to you yesterday, and I'm ever so sorry," he said.

"It's all right," I said. "I know you never work on Sundays, and there was nothing you could've done, anyway."

He planted his fists on his hips. "Thank you ever so much!"

"I mean, you've more than made up for it now!" I gestured toward the boxes.

He laughed away my discomfort at saying there was nothing he could have done. "This is the least I can do, wee Tinkerbell. Feed the body and hope it helps to nourish the soul."

"It does," I said.

"It nourishes my soul," said Ted, opening one of the boxes and taking out a cheeseburger. He noticed both Captain Moe and me giving him a quizzical look. "Well, it does!"

Captain Moe kissed my cheek. "I'll leave you two to your lunch. I hope you enjoy it."

"You know we will," I said.

As Captain Moe left, I sat down beside Ted and took my cheeseburger out of the box. First I inhaled the beefy-cheesy scent and appreciated the textures of the bun, the tomato, the onion, the pickles, the lettuce . . . it was a thing of beauty.

Then I took a bite. It was a thing of joy.

"You're right," I told Ted. "That really does nurture the soul."

We ate in silence for a few minutes, and then I told Ted more about Vera and Paul's visit to the shop.

"In addition to them scaring Julie into thinking they might cost her the job with Riley, Paul shared his theories about Marcus West's business burning," I said.

"Oh, did he, now?"

I nodded. "He thinks Mr. West burned his business to the ground to destroy evidence that he killed his partner, Joe Palmer."

"You didn't . . ."

"Of course I didn't. He did mention that Mr. West was missing," I said. "I hadn't read that in the newspaper account of the fire."

"That's because Manu asked Paul to keep it out of the paper for now. We have an APB out on West that includes the hospitals and morgues."

"Do you think Mr. West killed his partner?" I asked.

"I'm not sure," Ted said. "With him missing, it

could just as likely be that whoever killed his partner has eliminated West, too."

I glanced up and saw Vera and Paul approaching. "Speak of the devils . . ."

"Were you talking about us?" Vera asked with a smile.

"We were," I said. "I was just telling Ted Paul's theory about Mr. West setting fire to his business to destroy evidence."

Paul leaned forward and spoke in a stage whisper. "The case just got curiouser and curiouser. After Julie mentioned seeing the young woman in Riley's office, I got to thinking it might be Clara's stepdaughter's child. So Vee and I went to the funeral home and got a list of Clara's relatives."

Vera nodded.

"If the woman Julie saw *was* in fact Clara's step-granddaughter, then she very well might have been Erin Palmer," Paul said.

Ted pushed back his chair. "Wait a second. . . . Joe Palmer's widow is related to Clara?"

"By marriage," Paul said.

"I've got to make sure Manu knows about this," Ted said. "Will you all excuse me?"

"Of course," Vera said. "We're happy we could help."

Ted gathered our trash, gave me a quick kiss, and left.

"What do you think this means?" I asked.

"Oh, I have no idea," said Vera. "But I'm sure it means something."

Chapter Twenty

Before Paul and Vera left, Julie called.

"You'll never guess what just happened," she teased. "The bakery delivered the prettiest cake."

"Is that so?"

She chuckled. "Thank you so much. Will you and Ted please come by the shop this afternoon and share it with me?"

"I'll have to check with Ted to see what he's doing, but I'd love to," I said. "Hey, why don't we make a real celebration of it? Paul and Vera are here, and I can invite them. Of course, you'll want Amber to be there, and one of us could call and invite Riley, Camille, Keith, and Laura. It would be a wonderful way for you to get to know them a little better."

"That's a great idea! Are you sure you don't mind?"

"Mind?" I asked. "Any excuse for a party!"

"Thank you," she said. "I'll call Riley and invite her and her family."

"Cool. I'll be there around five," I said.

After ending the call, I turned to Vera and Paul.

"Would you like—," I began.

"I heard enough of your end of the conversation to know we're having a party to celebrate Julie's new job, and we are most definitely there," Vera interrupted. "Aren't we, darling?"

"We're there!" Paul echoed.

"I'll bring a bottle of champagne," Vera said. "We'd better be off. See you at the party."

After Vera and Paul left, I called Ted to ask him to come to the party.

"Sure," he said. "It's sweet of you to do that for her."

"Well, I know she's been really stressed since being laid off at the bank, and I think working with Riley will be such a good fit for her," I said.

"I'm following up a couple of leads on the cold case—which, thanks to Paul, you know more about than you should—but I'll be there as close to five o'clock as I can."

"You know I won't break your confidence on the cold case," I said. "I think Paul just had lots of information from five years ago, and then the fire last week caused him to start looking into it again. I'm not even sure he knew the murder of Joe Palmer was being reinvestigated until then."

"Babe, I'm not blaming you," he said. "In fact, I'm kinda glad it's out there and I don't have to be as careful what I say about it anymore."

"Did Manu know about Clara's connection to the Palmer family?"

"He did. He told me he was working on it but hadn't gotten that far interviewing the extended family members." Ted gave a bark of laughter. "He sourly reminded me that he had to take his head detective off the case. I told him he'd better just be glad *he* didn't speak to Clara on Thursday, or no one would be able to investigate."

"I think he should tell Nellie that you aren't a suspect in her sister's murder and that he's putting you back on the case."

"Yeah, well, I help out where I can . . . unofficially."

"Did anyone see the Crow?" I asked.

"Not yet, but our guys are still keeping a watch out for him. If you see him, stay in a crowded area and call me immediately. I don't want you dealing with this man alone. He could be dangerous."

"Yes, sir."

"Sorry," he said. "I don't mean to tell you what to do. I only want to keep you safe."

"I know. I love you."

"I love you more than you can imagine. And now Manu is looking at me weird, so I'll see you at five."

I grinned. "See you then."

I was explaining to two customers how blackwork was popular during the Renaissance when a court jester dressed in bright yellow with a yellow, green, and orange jester's hat with bells on the tips cartwheeled across the floor in front of the booth. The two women turned to stare at him.

His hat had fallen off his head during the cartwheel, but he picked it up, swept it in a wide arc, and bowed to us.

"Huzzah, fair ladies! Huzzah!"

The women looked at each other and then at the jester.

"Huzzah!" they said in unison.

"I am here with tidings from the king," said the jester. "He wishes me to invite all the merchants and villagers to the arrival of Her Royal Majesty Princess Fiona."

"I didn't realize King Duncan had a daughter," I said.

"Nay," said one of my customers. "I don't recall the Bard mentioning it in his play."

"Well, the Bard knoweth not everything," said the jester. "Princess Fiona was chosen to represent the royal family here today at a pageant at Tallulah Falls High School some fortnights ago. So please come out and herald her arrival."

"We certainly will," I said.

"Huzzah!" he shouted.

"Huzzah!" we replied.

He danced off to another booth.

I went back to showing my customers the blackwork patterns. I gave them the free patterns, and they bought some black floss and canvas.

After they paid for their purchases and moved on to the jewelry booth across the room, I went around the table to pop my head into Washerwoman Jan's booth.

"Hi," I said. "Did you hear the jester's announcement about Princess Fiona's arrival?"

"I already knew, thanks."

"Are you going?"

"No." She pursed her lips. "I believe I prefer to stay here and keep an eye on Nellie's booth. I'd hate for anything to happen to it."

"Are you upset with me, Jan?" I asked.

"No. I'm merely disappointed that I didn't get to see the fire juggler," she said.

"But I thought you were going out to talk with him."

"I was, but by the time I got there, he said some cop came along and made him put out the torches and juggle something less hazardous." She narrowed her eyes.

I imagined she'd heard Ted telling me he'd had the juggler douse the flames. Oh, well. I agreed a hundred percent. If the juggler wanted to throw around flaming torches, he needed to do so on-stage, not walking around among the crowd.

"Well, if you change your mind, I'll see you there," I said.

About half an hour later, I heard the trumpets blowing to announce the arrival of the princess. Several other merchants were already heading for the door, and I fell in behind them. The worst thing that could possibly happen to my booth had already happened. Besides, I didn't believe Washerwoman Jan was staying inside to oversee Nellie's booth. I thought she was simply being petulant about not getting to see the juggler with his torches on fire.

I stepped out into the sunshine and smiled at

the beautiful procession coming up over the grassy hill. The heralds came first with their long medieval trumpets. Next came the two knights on horseback. The heralds and knights wore white tunics with a blue Celtic cross on the front, and their horses were also draped in white with the cross on their chests. The bridles had tassels that alternated navy and light blue.

The heralds and knights were followed by a drum and fife corps that was undoubtedly from Tallulah Falls High School, where the princess had been crowned "some fortnights ago." They marched proudly and were seemingly unaffected by the camera flashes of many moms.

I smiled broadly at the joy and sweetness of it all.

Princess Fiona was a lovely girl with long reddish blond hair and light eyes. She was dressed in a lavender gown with gold trim, and she wore a tiara. As she smiled and waved to the crowd, I was impressed that some time-traveling orthodontist was working on straightening fair Fiona's teeth.

The princess's ladies-in-waiting followed. There were four—all pretty, fresh faced, and giggling.

There were lots more camera flashes. I even took out my phone and snapped a few photos of my own.

Four more knights and two lute-toting minstrels—neither of which was Paul—trailed behind the ladies-in-waiting.

Poor Jan. She doesn't know what she missed.

I turned to go back into the merchants' building and saw Jan duck back inside. Like one of the ladies-in-waiting, I put my hand over my mouth and giggled helplessly.

My happy mood carried right over into Julie's celebration. True to her word, Vera had brought champagne. For some reason I couldn't fathom, she'd also brought Muriel.

Muriel was a sweet soul who was hard of hearing and a regular in many of my stitching classes. However, she never seemed to know what was going on and was usually content to merely work quietly in the sit-and-stitch square without a word unless she had an embroidery-related question.

Ted came in, dropped a quick kiss on my lips, and handed a bouquet of mixed fall flowers to Julie.

"Congratulations," he said.

"Thank you," she said. "As soon as Riley and her family get here, we'll have cake, champagne, and fruit punch."

"May I try the champagne?" Amber asked.

"No, you may not," her mother said. "You wouldn't like it, anyway."

"I might," she said.

"Your mom's right," I said. "It's not all that great."

"You just aren't drinking the right champagne," said Vera. "This stuff is delicious. Can't Amber have just a sip?"

"No," Julie said firmly.

"When you're twenty-one, we'll drink a toast," Vera told Amber.

"Thanks, Ms. Langhorne."

Vera winked.

Muriel went over to the sit-and-stitch square, sat on a club chair, and pulled her blackwork project out of her tote bag. I wondered if she was simply wanting to work on her project or if she had mistakenly thought today was Tuesday. Either way, her cottony little head was bent over her work, and she appeared to be content.

Riley, Keith, Camille, and Laura arrived next. I held my arms out to Laura, and the precious baby reached for me. I took her from Riley and cradled her against my shoulder.

"She is so gorgeous," I said.

"She takes after her mom," Keith said, with an adoring look at his wife.

"I'm glad you thought Julie was the best candidate for the job," I said to Riley softly.

"She was the only person I interviewed," Riley said. "I believe she'll be great."

"She's never done paralegal work," said Camille. "To me, that's a plus. I can train her correctly from the start, and I don't have to worry about her having to overcome any bad habits ingrained in her by someone else."

"Is everyone ready for cake and champagne?" Vera asked. She looked at Amber. "Or some delicious punch?"

"Who invited Vera Langhorne?" The scorn dripped from Camille's words. She and Vera hadn't gotten along since Camille's husband al-legedly made a pass at Vera once at a party.

I bit my lip. "Sorry," I whispered. "She was there when Julie called me, and I didn't want to be rude."

"Of course not," said Camille softly. She raised her voice. "I'll take you up on the cake and cham-pagne, Vera."

Vera's lips tightened. "How nice to see you, Ca-mille."

I handed Laura back over to Riley. "I'll take Muriel a piece of cake and some punch. Be right back."

I got the cake and punch and took them over to Muriel. "Excuse me, Muriel."

She didn't glance up.

"Muriel?"

She raised her head. "Oh, cake! How nice!"

"Yes. It's to celebrate Julie getting a new job," I said.

"And punch!" Muriel said. "These are much better refreshments than those you usually serve."

I turned and was headed back to the counter when Mary Alice—known at the Ren Faire as Sis-ter Mary Alice—came through the door.

"Oh," she said, stopping just inside and putting a hand to her chest. "I didn't realize you were hav-ing a party."

"Please join us." I gestured toward Julie. "We're celebrating our friend's new job."

"Congratulations," Mary Alice told her. "I won't stay but a moment, though. I simply haven't had the opportunity to browse your booth at the

Faire, so I thought I'd pop into your shop." She smiled and wandered down the main aisle. "You have some marvelous things."

"Thank you," I said, trailing behind her. "Is there anything in particular I can help you find?"

"No, dear. I'm just looking." She reached the back of the store, turned, and inclined her head. "You must have been incensed when Nellie Davis's sister opened up a competing shop right next door to yours."

"Well . . . I wouldn't go that far. It upset me at first, but then I saw reason."

"And what was that?" she asked.

"I realized that if my store couldn't handle a little competition, then I must be doing something—or maybe a lot of things—wrong."

"Good point. Still . . . didn't the tiniest part of you"—she raised her thumb and forefinger, which were just shy of touching—"want to throttle her?"

I laughed. "That might be a bit of an exaggeration." Did Mary Alice believe I'd killed Clara? And, if she did, did others believe that, too?

She joined in my laughter. "I believe I will take you up on a glass of that champagne before I go."

I parked the Jeep in the driveway and waited for Ted to pull in behind me. We got out of our cars, called a "hello" to Angus, who'd jumped up and put his paws over the fence to woof a greeting to us, and walked hand in hand to the front door.

Ted opened the storm door while I took out my key. A tan envelope fell at his feet.

"Are you expecting something?" he asked.

I shook my head. "Who's it from?"

Ted took a pair of latex gloves from his pocket and slipped them on. He picked up the envelope by the corner. "It isn't labeled. Do you mind if I open it?"

"Of course not." I unlocked the door, and we went inside. "You obviously have some qualms about it."

"Don't you?"

"I do *now*."

"Do you have a letter opener?" he asked.

"Yes. Would you let Angus in while I get it, please?"

"Sure." He opened the back door, and Angus loped into the house.

Angus stopped to acknowledge Ted and then scampered into the living room. I turned and gave him a hug before going upstairs to get the letter opener off the desk in my office.

Angus went back to Ted. It was dinnertime, and Ted was in the kitchen. I heard Ted pouring kibble into Angus's bowl as I headed back to the kitchen with the letter opener.

Ted opened the envelope and took out a single sheet of tan paper.

I have information regarding the death of Joe Palmer. I can prove that Marcus West did not murder Palmer. I want to talk with Detective Nash. ALONE. If I see any other law enforcement officers, I will disappear. Meet

me at the back of the merchants' building tomorrow at
noon.

The Crow

"The Crow," I said. "He has to be Marcus West. He wants to come out of hiding."

"That could be the case."

"On the other hand, he wants to meet you alone behind the merchants' building." I paced in front of the kitchen table. "He might be trying to set you up! Do you think he's trying to set you up? What if this Crow isn't Marcus West after all—or even if he is—and he's out to get you?"

"Sweetheart, I'll be fine."

"So you're meeting him?" I asked. "Does that mean you're going to meet him? But not without backup, are you? You can't go in there blind."

Ted gently took my shoulders. "Babe. I'll be fine."

Chapter Twenty-one

I arrived at the Faire Tuesday morning trying not to appear nervous. I was also pretending not to look for the Crow. I was probably failing miserably at both, since I was, in fact, nervously looking for the Crow.

Either Ted was still at the police station preparing the undercover team who'd be near him when he met with the Crow, or else they were on their way here.

I walked slowly to the merchants' building. I wanted to give the Crow every opportunity to come up and talk with me, but I didn't see him anywhere. I wondered how he knew so much about me. I supposed it could be because Tallulah Falls was such a small town. Still, why had he fixated on me? Why hadn't he simply approached Ted directly if he had something he wanted to say to the police?

I supposed the Crow saw Ted and other officers of the law as a threat since he claimed he had information about Joe Palmer's murder. But why would he think I could help? Had he wanted me to pave the way for him with Ted?

I also wondered if the Crow had been the person who'd destroyed my booth. If so, what had he sought to gain by doing that?

I was full of questions this morning, but I had no answers whatsoever.

I walked into the merchants' building. Instead of going directly to my booth, I walked over to Clara's booth and thought back to the evening of her death.

Julie had said that Clara's funeral was today. I didn't know what time, and I knew that anything I could've done—sent flowers or food—would not have been welcomed or accepted by Nellie, and I didn't know any of Clara's other family members.

Granted, I hadn't known Clara . . . and she had despised me . . . but I had been the one to find her on that hard wooden floor. The image of her lying on her side beneath the overturned rocking chair with the uncompleted green scarf wrapped around her neck came into my mind. I shivered.

Had there been anything I could have done? Ted assured me that she was already dead by the time I arrived . . . but not even the coroner could be *that* precise about time of death, could he? Not if Clara had died between the time Nellie left for food and the time she returned.

I sighed and said a silent prayer for Clara's family.

Her booth was right beside the back door. I supposed that with it being in the corner as it was,

Clara's attacker could have come in and left by that door without being noticed by merchants who might've been in the building preparing their booths. I wondered if the door was usually kept unlocked.

I went to the door, pushed it open, and stepped outside. While I was out there, I looked for the Crow. It seemed plausible to me that he might be lurking, especially since he wanted Ted to meet him behind this building. I was the only one around. I turned and tried to reopen the door, but it had locked behind me. Perhaps it was to be used to exit the building only in an emergency.

I walked around to the front of the building and went back inside. Had the lock been picked on Thursday when Clara had been murdered? Or had it been picked when my booth had been vandalized? Or both? If the door automatically locked when closed, had Clara's killer been aware of that fact and used something to prop the door open in order to leave by the same door? Or had he been forced to leave by the front door?

I got back to my booth just as a school group was approaching. The teacher was a chipper woman with a dark blond bun and rose gold-framed glasses. She was wearing a red pantsuit. Her students appeared to be ten or eleven years old.

"Good morning," I said to them.

"Hello! I'm Mrs. McKinley, and this is my fifth-grade history class. Class, please say hi to the merchant."

"Hi," most of them said.

"It's so nice to meet you," I said. "I'm Marcy Singer, and I own the Seven-Year Stitch shop in town. I—"

"My grandma says your store's name is based on a dirty movie," said one little boy with unruly brown hair.

My eyes widened. "Well, I wouldn't say that."

"That Marilyn Monroe was one foxy lady," said a boy with dark hair and eyes as black as midnight. "That's what my dad says. And he knows about foxy ladies."

Just when I thought my eyes couldn't get any wider, the boy winked at me. This time, I thought my eyes would pop out of my head.

"Marilyn was a beauty, even though she was not considered thin by any stretch of the imagination," said a studious-looking girl with her hair in a ponytail. "In fact, by today's standards, she would be considered fat by Hollywood and the fashion magazines. We need to take back control of our self-esteem from the media and stop letting it dictate what is and what is not beautiful."

"Hear, hear," I said.

She smiled broadly. "My mom is a psychologist, and she's constantly fussing about stuff like that."

"Well, good for her. Tell her to keep fighting the good fight." I gestured to the booth behind me. "Let me tell you how my booth relates to this Ren Faire." I went into a discussion of blackwork in the Elizabethan era, and I believe Mrs. McKinley came close to relaxing for just a moment. She certainly had her hands full.

Before they left, I gave each student a flyer with information about blackwork on it.

"Stop by the Seven-Year Stitch and see me anytime!" I called after the students.

The black-haired boy turned, winked, and said, "Count on it."

"Cliff, come along!" called Mrs. McKinley.

I waved good-bye to the students with one hand and covered my smile with the other. Once they were out of sight, I released my pent-up laughter.

I paced the booth as the time drew near for Ted to meet the Crow. I hadn't seen Ted yet today. Nor, for that matter, had I seen the Crow. But I had expected Ted to at least come in and let me know he had arrived.

On the one hand, he wouldn't have wanted me worrying about him and the meeting. So he might've thought that if he didn't come in and let me know it was "fixing to go down," then I wouldn't think about it and he might get to meet with the Crow without any interference on my part at all.

Well, far be it from me to interfere in a police investigation!

On the other hand, what if there really was no backup? Or what if Ted had told his men to stay far away from the scene in order not to spook the Crow and to come only if there was an emergency? But what if the emergency happened so quickly that the men couldn't get there in time to stop it? Someone had to be looking out for Ted!

I jotted a quick note on the back on one of my flyers.

Gone to lunch. Be back soon!

I folded the flyer in half and set it up on the table. Then I crept over to the back door. I opened the door and peeped out. I didn't see anyone.

I stepped outside and closed the door as quietly as possible.

I stayed close to the wall and eased around the side of the building. Here I saw the court jester and a knight. Each was leaning against a fence enjoying a chat and a cigarette. The juggler was nearby, practicing with what I hoped were rubber or plastic knives.

Ted approached and rested nonchalantly against the side of the building. He checked his watch and looked around the perimeter.

I quickly ducked out of sight.

The next time I stole a glance at Ted, I saw the Crow approaching.

My breath caught in my throat. I didn't see *anyone* there to back Ted up! Maybe the knight could draw his imitation sword or the juggler could throw one of the plastic Ginsus or something, but where were the policemen? Were they on the other side of the fence?

Ted and the Crow began talking.

Suddenly, the Crow reached into his cloak. Was he going to bring out a gun?

I took off running toward them. I hadn't taken more than three steps when the juggler, the knight, and the court jester all pulled guns and yelled for the Crow to freeze.

Hmph. I felt silly.

I stopped and tried to go back to my hiding place, but it was too late.

"Get back here, Marcy," Ted said.

I sheepishly and very slowly started walking toward Ted.

"Mr. Crow . . . or Mr. West . . . or whatever you'd like to be called, we're taking you down to the station for questioning," Ted said, jerking the mask off the Crow and revealing a middle-aged man with thinning brown hair and pale skin. "You aren't being charged with anything at this time, but clandestine meetings between officers and suspects are not how we do things at the Tallulah Falls Police Department. We're going to take your formal recorded statement. Understood?"

The Crow nodded.

Ted waved the knight over, and he took the Crow by the arm. The knight, the jester, and the juggler started walking away with the Crow. Ted called that he'd be right with them.

He gave me a fierce stare. "What the hell did you think you were doing? You could've got yourself shot! Plus, you could be arrested for interfering in a police investigation."

"I was worried about you."

"I appreciate the sentiment, but I can handle

myself. If I couldn't, I wouldn't be in this job," he said. "I have to go. We'll talk about this later."

And then he turned and strode off.

I sighed. *Great. Now Ted's angry with me.*

When I went back to my booth, I was surprised to see Veronica there. She wore white linen slacks, a pale blue blouse, and blue and white espadrilles. She carried a large tote that matched her outfit. Upon looking closer, I saw that the tote had a mesh window.

"Ah, there you are!" said Veronica. "I was about to give up and leave."

"I'm glad you didn't," I said. "Come on around and sit down."

"All right."

Veronica and I went into the booth and sat at the table.

"You brought Clover with you?" I asked.

"I did. Would you like to see her?"

"Yes," I said.

Veronica opened the tote and took out the bunny. She supported Clover's feet as she handed her to me. I put the rabbit in my lap and petted her gently.

"Will you still let me come visit Clover if your son dumps me?" I asked.

"So that's the reason for the long face," said Veronica. "Of course, you may visit Clover, but I doubt you have to worry about Ted letting you go."

"He was pretty upset with me when he left

here." I explained to her about the Crow, their secret meeting, and my worry that Ted didn't have sufficient backup. "Like a fool, I thought I could provide him some help. Just about the time the three undercover officers drew their guns, I went running at the Crow."

Veronica threw back her head and laughed. "How delightful!"

"Your son was not delighted," I said.

"I think it's absolutely magnificent that a wisp of a girl like you with no police training whatsoever would throw caution to the wind and attempt to protect my supercop son," she said.

"He said I could be arrested for interfering in a police investigation."

She laughed again. "You must have scared him half out of his mind!"

"That wasn't my intention at all," I said. "I just had to make sure he was safe. I . . ."

"You love him."

"Yes, I do." I looked down at the top of Clover's head, not wanting Ted's mother to see the emotion in my eyes.

"And he loves you," she said softly. "He'll get over his angry spell. And if he arrests you for interference, I'll interfere and bail you out. Just don't tell him that. I'd hate for him to think the women in his life are plotting against him."

"I'll never tell," I said.

"I had my mind set on disliking you, Marcy. But the more I know you, the more I like you." She smiled. "I'm glad Ted has you."

"I'm glad he has you, too." I handed Clover back to her. "How are things going with Clover?"

"I have to use baby gates to keep her hemmed in most of the time," said Veronica, taking the rabbit and putting her back into the tote. "Her litter box is on one side of the room, and her food is on the other. She has these little sticks to chew on and a ball she enjoys playing with."

"So Clover *is* a girl," I said.

"Yes, the veterinarian determined that for me—although I felt she was female from the beginning. I don't know why. I suppose there's just something feminine about her." She smiled. "She's a great deal of company. I'm enjoying her very much."

"You'll have to bring her to see Angus one day," I said.

"I will. I thought it was touching how that big creature and this tiny one got along so swimmingly, didn't you?"

I nodded. "I was afraid Angus would accidentally hurt her the first time I brought her into the Stitch, but he seemed to realize he needed to be careful with her."

"Just as my son—when he calms down—will realize he needs to be careful with you," said Veronica. "I doubt he'll admit it, but when he thinks about it, he'll be proud of your bravery and honored that you care so much about him that you'd put your life in danger to protect him."

Blinking back tears, I leaned over and hugged her. I didn't tell her this, but I hadn't thought I'd like her when I first met her, either. She was downright intimidating. But I was so glad we were becoming friends.

I sure hoped she was right about Ted not staying angry with me.

Chapter Twenty-two

After Veronica left, I called Mom. I could always put her on hold and wait on customers if necessary, but things were rather slow this afternoon.

"Hello, darling," she said when she answered the phone. "Are you enjoying the Ren Faire? I'm so sorry I can't come up and spend a couple days with you."

"I'm not enjoying it as much as you'd think," I said. "I mean, there have been lots of great aspects to it . . . but some not so great . . . some downright awful."

"Spill it."

"Well . . . a lot of things have happened since we talked last." I cleared my throat. "You remember that on Thursday I was going to sneak a peek at Clara's booth?"

"Yes. What happened? Was it set up like the Stitch, too?" she asked.

"No, not so much. When I arrived, Clara was lying on the floor beneath an overturned rocking chair. She'd been strangled to death with the scarf she was knitting."

"Marcella Singer! Why didn't you call me before now?"

"I don't know, Mom. For one thing, I didn't want to worry you."

"So who killed her?"

"The police don't know yet," I said. "There weren't that many people here, and no one seems to have seen anything." I quickly weighed whether to tell her about my booth getting trashed. *Not.* That was definitely not something Mom needed to be concerned about.

"Anyway, Clara's funeral is today, and I feel so bad about everything," I continued. "I want to do something to recognize her passing, to commemorate her life—no matter how bitter she was toward me—but I know anything I would do for Nellie or any flowers I would send to the funeral home, Nellie would merely throw away."

"I'm sure you're right about that," Mom said. "To do anything at all, you'll have to remove Nellie from the equation." She was silent for a second. "Maybe you could wait until next week and put some fresh flowers on Clara's grave. Or you could send an anonymous card to other members of Clara's family to express your condolences."

"Both of those are good ideas," I said. "Thanks. I'm not trying to be two-faced about Clara. I don't *like* her now that she's gone, and I'm not going to pretend we were ever even civil, much less friends. But she's dead, and I'm the one who found her. I can't help but feel bad about a life lost. No matter how she treated me, she was loved by Nellie and the rest of her family."

"I hope she was, darling," said Mom. "But sometimes you just never know. It's as likely to have been one of them who killed her as anyone. Let's move on to a happier subject. How are things going with Ted?"

I didn't say anything.

"Marcella? Has something happened?"

"Well, there was this shady character who called for a private meeting with Ted," I began.

"You didn't . . ."

"I did. I was afraid he didn't have sufficient backup, and . . ." I blew out a breath, and then I related the entire story—almost—about the Crow. I left out how he'd approached me twice and had left the note for Ted at my house. I left in the parts about my choice to run to Ted's rescue as his team moved in with their guns drawn.

Mom said a few words I rarely hear her say. They were not nice words.

"No wonder he's upset with you! Not only could you have gotten yourself killed, you made him look like a fool! You acted like you didn't trust him to take care of himself!"

"I didn't mean it that way," I said.

"I don't care how you meant it," she said. "That's how it was! You need to apologize and assure him you'll never do anything that stupid again."

"Mom! You're supposed to always be on my side!"

"I *am* on your side. But I also realize when

you've done something stupid that you need to make amends for."

"Well, at least Ted's mom understood my actions," I said. "She thought it was *magnificent* that I cared about Ted enough to risk my life for him."

"I don't care how *magnificent* she thinks it is," Mom said. "It was foolhardy. Ted knows it, I know it, and deep down you know it."

"Fine. Okay. Look, I see a customer coming, Mom. I'll talk with you later," I said.

"I'm sorry I came down on you so hard. But you're my only child. I adore you, and I couldn't bear it if anything happened to you."

"I know. I love you, Mom."

"I love you. Call me later."

I promised I would and then ended the call so I could go wait on my imaginary customer . . . and feel guilty because the customer *was* imaginary and that I'd simply wanted to get off the phone with my mother, who was not telling me what I wanted to hear.

Over the next couple of hours, I soothed my bruised feelings and admitted to myself that Mom was right. Mom was almost always right. It was a trait that could be downright irritating at times. But she'd been around a lot of different people at different stages in their lives, and she'd learned so much about human behavior.

Anyway, traffic into the merchants' building had picked up, and I'd been selling rather steadily. Interacting with customers and talking about embroidery always put me in a happier frame of mind. During the few lulls I had, I'd worked on embellishing a poet's blouse that a woman had ordered yesterday afternoon. Leaving the one remaining shirt on display and taking orders had been an excellent idea.

I was so busy when Ted came in that I didn't see him standing by the side of the booth until the three ladies I'd been waiting on left.

As soon as I saw him, I came out from behind the table. "I'm so sorry! I didn't mean to behave so recklessly. And I wouldn't embarrass you for anything in the world!"

He took my face in his hands and kissed me passionately. "I'm sorry, too. I understand why you did what you did. But you have to realize that I can't do my job effectively if I'm having to look over my shoulder to make sure you're safe."

"I know that," I said. "I'm sorry. I made a huge mistake, and it'll never happen again . . . probably." Hey, I didn't want to lie. I couldn't be a hundred percent *sure* it wouldn't happen again.

He chuckled. "*Probably*. I guess that'll have to do for now."

"Did the other guys give you a hard time about it?" I asked.

"A little . . . but not much." He lowered his voice and led me back inside the booth where we wouldn't be overheard. "We were all too busy with Mr. West."

"So it *was* him. Did he have the evidence he claimed to have?"

"He had some of it," Ted said. "In fact, he was taking a USB drive from his pocket when everyone sprang into action."

Including me. Neither of us said it, but it was the truth. I could've gotten myself shot over a USB drive.

"So you took this USB drive, questioned the man, and released him?"

"Not quite. Some of our guys are currently assessing the authenticity of the files on the drive," he said. "They could have been produced in order to give Mr. West an alibi and to give us another viable suspect. For now, our *Crow* is in protective custody."

"That's one way of keeping him from flying the coop." I groaned. "Sorry—that was so bad. I realized it when it was about halfway out of my mouth, but I couldn't stop it in time."

Ted grinned. "It's all right. I'm off to interrogate our suspect now. I just wanted to come by here first to make sure . . . you know, that we're okay."

I drew his head down to mine for a kiss. "I think we're okay. Do you?"

"Oh, yeah. We're better than okay." He frowned. "You've got the big class tonight, right?"

"The blackwork class, yes," I said.

"Do you mind if I meet you at your house after class?"

"I'd mind if you didn't. It'll be the best part of my day."

After Ted left, I called Mom and quickly told her everything was fine. She didn't make me admit she'd been right all along, and she spared me the *I told you so*.

Once I'd cleared the air with her, I worked on the blackwork trim on the shirt and thought about Mr. West. Why did he call himself the Crow? Was it the costume? Or was it something else?

I wondered if the files on the USB drive implicated Lacey Palmer in the murder of her husband and Mr. West's business partner, Joe. If so, were the files legitimate or were they inventions of Mr. West to throw blame onto someone else? After all, he and Lacey had been the two prime suspects in Mr. Palmer's murder.

If Mr. West's information was legitimate and Lacey Palmer killed her husband, could that make her a suspect in Clara's murder? After all, Lacey was Clara's stepdaughter. Paul had suggested that Clara had been doling out Mr. Palmer's money to her own children but not to his. It was only natural that Lacey would want her children to benefit from her father's estate instead of Clara's children. After all, Clara's children had no biological ties to Lacey's father. With Clara out of the way and no longer executor of the estate, everything would revert to Mr. Palmer's biological children.

Still, I couldn't shake the feeling that a man had murdered Clara. For one thing, she was a stout woman. If she'd been fighting for her life, she'd have struggled like crazy. And she'd have screamed . . . wouldn't she? She would if she could have. Had she not been aware of her attacker until it was too late?

I wondered how Lacey Palmer's husband had been murdered. I'd have to ask Paul.

I picked up the phone and called Vera.

"Hey, Marcy," she said. "What's up?"

"I was wondering if you could do me a favor. Would you mind asking Paul how Lacey Palmer's husband was killed?"

"No. I'll call him right now. Wait, you're thinking maybe she killed Clara so her kids would have access to her dad's estate, aren't you?"

"It's a possibility," I said. "I know that both she and Mr. West were suspects in Mr. Palmer's death . . . and if she did kill her husband, then she might be more willing to kill again."

"Good thinking," Vera said. "And that Mr. West hasn't turned up yet, either."

I didn't dare tell her that he had. "If you don't mind, call me back when you know something."

"It's almost time for the blackwork class," she said. "If you don't hear from me before then, I'll come early and let you know what Paul dug up."

"That'll be great. Talk to you soon."

As it turned out, I didn't hear from Vera before the blackwork class. I'd quickly gone home and fed Angus, but I'd had a couple last-minute customers at the festival, so I hadn't even had time to change out of my noblewoman's dress before heading to the Stitch for class.

When I arrived at the shop, Vera was waiting for me in her BMW. She got out and went with me to the door.

"Lacey Palmer's husband was poisoned," she told me as I unlocked the door.

"So even if she *did* kill her husband, the same method wasn't used on Clara."

We went inside, I turned on the lights, and we sat down on the navy sofa facing the window so we could see when the other students began arriving.

"That still doesn't mean that she didn't murder them both," Vera said. "Maybe she wanted to mix it up—afraid she'd draw too much suspicion if she did away with two of her enemies in the same way."

"Do you think Mr. West could have had anything against Clara?"

"I don't know. Had he met her?" Vera started to laugh and abruptly stopped herself. "I'm sorry. That was ugly. I'd forgotten that Clara's funeral was today."

"I was thinking about that earlier," I said. "Did you go?"

She shook her head. "I sent some flowers, but I didn't go to the service. I hadn't met Clara but a time or two, and I don't know any of her family members except Nellie. But back to your original question, I think Paul is digging into the possibility that Lacey had something to do with Clara's death. I'll let you know what he uncovers."

"It's just weird that two people die within a five-year time frame and that they're closely connected," I said.

"And it could merely be a coincidence," Vera

said. "According to the Internet, we're all just six people away from getting to know Kevin Bacon . . . or something like that . . . so those two murders might not be connected at all."

I was able to hide the smile brought about by Vera's lopsided explanation of six degrees of separation. "Maybe not. But it seems that in Tallulah Falls, everything ends up being connected in some way or another."

"That's true enough, I suppose."

Her phone rang from the recesses of her purse.

"Excuse me," she said as she rummaged for the phone. "This is Paul. He might have some more information for us."

I bit my tongue to keep from asking, "Are you sure that's Paul? It might be Kevin Bacon."

She located the phone and answered with, "Hey, there, precious!"

That convinced me that she was positive it was Paul.

"What? No!" Her eyes flew to mine. Her expression of fear chilled my blood even though I had no idea what was going on.

"If you do go over there, you be careful," she said. "You're there to get a story, not to play the hero. Remember that."

When she ended the call, she didn't return the phone to her purse. She sat there fidgeting with it as if it were a giant worry stone.

"Vera, what is it?"

"Paul heard over the scanner that shots have

been fired and that immediate assistance is requested at a residence," she said quietly. "He
knows it's Marcus West's residence because he
looked it up. He's going over there to see what's
happening."

Chapter Twenty-three

My first instinct upon hearing that there had been a shooting at the very place Ted had been going this afternoon was to rush over. But I'd learned my lesson. I knew I must trust Ted to do his job. My job was simply to pray that he and the rest of his crew were safe.

The other students were starting to come into the Seven-Year Stitch, so I whispered to Vera to quietly let me know if she heard anything from Paul.

Then I greeted the students, offered them water, and helped them get settled in to stitch. Throughout the class, I kept glancing at the clock. When I wasn't looking at the clock, I was trying to catch Vera's eye. When I did, she'd give a slight shake of her head to let me know she hadn't heard anything. It was all I could do to concentrate on the blackwork class long enough to help my students.

I was relieved when the class was over.

Vera waited while I tidied up and locked the doors.

"Must've been nothing," she said as we walked out onto the street. "If it had been, Paul would have called and told me something."

"You're probably right," I said. "Ted is supposed to meet me at my house. He's probably there now with Angus."

"Yeah. . . . See you tomorrow!" She got into her car and waited for me to get into the Jeep and start it before she drove away.

When I got home, Ted wasn't there yet. I tried to tell myself that the report of the shooting that Paul had heard over the scanner had been a mistake . . . or that he'd had the wrong address.

I went through the house and let Angus in the back door. I'd fed him before going to the blackwork class, and now he was ready to play. He picked up his green dragon and gave it a vigorous shake. Then he threw it and ran to snap it up again. He came and stood before me. I played tug-of-war with him over the dragon, and then I let him win. He ran off to the living room with it.

I checked my phone to see if I'd received any messages or texts since I'd looked five minutes earlier. Nothing.

I went into the living room. Angus was lying by the hearth chewing on the dragon. I curled up on the sofa and turned on the television. Maybe there was something on the news.

I knew that if something had happened to Ted, Manu would have called me—or even delivered the news in person. Ted was fine. Everything was all right. That was so easy to say and so hard to believe.

Suddenly, headlights lit up the living room curtains. I looked out the window. It was Ted.

Thank You, God!

I hurried to the foyer and threw the door open. When Ted walked in, I hurled myself into his arms.

"I'm so glad you're okay. I've been worried out of my mind about you," I said.

He had his arms around me, and I was stuck to him like a leech, so he closed the door with his foot. "Let me guess. You heard something."

"I heard there'd been a shooting at the West house. Paul heard it over the scanner and went to see what was happening."

"Sometimes I hate that civilians can monitor police scanners," Ted said.

"So is it true?"

He nodded, and I saw how tired he was.

"Come on," I said. "Let's get you in here in the living room." I took his hand and almost bumped into Angus, who'd also come to greet Ted.

Once Ted had removed his tie, unfastened the first couple buttons of his shirt, and sunk onto the sofa, I offered him something to eat.

"I am a little hungry," he said. "But I don't want you to go to any trouble. A peanut butter sandwich would be super."

"You know I'm always prepared for guests. Not that you're a guest . . . just that I can throw something together in a hurry—something better than a sandwich. I'll be right back."

Although I was anxious to know what had happened at the West house, all that mattered at the moment was that Ted was fine . . . and hungry. He'd tell me what he could later on.

I preheated the oven and took some spanako-pita from the freezer. I put the savory spinach pastries on a cookie sheet and found some bacon-wrapped filet mignon hors d'oeuvres to go with them. They, too, went on the cookie sheet while I warmed cheesecake bites and chocolate chip cookies in the microwave.

Once the food was ready, I put everything on a large tray and took it into the living room. Ted was on the sofa with his eyelids drooping.

"Are we having a party?" Ted bit into a spana-kopita. "This is delicious . . . hot, but tasty."

"I'm glad you like it," I said. "And, as a matter of fact, we *are* having a party. We're celebrating the fact that you're all right. I know you're put in dangerous situations every day, and that's just the nature of your job. I also know you're good at your job, and that whatever situation you're put in . . . you'll handle it."

He grinned and handed me a spanakopita on a napkin. "There. Eat that." He got himself another. "You're fishing."

"I'm not!" I blushed. "Maybe I'm fishing a little. But I realize that you might not be able to tell me anything about the shooting . . . or even if there *was* a shooting . . . and that's okay."

He chuckled, finished off the spanakopita and licked his fingers. "You're adorable."

I huffed. "Are you going to tell me or not?"

"Not." He popped a bite of filet mignon into his mouth. "Oh, this is good, too. I like your thrown-together dinner party fixings."

"Thank you." So he wasn't going to tell me. No big deal. I understood all about confidentiality and all that.

Given my frustration, I went right for the cheesecake.

"Fine. I was just testing you to see if you could stand not knowing. Well done," he said. "Some-one drove by Marcus West's house this afternoon and fired off a couple rounds. We were all inside, and no one was hurt. In fact, no windows were even broken. Either our shooter was a lousy shot or the person was only hoping to scare West."

"So he's no longer a suspect in Mr. Palmer's murder?" I asked.

"We haven't eliminated him yet. I don't think he had anything to do with the shooting at his house because he was with us the majority of the day." He tossed Angus a bacon-wrapped filet mi-gnon bite.

"Wait. Why would he have anything to do with a shooting at his house?"

"To throw us off . . . to further convince us that he's innocent," he said.

"Your job is really complicated." I ate another cheesecake square.

"It can be." He smiled. "You just have to always make sure you're seeing the complete picture. You can't take anything for granted."

"So, now what?" I asked. "Are your guys guarding him at his home?"

He shook his head as he took a chocolate chip cookie from the tray. "Mr. West has been moved to a more secure location outside of town. The security team left with him as soon as we were certain there was no longer an immediate threat. I stayed behind and convinced Paul to downplay the incident in tomorrow's newspaper."

"How did you manage that?"

"With the promise of an exclusive once we break the case." He ate the cookie. "Still, I'm eager to see what Paul *does* say in tomorrow's news."

On Wednesday morning, Ted arrived about an hour before he had to go in to work. He had a copy of the *Tallulah Falls Examiner* under his arm.

I'd already prepared breakfast—blueberry muffins with streusel topping, scrambled eggs, bacon, and biscuits.

"Wow, everything smells and looks wonderful," Ted said. He tossed the paper onto the table, gave me a kiss, and then nuzzled my neck. "Especially you."

"Thank you," I said. "I'm back to wearing my saucy-wench costume today." I was wearing the blue skirt, peasant's blouse, and black corset vest.

"I like your saucy-wench costume." He poured us both some coffee and put the cups on the table.

We sat down and filled our plates. I'd already

given Angus a biscuit, an egg, and a couple slices of bacon, and he was outside playing in the yard.

Ted opened the paper and spread it out between us. "Front page. Headline—'Drive-by?'"

"Well, it isn't every day that there's a drive-by shooting in Tallulah Falls."

"Yeah, but putting the column on the front page and putting 'Drive-by?' as the headline is *downplaying*?" he asked.

"Let's read it before we get too upset."

An incident early yesterday evening had Tallulah Falls residents on edge.

"I was sitting inside watching the early news and heard BAM! BAM! BAM!" said Roger McCormick. "It scared me half to death."

When questioned about what he thought the noise was, Mr. McCormick said it sounded like a gun going off. I asked him if he saw a gunman. He said he didn't and that he guessed it could've been a car backfiring or something, but he admitted that "you never can tell these days."

While many area residents heard the sound, no one actually saw what occurred.

I spoke with officials of the Tallulah Falls Police Department shortly after the popping sounds were heard, and I was assured that the residents of Tallulah Falls were in no immediate danger. While I wasn't told definitively what generated the noises heard by Mr. McCormick and other residents, I was told that the matter is under investi-

gation. The *Tallulah Falls Examiner* will follow up
this report as soon as more details are known.

Ted blew out a breath. "Well done, Paul."

"That was an excellent cover," I said. "If the
shooter reads this, it will be apparent that his—or
her—efforts to either kill or scare Marcus West
failed."

"I wouldn't go that far," said Ted. "West acted
scared half to death. But if the evidence he has on
that flash drive is legitimate, then we'll need him
to testify against Lacey Palmer."

"Tell me about Lacey Palmer," I said. "I know
you told me before I knew the names of anyone
involved that she got a sizable settlement from the
insurance company when her husband died. And
Vera told me that Joe Palmer was poisoned. What
kind of poison was used? I mean, if there was any
question of the wife being suspected in her husband's death, then why did the insurance company release the money?"

"Like us, they couldn't prove the poisoner was
the wife." He took a sip of his coffee. "See, the
poison discovered in Palmer's system was eth-
ylene glycol—antifreeze. In the days before his
death, Palmer had become sick enough to go to
the emergency room. That day he'd had his typical breakfast at home and lunch at work. He
hadn't noticed anything unusual about his food
at either place."

"So he could have been poisoned at either

place," I said, pinching off a piece of blueberry muffin and popping it into my mouth.

"Right. Both his wife and his partner had motive, both had means, and both had opportunity," he said. "We have to get good solid evidence against one of them—in this case, the widow—to take to the district attorney before he can indict, much less convict. We didn't have that five years ago. But with West's help, we might have it now."

"What about Clara?" I asked. "Do you think it's possible that Lacey Palmer had anything to do with Clara's death?"

"Manu says she has a rock-solid alibi for the entire day of Clara's murder."

"And West? Is there anything that might tie him to Clara?"

Ted smiled slightly. "Why are you so determined to put those two murders together?"

"I just want to solve—I mean, I want *you* to solve—Clara's murder," I said. "I can't begin to put it behind me until that's done. I mean, I keep asking myself if Clara's killer is the one who trashed my booth . . . if that person is out to get me, too. I mean, for all I know, it's another embroidery shop entrepreneur whose intention was . . . or *is* . . . to take us both out."

Ted put down his fork and took my hand. "Don't be afraid. You have plenty of security surrounding you right now."

"Right now. But who's to say this person isn't biding his or her time for another opportunity to strike?"

"Do you really believe the person who killed Clara is out to get you, too?" he asked.

"I don't know," I said. "Maybe. Whoever vandalized my booth was vicious and cruel. That person meant to hurt me, and did."

"I realize that, babe, and I'm sorry." He raised my hand to his lips and kissed it. "And if there's a connection, trust me, I'll find it."

"I know you will."

"And I'll find Clara's killer," he said. "I promise."

Chapter Twenty-four

When I got to the Renaissance Faire Wednesday morning, I met Amelia and Herodias as I was heading to the merchants' building. The young redhead wore her typical black ensemble, but today she also had on a light blue jacket. The jacket had a yellow patch with the logo osoc over the left breast.

"Good morning," I said.

"Hey," Amelia said. "I heard about your booth. That's rough."

"Yeah, it was very upsetting . . . as you can probably imagine."

"Is everything okay now? Was everything replaced?" she asked.

"Not everything." I explained how I'd hand-embroidered several shirts in Elizabethan-style blackwork. "The vandal ripped those to shreds."

"That's terrible! Were *all* the shirts ruined?"

"All but one," I said. "I saved it to use as a demo, and a few people have ordered them based on that shirt."

"I'd like to see it," she said.

"Sure. Just stop by the booth whenever you have time."

"I have time now. Herodias and I will walk with you if you don't mind."

"I don't mind at all." I smiled slightly. "Seeing you with Herodias makes me miss Angus even more. I'll be glad when this festival is over and everything gets back to normal. I usually take Angus to work with me every day. I wonder if he's confused by having to stay home all of a sudden."

"I doubt it," she said. "He still sees you when you get home, and I'm guessing you shower him with attention. That's likely good enough for him, you know? Animals typically don't have the insecurities and need the reassurances that we people do."

"Lucky them."

She laughed. "True. And you always know where you stand with an animal. Unfortunately, that can't be said with most people."

I wouldn't have said anything to Amelia for fear it might've hurt her feelings, but I had no clue where I stood with Herodias. The bird might be okay with me, or it might try to claw out my eyes any second now—I just didn't know. So you might always know where you stand with an *animal*, but I wasn't too sure about falcons.

"Here we are!" I opened the door to the merchants' building and led Amelia to my booth.

"Cool." She glanced over at Clara's uninhabited booth. "Does that bother you? Being right next to the booth where that woman was found?"

"Not really. I try not to think about it." I didn't remind her that I was the one who found Clara's body. I handed her the shirt with the blackwork-embellished collar and cuffs. "I had ruffled Elizabethan collars and cuffs with blackwork, too, but none of those survived."

"This is really pretty," said Amelia. "I hope the police catch whoever did this to you."

"I hope they do, too. I can't imagine who would do such a low-down thing."

"This shirt is my size," she said, handing it back to me. "Are you planning on selling it?"

"I'm going to sell it the last day of the Ren Faire," I said. "Quite a few people have asked to buy it, so I tell them that whoever gets here first can have the shirt."

She smiled. "Then I have a fairly good chance." She looked around the merchants' building. "It looks like there's some interesting stuff in here. I should look around and see what I've missed by not coming in here before now."

"Yes, you should," I said.

Amelia wandered into Nellie's booth, and I tidied mine in preparation for the morning visitors—hopefully, customers.

I was surprised to see Nellie come into the building. She was headed straight for her booth. She wore her usual Parisian artist–inspired getup of a black turtleneck, black cigarette pants, and black ballet flats. All she was missing was the beret on that unruly white hair. Still, she looked pale and gaunt. I felt a stab of pity for her.

"Nellie, do you have a second?" I asked as she walked by my stall.

"What do *you* want?" she asked.

"I just wanted to say that I know Clara's funeral was yesterday and to tell you that if there's anything you need . . . anything I can do for you . . . just ask."

Nellie balled up her fists. As she came closer to my booth, I could see that she was shaking.

"You've already helped me more than you could ever know." Her lips curled into a snarl. "You know when? The night I came in here and tore your stupid booth to shreds!"

I gasped and tears pricked my eyes.

"Yeah, that's right! *I* did it! I took the scissors to those ugly shirts; and as I did, I imagined all the hours you'd put into them . . . and I hoped you'd pricked your fingers over and over . . . making it hurt even worse that it was all for nothing! But you know what? Your loss is *nothing* compared to mine. *Nothing!*"

Amelia came around the side of the booth. "Hey! Back off, lady!"

At about the same time that Amelia stepped up, the undercover-cop-slash-knight crossed the room.

"Ms. Davis, did I just hear you confess to vandalizing Ms. Singer's booth?" asked the knight.

"No, you didn't!" Nellie cried.

"Yes, you did," Amelia said. "I heard it, and I'd say these people did, too."

A crowd was beginning to gather around my booth, and many of the spectators nodded in agreement with Amelia.

"Ms. Davis, I'm taking you to the police station for questioning," said the knight.

"I refuse to go!"

"If you refuse to go, then I'll go ahead and arrest you here and now," he said.

She huffed. "I didn't do anything wrong."

The knight motioned to a man who was dressed as a minstrel. When the minstrel joined us, the knight instructed him to take the statements of everyone in the merchants' building.

As the knight led Nellie away, the minstrel took a notepad out of a leather pouch attached to his belt.

"I'm Officer Newland," said the baby-faced minstrel. "Tell me exactly what happened here."

Officer Newland was looking at me, but Amelia jumped in with her version of the tale.

"Okay, I'd just stepped into that aromatherapy booth when I heard Marcy here asking somebody if there was anything she could do," she said. "Somebody's funeral was yesterday."

"It was Nellie's sister, Clara," I said. "Clara was the woman found dead in her booth on Thursday evening."

"Was she"—her voice dropped to a whisper—"the *not so nice* woman with the sweet bunny?" Amelia asked.

I nodded.

"I guess that woman and the one who was here a minute ago were a lot alike," she said. "I hope the one was at least nice to the bunny. She seemed like a sweet little thing."

"Could we get back to what happened here this morning?" asked Officer Newland.

"Yeah, sure," said Amelia. "After Marcy asked if there was anything she could do, the older woman began yelling about how much pleasure it gave her to destroy Marcy's booth."

Officer Newland looked at me, and I nodded.

"That's basically it," I said.

"Still, I want to take everyone's statement individually," he said, turning to the crowd. "Go back to your booths if you're a merchant. If you're here shopping, then please stay in this area until I get your name and information and take your statement."

He drew Amelia aside slightly and finished questioning her.

Afterward, she came by the table where I was sitting. "Hey, I'm sorry about everything. I am glad they caught that old bat, though. She'll pay for what she's done."

"Thanks."

"Ms. Singer, may I take your statement now?" asked Officer Newland.

"Of course," I said. I told him what had happened that morning. I also reiterated that Manu had instructed the crime scene technicians to take photographs of the damage done, and I gave him the estimate of loss I'd prepared for the insurance company.

He asked me a few additional questions—had I known Nellie Davis long, that type of thing—and then he went to take the statements of the other bystanders.

About half an hour after Nellie had been taken away by the knight in shining armor—actually, he'd been wearing chain mail—Ted called.

"Hey, babe, how are you? Why didn't you call me?"

"I'm okay. I've been giving my statement to Officer Newland," I said. "Besides, I knew you'd call once Sir Officer of Tallulah Falls brought Nellie in."

"Deel," Ted said.

"What?"

"The knight. His name is Officer Deel. Anyway, Nellie has been arrested and charged with criminal trespass and criminal mischief."

"Criminal mischief?" I asked. "That makes her sound like a naughty little scamp who toilet-papered my lawn or something. I mean, I realize she just lost her sister, but . . ."

"Trust me. Criminal mischief is a serious crime in the state of Oregon," he said. "She could be charged with jail time and a steep fine."

"Jail time? How much?"

"Not much . . . and since it's a first offense, she'll probably get off with probation since her lawyer will plead that she was grieving over the loss of her sister, et cetera," he said. "But your insurance company will go after her for compensation of your damaged property."

"She has a lawyer?"

"Apparently," said Ted. "She's waiting at the station until he arrives and gives her advice."

"I still can't figure out why Nellie would do such a horrible thing to me," I said. "While it's true that we've never been friends, I never actually thought she was my bitter enemy. Do you think she truly believes I'm responsible in some way for Clara's death?"

"I don't have a clue what's going on in Nellie's head, Inch-High. And what does it matter what she thinks? You know the truth. And you know you did nothing to deserve that woman's wrath. Try to let it go."

"Okay. I'll try."

"I'll be there soon with lunch," he said.

"Let's meet somewhere. I'm leaving here early today so Julie can start her training with Riley and Camille. I told her I'd be at the Seven-Year Stitch at one thirty this afternoon."

"Pizza place at noon?"

I laughed. "How could I say no when you sound so hopeful?"

After I spoke with Ted, I noticed Officer Newland making his way around the booths, talking with all the merchants. He must've finished with the shoppers.

I suddenly had an influx of business. Some people, no doubt, wanted to see how I was holding up after Nellie's outburst. But some seemed genuinely interested in my products.

Sadie stormed into the merchants' building and over to my booth. She stood there tapping her foot, with a tight grimace that she was trying to pass off as a smile.

I excused myself from two ladies who were looking around my booth. "I'll be just outside the stall if you need me."

"I take it you heard," I said quietly to Sadie.

"Yes, I heard. I want to throttle that old hen! How dare she do such a thing to you?"

"What got me was how gleeful she seemed about the whole thing," I said. "She told me that it had helped her to rip my things to shreds." I glanced down at the floor. "I know she's grieving, but how does hurting someone else help her?"

Sadie pulled me to her in a big-sisterly hug. "I wish Nellie Davis would just leave Tallulah Falls. She's a hateful, bitter woman, and no one is going to want her around when they hear what she's done."

I gently broke out of the hug, knowing it would make me cry if I accepted Sadie's sympathy. "I'm all right."

"You're better than all right. And you're way better than her," she said. "You might have lost some *things*, but you have more of all the things that count than Nellie Davis will ever have."

I nodded. "I know. Thanks, Sadie."

"I'd better get back. See you later."

"See you," I said.

After my two customers paid for their purchases and wandered into another stall, I called Ted back.

"Hi," I said. "Can you keep Nellie there until I get there?"

"Yes," he said. "She's in an interrogation room right now with her attorney."

"Make her stay until I get there. I'm coming to talk to her. She and her attorney have to grant me that, don't they?" I asked.

"I can't make any promises, but I'll see what I can do."

Ted met me at the door of the police station. He pulled me into his office, closed the door, and after giving me a kiss, told me that he'd persuaded Nellie's attorney to let me have a word with her. "The attorney is hoping that by talking with you, Nellie will show remorse and he can use that to have a judge give her a reduced sentence."

"If she shows any remorse, she deserves an Academy Award," I said. "And I want to talk with her alone . . . without the lawyer present."

"I'll see if he'll allow it." Ted ushered me into an interrogation room.

He came back a few minutes later and informed me that I could speak with Nellie. An officer would be in the room to ensure that no physical altercations took place, and Nellie's attorney would be with Ted and Manu on the other side of the one-way glass.

"If anything is said that the attorney deems inappropriate, he'll stop the interview immediately," said Ted.

"Fair enough."

Within five or ten minutes, Nellie came into the room accompanied by a female officer I'd never met.

Nellie sat down across the table from me. "Are you here to drop these outrageous charges?"

"No."

"Then why am I talking with you? Now that Clara is dead, I have *no one!*" She took a deep, shuddering breath and looked down at the table. "Of course, when life was good for Clara, I didn't have her. I don't even know Clara's family. I only met her second husband once. I haven't seen Clara's boys since they were small."

"Then don't you think this is a good time to reconnect with them?" I asked. "One of Clara's stepgranddaughters came looking for her on Friday. They must've been close. Maybe you could help fill the void left by Clara's death."

"Clara wasn't close with any of her late husband's granddaughters," said Nellie. "At least, I don't think she was. She didn't speak of any of his family members favorably."

"How many are there?"

"There are three granddaughters, I think. What's it to you, anyway? You think I'm going to get all mushy about people I don't even know?" she asked. "They don't know me, and they don't want to. I feel the same way about them. Now that Clara's dead, I've got no one . . . and it's all your fault."

"Nellie, do you truly believe I had anything to do with Clara's death?"

Her lips trembled, and she closed her eyes. "No . . . but you didn't save her."

"I couldn't," I said.

"How do you know?"

"I did everything I could. I called Ted, and he

got the paramedics there right away." I tried to take her hand, but she pulled it back as if I'd burned her. "I wouldn't have let your sister lie there and die if I could have helped it."

Nellie's tears dripped onto the table.

"Please say you believe that much, at the very least," I said.

"She's gone," Nellie whispered. "My sister is gone, and I'm alone . . . again. Just get out of here and leave me alone."

Chapter Twenty-five

I took a steadying breath and walked out of the interrogation room. Ted met me in the hallway.

"You okay, babe?" he asked.

"I'm fine," I said. "Let's go to lunch."

He nodded. He opened his mouth to say something, but I shook my head slightly. I didn't want to talk about Nellie . . . didn't want Ted to ask me again if I was all right. . . . I knew I'd get upset about this whole ordeal again later. But for now I had to keep it together. I had a business to run and then a class to teach. I didn't have time to . . . well, to rehash the same sorrows I'd already dealt with earlier in the week.

"I'll meet you there." I stood on my tiptoes and gave Ted a quick kiss.

Upon walking into the pizza parlor, I was happy to see at least one other person in Renaissance Faire garb. Still, I was glad I'd brought a change of clothes to put on after I got to the Seven-Year Stitch. I didn't want to spend the rest of the day looking as if I'd just stepped off a cocoa box.

Ted put his hand at the small of my back. I tensed slightly, afraid he was going to ask if I was all right, but then I relaxed when he made small talk about how good the pizza smelled and how hungry he was.

The hostess came and seated us. When we ordered the buffet, she told us she'd get our drinks—water for both of us—and that we could help ourselves.

I'd always thought buffets were such fun. They gave you an opportunity to try things you wouldn't order otherwise. I always selected at least one small slice of ham and pineapple pizza at the buffet. I didn't like it enough to have it often, but I enjoyed it on occasions like this.

There was also a chicken Alfredo pizza on the buffet. I'd never tried that, so I got a small slice of that also. Then, to be on the safe side, I got a slice of sausage pizza and a breadstick.

When I returned to the table, I saw that Ted had already sat down and that Paul Samms was standing there talking with him. Today Paul had ditched his minstrel's clothing for a gray silk suit.

"Hi, Paul. Where's Vera?" I asked.

"She went up to Portland to do a little shopping," he said. "She's going to be livid when I tell her it was Nellie who vandalized your booth at the festival."

I glanced at Ted as I sat down at the table.

"Paul heard about Nellie's arrest over the police scanner, and then he called her attorney," Ted said. "The attorney is going to meet with Paul and give him a statement for tomorrow's *Examiner*."

"Pure damage control is what he's doing," Paul said. "And I can't say that I blame him. Residents of Tallulah Falls are going to despise Nellie when they learn what she did out of malice and spite. She might even need to pull up stakes and relocate after this fiasco."

"Won't you have a seat, Paul?" I asked.

"No, dear, but I appreciate your asking. I was just leaving. I'm sorry it was Nellie who trashed your booth, but I am glad you got some closure over it."

"Thanks," I said. "You say the lawyer will be doing damage control. What do you think he'll say?"

"He'll say that Nellie was overcome with grief about her sister's death and that she lashed out without even realizing the magnitude of her actions," he said. "I could write the article for you now, have you keep it until after I meet with the attorney, and I probably wouldn't have to change but a word or two before the piece went to press."

"Maybe it *was* her grief that made her do such a horrible thing." I took a sip of my water.

"Marcy, don't look so sad," said Paul. "The woman did this to herself."

"I know, but I can't help feeling sorry for her . . . at least a tad. I think Nellie must've had a very sad life."

"Or maybe she's just mean and deserves what she's got coming to her." Paul looked at Ted. "Am I right?"

"You could be right, Paul," he said.

Paul glanced at his watch. "Gotta run, folks. See you soon."

Ted and I ate our pizza in silence for a few moments. The chicken Alfredo slice was interesting, better than I'd thought it would be.

"Do you agree with Paul that the whole town will turn against Nellie?" I asked.

Ted wiped his mouth on his napkin. "Maybe for a while. But she runs the only aromatherapy shop in Tallulah Falls and she seems to have a fair amount of traffic, so her customers won't hold anything against her for long." He shrugged. "Who knows? Maybe Nellie will take this entire incident as a wake-up call."

"Because she's having to suffer the consequences of her actions?" I asked.

"Yeah. And maybe she'll learn that you have to be a friend to have a friend. I mean, that's stuff everybody else finds out in kindergarten, right?"

I smiled. "Right. But if that lesson hasn't hit home to her yet, I don't think it ever will."

I felt slightly better as I walked into the Seven-Year Stitch.

"You're early," said Julie.

"I know." I held up the pink-and-white-striped tote bag I was carrying. "I wanted to change clothes before you left."

"I don't blame you. As cute as that is, I can't imagine it would be all that comfy."

"It isn't." I went into the bathroom and changed into jeans and a heather gray sweater set.

When I came back into the shop, Julie told me she was sorry to have to take me away from the Renaissance Faire.

"Don't worry about that," I said. "The whole Ren Faire experience has been a bit of a letdown for me. And to think I'd been so excited about it."

"You've just had some horrible luck, that's all," she said. "If you hadn't been the one to find Clara . . . and then if that vandal hadn't chosen your booth to trash . . . then it would have been fun."

"It was Nellie," I said.

"What?"

"It was Nellie Davis who demolished my booth. She came into the merchants' building today and confessed to the whole thing."

"You're kidding," said Julie.

"I'm not. She started ranting and raving, and then one of the undercover police officers took her away. She's been charged with criminal trespass and criminal mischief."

"Wow. . . . Did she say why she did it?"

"She seemed to think there might've been something I could've done for Clara," I said. "I don't think she believes I did anything to *hurt* Clara . . . but she certainly doesn't think I did anything to help her, either."

"You did your best, and you know that," Julie said. "Try not to think about it."

"And you try not to think about anything except learning this new job," I said with a smile. "But I know you're going to do great."

"I wish I had as much confidence in myself as you have in me."

After getting my reassurance that she looked fine, Julie left.

"Don't be nervous!" I called after her. I knew I was wasting my breath, but I really did know she'd do well. She seemed to catch on to new skills quickly, her personality appeared to be in sync with Riley's, and she enjoyed learning things.

I sat down on the stool beside Jill.

"Hi, there," I said to the mannequin. "Have you missed me?"

Some. I'm sorry you've had such a sucky experience at the Faire. I'd hoped it would be more pleasant for you.

"And I'd hoped the very same thing!"

See how often my imaginary friend and I were on the same wavelength? No, I didn't think she was real . . . and that made her all the more fun to chat with on occasion. Real people seldom said what you wanted to hear.

The bells over the door jingled, and a young woman with shoulder-length blond hair walked in.

"Hi. Welcome to the Seven-Year Stitch. May I help you find something?"

"Just browsing at the moment, thanks," she said.

She walked around the store looking at the displays more than at the products. But that was okay. A lot of people did that . . . at least, at first.

"Did you do all these?" she asked.

"I did."

"They're really pretty. You must have a lot of patience."

"Some days," I said. "But I find stitching relaxing."

"That's good." She frowned. "What's with the rough-looking bear?"

She'd noticed the Kodiak bear that Vera had given to Angus some time ago. Surprisingly, the bear had lasted much longer than I'd anticipated.

"That belongs to Angus, my Irish wolfhound," I said. "He's at home today . . . for now, anyway. I'm planning on bringing him to class with me this evening."

She nodded. "By the way, I'm Erin Palmer. I understand you found my grandmother last week."

I gasped. "That's right. I did. I'm sorry for your loss."

"How did you find her?" Erin asked. "I mean, what condition was she in? Did she appear to be in any distress?"

I paused, then said, "Well . . . when I found her, she was lying on her side on the floor. The rocking chair she'd been sitting on was kind of on top of her. I didn't know what had happened, and I was afraid to move her. I didn't want to hurt her worse somehow."

"Sure. Was she awake?"

"No. She was unconscious. May I get you a bottle of water, Erin?"

"No, thanks. I'm fine," she said. "So . . . when you got there, she wasn't suffering."

"She didn't appear to be. Were you and Clara close?"

"Not very. I actually didn't know her all that well." She lifted and dropped one shoulder. "Still, when someone is family, you have questions . . . or I do, anyway. Clara married Granddad about three years before he died. I was away at college for most of the time they were married."

"I understand your grandfather hasn't been gone that long," I said. "As I said, I'm sorry for your loss."

"Thank you," said Erin. "What happened to Clover?"

"Clara's sister, Nellie, gave Clover away. Why? Did you want her?"

"No. I have allergies," she said. "I just want the poor little thing to have a good home somewhere."

"Well, the woman who has Clover now dotes on her," I said. "I think Clover will be happy."

"Good. I didn't want her to end up in a Crock-Pot or something."

That was a gruesome thought. I realized some people ate rabbit, but surely not rabbits with whom they are—or I am—personally acquainted. The thought of anyone eating little Clover made my stomach churn.

"Were any of your grandfather's family members close to Clara and her sons?" I asked.

"Not really," said Erin. "My older sister got married and went to work for a nonprofit conservation society, so she wasn't around much. My younger sister still lives with our mom, and Mom doesn't like Clara. She never approved of Granddad marrying—in Mom's words—'that old gold digger,' so they didn't visit Granddad and Clara very often, either."

"What about Clara's sister, Nellie? Do you know her?"

"I didn't even know Clara *had* a sister until the funeral," Erin said. "I'm being honest—we didn't have much to do with Granddad, his wife, or her family. That's sad to say . . . especially now that both Granddad and Clara are gone . . . but that's just how it is."

Chapter Twenty-six

An elegant woman with salt-and-pepper hair pulled into a French twist walked into the Seven-Year Stitch not long after Erin Palmer had left. She wore a burgundy suit and black pumps, and she carried a black envelope clutch.

"Good afternoon," I said. "Welcome to the Seven-Year Stitch. Is there anything I might help you with?"

"I hope so," she said. "My grandmother was from Bulgaria, and she embroidered some beautiful pieces. She's gone now, and I've been thinking about her and that style of embroidery for quite a while. Do you have any pattern books for Bulgarian embroidery?"

"I don't have any in stock," I said. "But if you'll have a seat, I'll grab my laptop and we'll see what my distributors might have available."

"Thank you." She walked over to the sofa that faced away from the window and sat down. "You have a lovely boutique."

"Thanks!" I went into the office and got my laptop. I brought the computer to the sit-and-stitch square and sat on the club chair adjacent to the customer.

To make conversation while the laptop was booting up, I said, "I didn't even realize there *was* a distinct form of Bulgarian embroidery."

"Oh, yes. One of the main things that sets it apart from other styles is that everything is outlined in black," she said.

I typed in a distributor's Web address.

"And there are styles that correlate to different regions," she continued. "There's the Samokov, the Gabrovo, and the Sokai."

"What region was your grandmother from?" I put *Bulgarian embroidery* into the site's search engine.

"She was from Gabrovo."

"Have you ever been there?" I asked.

"No," she said. "Maybe someday."

I told her that this distributor had two books, one on different styles of Bulgarian embroideries and one that was a reproduction of a pamphlet of Bulgarian embroidery created in the late 1800s.

"Oh, I'd like both, please."

"All right. I'll order them right now, and they should be here Friday," I said. "You can either leave me your number so I can call you when the books arrive, or you can call me to find out whether they're here or not."

"I'll leave you my number." She took a card from her purse and handed it to me. "But I'd like one of your business cards as well."

I hopped up from the club chair and got her one of my cards from the holder on the counter.

She rose and extended her hand. "Thank you so much. I'm really looking forward to getting the books."

I shook her hand. "I'll look around at some other sites, and if I find anything else I think you'd be interested in, I'll let you know."

She thanked me and left.

I checked other distributors for books on Bulgarian embroidery. I found the same ones, and I made note of one other that I came across. I'd call and tell her about it later.

Since I was already on the Internet, I checked my social media sites. Riley had put up some adorable photos of Laura in her faerie costume. There were a few memes that gave me a chuckle, and there were a couple links to embroidery-related blog posts that I clicked through and read. One of the blogs had a picture of a woman who reminded me of Amelia. She had certainly rushed to my defense when she'd heard Nellie berating me.

Thinking about Amelia, I decided to learn more about falcons. Was that Herodias as mean as she looked? I'd somehow begun to think of her as the equivalent of an attack dog. She loved her owner but would harm anyone else on command. I doubted she was a people person . . . er, falcon. But maybe I was misjudging the bird.

I found a site dedicated to birds of prey, and I read aloud from the page to Jill:

"Falcons are part of the family Falconidae. Males are called tiercels and are smaller than the females. Types of falcons include the gryfalcon—that seems appropriate, don't you think, Jill? Grrrrr . . . falcon." I giggled at my silly joke. "I think our site is a school science page or something. Anyway, back to types of falcons, there are merlins—cool—lanner falcons, forest falcons, and laughing falcons. Huh. Wonder whether I should tell Herodias a joke to see if she laughs."

I skimmed on down the page. When I read how falcons kill their prey, I quickly closed the tab.

"Eww, Jill, I'll spare you that. As it is, I'm sure I'll have nightmares of Herodias ripping me apart tonight." I had no idea why I was frightened of that bird. I usually loved all kinds of animals. I'd even held a ball python at a fair once that was longer than I was tall. Granted, that wasn't saying much for a lot of things, but a snake well over five feet long was pretty large in my book.

I remembered the patch on Amelia's blue jacket. It was yellow and had black letters: osoc. I wondered what the acronym stood for. I was guessing one of the *O*s stood for *Oregon*. So I did a search for *Oregon SOC*.

The best match was *Oregon Society for Ornithological Conservation*. I clicked on the link.

This OSOC was a nonprofit conservatory group. I remembered Erin saying her sister worked with a nonprofit group. What were the odds? Was it possible that Amelia was Erin's sister? Could it be that the conversation between Amelia and Clara on Thursday hadn't been random but that Amelia had gone to talk with Clara about her grandfather's estate?

But if that were the case, why hadn't Amelia admitted to being Clara's step-granddaughter? Had she been afraid she'd be accused of the murder? Or was she simply ashamed because Clara had been so hateful to everyone?

I called Ted. He didn't answer, so I left him a voice mail: "Hi, sweetheart. I'm calling to ask you if Erin Palmer has a sister named Amelia. Give me a call back when you have time, okay? Thanks. I love you."

I ended the call, put my phone on the table, and turned off the laptop. I retrieved my tote bag from behind the counter and took out the poet's shirt I was embellishing with blackwork. As I worked, I thought about the shirts I'd sold Friday and Saturday before Nellie had wrecked my booth. I was grateful that not all the shirts had been destroyed and that some were being enjoyed by festivalgoers. I saw one on a woman today—she was wearing the shirt with a black skirt and riding boots.

I thought again about my conversation with Nellie . . . how bitter she was . . . not just toward me but toward almost everyone. She wanted nothing to do with Clara's family. She presumed they didn't want anything to do with her, either, but wouldn't it be worth it to at least find out?

I wondered about Nellie's past. Had she ever married? She spoke about Clara not being close to her when life was good. She'd acted as if Clara wanted to be with her only when she wanted something or had no one else.

I shook my head, as if to clear the thoughts of Nellie Davis out of it. I preferred to think of more pleasant things. Nellie's problems weren't my problems. I *had* a couple problems, thanks to Nellie—namely the destroyed pieces I'd worked so hard to complete—but they were nothing I couldn't overcome.

It was too quiet in here. With so many people at the Ren Faire or at work, and the fact that it was the typical three o'clock slump, the Stitch was so still I could've heard my pin drop . . . literally. I set my project aside and booted the laptop up again. What I needed was some music.

I was scrolling through my playlists when I heard a scream pierce the silence. I froze and listened intently . . . desperately hoping my imagination was playing tricks on me.

I got up and went to the window. I didn't hear anything else. I didn't see anyone outside on the sidewalk. Maybe I *was* hearing things . . . or maybe it had been a strange bird cry . . . or something. I decided to peep out the door just to make sure.

I looked toward MacKenzies' Mochas. I saw a couple people walking toward the coffeehouse, but they looked normal and content. I looked in the other direction—toward Knitted and Needled and Scentsibilities. My heart sank. A skinny, black-clad body was crumpled on the sidewalk.

Oh, no. Not again!

I sprinted up the sidewalk. "Nellie!"

She lifted her head. She was sobbing. Her face was bruised, and her red-framed glasses were broken.

"May I help you up?" I asked.

She nodded, rolled over, and pulled herself into a sitting position.

I bent and put one arm around her bony shoulders. I took her right hand in mine. "On three, we'll stand and walk to the Stitch . . . all right?"

Again, she nodded.

"One . . . two . . . three . . ." I pulled her as gently as I could while still being effective enough to help her stand.

It worked. She stood shakily and walked with me to the Seven-Year Stitch.

"What happened?" I asked.

She didn't answer. She merely sobbed.

I walked her into the store and sat her on the sofa facing away from the window. "Stretch out there or put your feet up on the ottoman while I call the police." I handed her a couple of tissues from the box on the counter.

I called Ted, but he still didn't answer. I called Manu.

"Chief Manu Singh," he answered.

"Hi, Manu. It's Marcy Singer." I quickly explained how I'd found Nellie. "I'll be right there," he said. "I'll have the paramedics meet me. Try to keep her calm."

"I'll do my best." As if I could possibly be a calming influence on Nellie Davis.

I ended the call and put the phone in my pocket.

"Can I get you a bottle of water or something?" I asked Nellie.

She shook her head.

"Where are you hurt, besides your face?" I was trying to look her over, but she'd drawn herself up into a ball and was rocking back and forth.

She took off her glasses and placed them on the coffee table. "I just went in through the back to check on things. I didn't lock the door behind me because I wasn't going to be but a few minutes."

"And someone came in behind you?" I asked.

"He was dressed up in a black cape that covered his entire body, and he wore a gold mask with a long nose." She breathed raggedly. "He whispered something about Clara. I should have been more scared . . . but instead I was angry. I reached for that mask. That's when I got hit in the face." She started crying again.

I sat down beside her and put my arm around her. "You're safe now. Manu and the paramedics are on their way."

"Thank you." She dabbed at her eyes with the tissues. "I didn't lock either of the doors back."

"Whoever did this to you might still be in your shop," I said. "We'll have Manu investigate and then lock the doors for you."

She nodded.

"Do you know why someone would do this? Do you think it was a robbery?"

"No . . . he had to have followed me to the store. And he spoke about Clara," she said. "I think it was whoever killed Clara . . . and he thinks I know who he is."

"Do you?" I asked.

"I don't think so."

"Nellie, what were you and Clara arguing about Thursday evening?"

"About the money . . . she was spending too much."

"Are you talking about the money from her late husband's estate?" I asked.

"She used it to open her shop," she said. "Now it's almost gone. I warned her they'd all be mad over it—her kids, his kids . . . everybody."

"Maybe she was looking at it as an investment," I said.

"She said it was hers . . . that she'd earned it caring for that hateful old man for three years."

It was then that Manu, a couple of paramedics, and two deputies came into the shop.

The paramedics hurried to Nellie's side and began examining her.

"Has she said much?" Manu asked me quietly.

"Surprisingly, yes," I said, thinking Nellie must've been fairly addled to have been willing to talk to me. "She thinks the person who attacked her might be the same person who killed Clara."

"Has anyone gone into Ms. Davis's shop since the time of the attack?" he asked.

"Not that I know of."

He motioned the two deputies over and instructed them to proceed with caution but to ex-amine Nellie's shop for evidence. "I'm guessing her attacker is long gone, but, hopefully, you'll find something."

"She told me the man who attacked her was wearing a black cape and a gold, long-nosed mask," I said. "She said the cape completely disguised the person's body."

Manu frowned slightly. "Ms. Davis, do you feel up to talking with me?"

"We really need to get her to the hospital," said one of the paramedics. "I believe she has a concussion, and she should have an MRI."

"All right," said Manu. "I'll touch base with my deputies and meet you there."

The paramedics went to get the stretcher from the ambulance.

Manu stooped down in front of Nellie. "Ms. Davis, can you describe your attacker?"

"No. He wore a cape and a mask," she said.

"Are you sure it was a man?" he asked.

"No. I don't know. He was all covered up. But he hit me . . . with his fist," she said. "What woman would do that?"

"Plenty," said Manu. "You'd be surprised. Did you notice any tattoos on the attacker's hands or arms?"

"No."

The paramedics returned with the stretcher and gently lifted Nellie onto it.

"I'll let these gentlemen take care of you now," Manu told Nellie. "I'll be at the hospital to check on you and to talk with you in just a little while."

"Do you have an extra pair of glasses?" I asked Nellie. "I imagine one of Chief Singh's deputies would go to your house and get them for you."

She nodded. "My keys are in my purse . . . in the shop somewhere."

"We'll take care of it," said Manu. "Where are your glasses, Ms. Davis?"

"In the medicine cabinet in the master bathroom."

Manu patted my shoulder as the paramedics wheeled Nellie out. "That was good thinking. I didn't even consider asking her about a spare pair of glasses."

I wanted to ask Manu a question, but I hesitated.

He seemed to have read my mind. "It couldn't have been West. He's been under police security all day."

"Apparently whoever attacked Nellie doesn't know that," I said.

He nodded. "It does look as if the attacker went to a lot of trouble to implicate Mr. West. There are other ways to conceal one's identity than with a gold mask and a black cloak."

Chapter Twenty-seven

My hands were shaking too badly to resume the blackwork, so I paced near the sit-and-stitch square. I was relieved when Ted arrived.

"I just heard," he said as he came through the door. "I was in a meeting and had my phone turned off. Are you all right?"

"I'm fine. It's Nellie I'm concerned about. Apparently, her attacker hit her right in the face." I shook my head. "Who strikes an old lady? In the *face*!"

"The deputies Manu brought with him are still combing through her shop. Hopefully, they'll find something."

"Did Manu tell you the attacker was dressed as the Crow?" I asked. "Do you think Mr. West sent someone to hurt Nellie? Or was the attacker trying to frame him, unaware that he's currently under police protection?"

Ted took his phone from his jacket pocket and punched in a number. "Hey, it's Nash. Has West made any personal calls? Ask him if he has a beef with someone named Nellie Davis. Yeah, I'll wait."

While Ted was on the phone, I stepped into the office and got us both a bottle of white grape juice.

"Okay . . . yeah . . . let me know what you find out." He ended the call, uncapped the bottle, and took a drink. "West acted as if he wasn't familiar with the name Nellie Davis. When told she was Clara's sister, West said basically that Nellie's attack must be connected with Clara's death but he doesn't know how or why."

"We know that much," I said. I opened my bottle of grape juice and took a long, refreshing drink. "And the only suspect we're positive *didn't* attack Nellie is Mr. West, because he's been guarded by police all day . . . right?"

"Right. He hasn't made any phone calls today either, so he didn't order someone else to do it," Ted said. "The deputy I spoke with said they'd ordered a pizza and played cards all day."

"Wow. Good work if you can get it." I took another drink of my juice.

"Why don't you cancel this evening's class?"

I hesitated.

"Look, Nellie's attacker hasn't been caught and probably won't be caught tonight," he said. "Your booth at the Ren Faire was singled out. I don't want you or your students put in harm's way by this nut job."

"You're forgetting that Nellie is the one who trashed my booth," I said. "Since *that* nut job is in the hospital, I don't think my students and I have anything to fear tonight."

"I'm not forgetting about Nellie trashing your

booth. I'm just wondering if she really did it. I still can't wrap my mind around a woman her age coming out in the middle of the night to sneak onto the fairgrounds, pick a lock, and destroy your booth."

"Then why did she confess?" I asked.

"I don't know, Inch-High. I just have a bad gut feeling about all of this. And don't forget there *is* still an attacker out there," he said. "There's no guarantee he won't be back. If he targeted Nellie because of Clara, you can bet he's aware that you found Clara's body."

"Okay, okay. You're right," I said. "I don't want to be responsible for any of my students getting hurt. I'll reschedule the class."

I went to the counter and got the roster for tonight's class, sat on the stool, and began calling my students.

Ted set his juice on the counter and gestured to let me know that he was going up the street to Nellie's shop to see how things were going with the deputies.

When he came back, I was just finishing up my last call.

"So what did you learn?" I asked.

He shook his head. "They can't find a thing."

"But the attacker was dressed in the same costume Marcus West wore at the Renaissance Faire," I said. "That has to mean something."

"I believe you're right that the attacker meant to throw suspicion on West." He took out his phone, called his deputy, and asked him to find out who knew how West was disguising himself at the Ren Faire. "Let me know what you learn. Thanks." He ended the call and returned the phone to his pocket.

"Why don't we go ahead and get out of here?" he asked. "You've had a rough day."

I gave him a wan smile. "I *am* ready to get out of here." I got up off the stool and went to the office for my tote bag and purse.

"Want me to drive you?" Ted asked. "We can always come back for your Jeep later, or we can have Blake and Sadie bring it home."

"No, I'm good," I said. "Thanks, though."

He put his hands on my shoulders. "You were pretty shaky when I got here. Are you sure you're okay to drive?"

"I'm fine. Besides, I thought maybe we could take Angus to the beach later. We'll definitely need the Jeep for that."

"All right." He gave me a kiss. "I'll be right behind you . . . unless you want me to stop for Chinese takeout."

"I could go for some Chinese . . . and I certainly don't want to cook tonight." I locked the doors. "See you in a few."

I was kind of glad for the opportunity to decompress at home alone for a little while. I adored Ted, but I didn't want him to know how scared I'd been during the whole episode with Nellie. It had also crossed my mind, as it had Ted's, that Nellie's being the one who'd demolished my booth was a little too convenient. On the other hand, though, I couldn't imagine Nellie covering for anyone. I mean, why would she?

When I got home, I went through the house and out the back door, where I sat down on the swing. Angus gladly came over, crawled up onto the seat beside me, and stretched out across my lap. I gently moved the swing back and forth and petted the dog.

Unlike Ted, Angus wouldn't try to fix anything. He would just let me sit here until I felt better. I could talk if I wanted to, but I didn't have to. I could cry . . . or not. It was up to me. Whatever I wanted to do was all right. Angus was an excellent therapist.

I stayed there until I heard Ted's car pull into the driveway. Angus got up off the swing and went to peep over the fence.

I got up and opened the door. Angus left the fence and came to go in ahead of me.

"I haven't fed him yet," I said to Ted. "I went outside and lost track of time while sitting on the swing."

"Good," said Ted. "That's what you needed to do."

I filled Angus's bowl with kibble, but he wasn't particularly interested. He knew Ted had something better in those funky little boxes with the wire handles. He kept sniffing the air and moving around the table.

"Sorry," I said. "He probably won't eat his dinner until we're finished with ours."

"That's fine. A little moo shu pork won't hurt him." He looked at Angus. "Right, buddy?"

Angus opened his mouth and panted, making it look as if he were laughing because he and Ted had put something over on me.

I smiled and shook my head. "You're gonna spoil him, you know?"

"Well, it's a good thing I came along when I did, then," said Ted. "Because this is one of the most unspoiled dogs I've ever seen. If any dog could use some spoiling, it's this one."

"Touché," I said. "But you'll spoil him *worse*. How's that?"

"We guys have to stick together. Right, Angus?"

Angus gave him a dopey look and sat beside him, obviously waiting for a treat.

After dinner, we took Angus to the beach. Ted and I were walking hand in hand while Angus ran ahead of us and explored everything.

"Did Manu mention how Nellie is doing?" I asked.

"She's going to be fine. They're keeping her overnight because she does have a concussion, but there wasn't anything major wrong."

"That's good."

"I wish she'd gotten a better look at her attacker. Maybe then we could figure out how that person is linked to Marcus West," said Ted.

"Does anyone know why Marcus West would choose to call himself the Crow? I mean, he could've called himself El Doctoro or whatever the Italians call the costume . . . but he didn't have to call himself anything at all. What was the point?"

"I don't know. I haven't heard anyone say why he did it. Let's try to reason it out. What do we know about crows?"

"Well . . . they're very intelligent birds," I said.

"They'll eat almost anything, including carrion," said Ted.

"Um . . . ew . . . I don't think Marcus West was trying to convey that he'll eat roadkill," I said. "Or at least I *hope* that wasn't his intention."

Ted chuckled. "I've heard they tend to be tight with their families."

"Are you serious?"

"Yes! You think I'd make that up?" he asked.

"Sometimes I can't tell with you."

"The young stay with their parents up until they're about six years old," he said.

"So you think West might've been making a statement about family by calling himself the Crow?" I asked.

"Wait . . . I've got it. There's a comic book character called the Crow. The series was created by James O'Barr," Ted said. "The Crow avenges wrongful deaths."

"Like Joe Palmer's," I said.

"Exactly."

Ted's phone rang. He checked the screen. "It's one of the deputies with West."

"Take the call." I walked on ahead to see what Angus had found.

He was studying a flat rock that was shaped like a lopsided heart. He sniffed at it and then slapped it with his paw.

"Do you like that rock?" I asked.

He looked up at me, tilted his head, and then looked back down at the rock. He gave a playful bark.

I picked up the rock and brushed the sand off of it.

Satisfied that he'd done his job—whatever that might be in this instance—Angus happily trotted off to see what else he could discover.

I zipped my jacket, leaned against the retaining wall, and looked out at the ocean. It was a beautiful evening. The waves crashed against the shore, leaving the sand slick and foamy in their wake. The sky was a brilliant blue except for the yellow, orange, and gray where the sun was lowering itself into the sea. A cluster of wispy clouds hung overhead as if they'd gathered to watch the sunset.

Ted came over to me. "Do you have any idea how beautiful you look standing there?"

I smiled. "Not a clue."

He showed me the photo he'd just snapped with his phone.

I laughed, and he pulled me into his arms for a kiss.

"I found out a bit more about our friend Marcus West," he said.

"Oh?"

"He opened up to the deputies about what happened the day of the fire. He'd gone to run an errand of some sort, and when he came back, the office was in flames. He hurried home—well, one street over from his home because he was being careful—and gathered up some things."

"So he knew from the moment he saw the fire that it was arson?" I asked. "He didn't even consider that it could've been an accident?"

"Apparently not," said Ted. "He said he gathered what cash he had on hand, got some clothes—including the Crow costume—and called a cab. He had the cab pick him up—"

"Let me guess," I interrupted. "One street over?"

"You got it. The cab took him to a hotel, where he checked in as Mark Crow. He told the deputies that dressing up as the Crow and attending the Ren Faire allowed him to talk with people anonymously, find out what was being said about the fire, and learn what people thought had happened to Marcus West."

"And what about Clara?" I asked. "Does he know anything about her murder?"

"He says he doesn't know anything definitive, but he believes Lacey Palmer is somehow involved."

"But you said Lacey Palmer has an ironclad alibi for the evening of Clara's murder," I said.

"She does," said Ted. "But West thinks she's highly manipulative . . . that she could get someone else to do her bidding so the murder can't be pinned on her."

"Just like she did in the case of her late husband," I said.

"If West's story pans out, then yes."

"How soon will it be before you'll know whether West is telling the truth?"

"It shouldn't be long," Ted said. "I'd say another day at most."

"Good. I'll be glad when this whole mess is over with," I said. "Who did he trust with his identity?"

"No one. He says the only people who could've seen him when he was unmasked were the desk clerks at the hotel—but he insists he took precautions against that—and maybe someone at the Ren Faire when he'd taken his mask off to eat or drink," he said. "He says he tried to hide during those instances, but it's possible someone saw and recognized him."

"If I didn't know the juggler is a police officer, I'd be suspicious of him," I said. "That one day when I was trying to get the Crow to talk with you, the juggler came and got right between us to get me to light his torch. After the Crow got away, I thought maybe they were working together."

"That juggler wasn't our guy," said Ted. "The guy that I made douse the torches that day was *not* our undercover officer. A cop wouldn't have been so reckless. Looking back, though, I guess they do look alike . . . same build . . . same hair color. . . ."

"Well, the only time I saw *your* juggler was when I thought the Crow was pulling a gun on you and the juggler and the knight were there to back you up," I said. "I didn't look that closely at him. I merely assumed he was the same guy."

"We need to find that juggler and see what he knows," said Ted. "I'll call Manu and have him meet me at the Ren Faire." He whistled, and Angus trotted back to us.

"Want me to come, too?" I asked. "I can identify the guy."

"A second ago you thought he was our undercover officer."

"Good point. I'll stay home and leave the investigating to you this time."

Chapter Twenty-eight

While Angus and I were waiting for Ted to return from the Ren Faire, I turned the television on and began scrolling through the channels. *Once a Queen*, a movie Mom had done the costuming for, was playing. It was halfway through, but I knew the film by heart. It was a good one, plus I could reminisce about all the stories Mom had told me while she was working on the set.

I put the television on the channel where *Once a Queen* was playing, and I covered up in a green fleece throw. Angus lay down beside the sofa, and before long I heard him snoring.

Once a Queen told the story of a queen named Kathleen who wanted a better life for her younger sister, Esme. The queen's marriage had been arranged and most of her life had been mapped out for her. She saw that her sister Esme could have opportunities that she herself could never have, and she used her position and power to give Esme everything she wanted ... or everything she *thought* Esme wanted.

In the end, Esme resented Kathleen's interference. She'd wanted to live her own life, not the life Kathleen had envisioned for her. In a very real sense, Kathleen had dominated Esme's life and created the same situation for Esme that Kathleen had despised. It was sort of a take on what the Bard had said of Othello: one who loved not wisely but too well. In trying to give Esme everything, Kathleen had taken away her sister's freedom and her choices.

I sat thinking about the movie long after the credits ran and the next movie began. Something about the sisters was nagging at the back of my mind.

Everything about Clara's murder and Ted's cold case circled back to Lacey Palmer: Five years ago, her abusive, philandering husband dies and leaves his wife a rich woman. A win-win for Lacey. Marcus West's building burns to the ground, and then he comes to the police claiming to have damning evidence against Lacey. While he's in protective custody, someone dressed in a way to cast suspicion on West beats Nellie Davis and threatens her. Clara won't turn over Lacey's father's money to Lacey's children. Clara winds up dead.

Since Ted claimed that Lacey had an airtight alibi for the Thursday evening when Clara was murdered, I was beginning to wonder if Lacey had an accomplice—maybe a sister, or a brother—who was more than willing to help her get the justice they both felt she and her family deserved.

When Ted got back, he informed me that the juggler was nowhere to be found.

"When Manu and I got there, it was nearly closing time," he said. "We'd called ahead and had our guys searching for the juggler, but they had been unable to locate him. We did a quick search of the grounds, but we didn't have any luck. We're going to try again tomorrow. If you see the juggler in the morning when you get to the Ren Faire, don't approach him or interact with him. Simply go to your booth and give me a call."

"Okay," I said. "Crazy thought here—do you think he could be Lacey Palmer's brother?"

He frowned. "Lacey Palmer has a brother?"

"I don't know. Does she?"

"Not that I know of," he said.

"Wouldn't that be in the cold case file?"

"No. Her siblings—or lack thereof—had no bearing on the case."

"That you know of," I said. "Just check and see if she has any . . . please."

"Sure, Inch-High. You want to share your theory with me?"

"Not yet. You'd think it was too"—I waved my hands—"out-there."

He held open his arms. "Well, tonight I'd rather you be in here."

I happily snuggled into his embrace.

On Thursday morning, I considered going to check on Nellie. But on the one hand, I thought they'd probably examined her and then let her go home by then. And on the other hand, whether she was still at the hospital or not, she probably wasn't on powerful enough drugs to consider being nice to me. So I went on to the Ren Faire.

I saw the juggler from a distance as soon as I walked through the gate. Today he was juggling plates. I wanted so badly to try to engage him in conversation, but Ted had advised against that. Besides, I didn't want to wind up getting brained by a plate.

I got out of the stream of pedestrian traffic entering the fairgrounds and called Ted.

"Good morning, beautiful," he said.

"Hi. I see the juggler," I said quietly. "He's juggling white plates near the stables."

"Thanks, babe. I'll alert our undercover officers. Stay safe, and I'll see you soon."

After talking with Ted, I headed toward the merchants' building. Along the way, I heard someone call to me. Turning, I saw that it was Amelia. I was surprised that Herodias wasn't with her.

"Hi, there," I said. "How are you today?"

"Great," she said.

"Where's Herodias?" I asked.

"I haven't taken her out of her cage yet. I leave her here at night, locked inside one of the buildings."

"Don't you worry about her?"

"Nah. I'm one of the last to leave and one of the first to get here every morning," she said. "Leaving her here gives us both a break from each other."

"Pets can be a huge responsibility," I said.

"True, but, hey, they're nicer than a lot of family members, right?" She laughed. "At least, that's the case with me and Herodias."

"I know the feeling," I said, glad she had given me an opening to ask about her family. It suddenly struck me that in all of yesterday's excitement, Ted never did say whether Erin Palmer had a sister named Amelia. "Do you have brothers or sisters, Amelia?"

"One of each—an older sister and a younger brother," she said. "I wouldn't take anything for either one of them, but they can try my patience sometimes, you know?"

I nodded. "Your sister's name isn't Erin, is it?"

Amelia frowned. "No. Why?"

"I met a young woman named Erin the other day, and she just reminded me of you." Sure, Erin appeared to be younger than Amelia, but I wasn't done fishing yet. After learning that Amelia was in a conservation group and that Erin's sister was also, I'd convinced myself that they were siblings.

She smirked. "Poor girl."

"Actually, she was very attractive . . . as are you," I said. "I'd better run. I have a shirt I need to get finished by the end of the day."

"Good luck!"

I walked into the merchants' building and was glad to see that Sister Mary Alice was manning Nellie's booth rather than Washerwoman Jan. Jan had been cool toward me ever since she'd missed seeing the juggler with the flaming torches.

I put my purse and tote bag under my table, and then went over to talk with Mary Alice.

"Hi," I said as I stepped into the booth.

"Hey, Marcy. How're you doing this morning, hon?"

"I'm fine. How about you?"

"Doing well, all things considered," she said.

I noticed a prescription bottle on the table in front of her. "Are you sick?"

"No, it's just my blood pressure medicine. I have to take it every day with breakfast," she said. "Wasn't it Bette Davis who said, 'Growing old is not for sissies'?"

"I believe it was," I said with a smile.

"So what's new with you? Things are bound to be better now that you have your booth fixed up and all," she said. "I've not meant to eavesdrop, but I've heard you take a lot of shirt orders."

"Yeah, that's going well. Also, I was lucky to have sold several on Friday and Saturday before the vandal got to them on Saturday night," I said. "Some people have admired those shirts on the wearers and have come by my booth to place orders."

"That's good." She shook her head. "I still can't get over Nellie doing such a thing."

"Neither can I. Did you hear what happened to her yesterday?"

"I don't think so," she said.

"She stopped by her store, and she was attacked," I said.

"Was she hurt badly?"

"The attacker punched her in the face and broke her glasses." I winced at the memory of Nellie's bruised face. It most likely looked even worse today. "Anyway, she was taken to the hospital and someone mentioned she had a concussion. I haven't heard whether they've released her or not."

"It wasn't you, was it?" Sister Mary Alice asked.

I gasped. "No!"

She laughed. "Relax, hon. I'm joking!"

"Oh . . . of course."

"Although I wouldn't have blamed you if you had roughed her up," she said. "If she'd torn up something of mine—something I'd worked as hard on as you had the things in your booth—I'd have wanted to punch her."

"I guess that thought *did* cross my mind," I said. "But still . . . she's so old . . . and frail. How could someone *do* something like that to her?"

"Marcy, let me give you a piece of advice. From what I've seen of Nellie Davis, and knowing what she did to your booth, I imagine she did something to provoke that attack. Never let someone's age—especially someone's advanced age—make you underestimate what they're capable of. And, if she had it coming, there are people who don't care a whit about age, sex, or size. Justice is justice."

Sister Mary Alice went from looking dead serious to laughing. "How's that for a nun with some street cred, kiddo?"

I laughed. "Pretty good! You had me going. I'd better get next door and get to work. Talk with you later."

I went back to my booth, sat down at the table, and got out my tote bag. I took out the shirt I was embellishing and began to embroider.

Justice is justice.

It wasn't just street cred. Mary Alice had meant what she said. That didn't make her a bad person, though. So why did I have a bad feeling pricking at the back of my neck?

I texted Ted: *Did you ever find out whether Lacey Palmer had any siblings?*

I knew I was being ridiculous. Mary Alice was simply making small talk and probably trying to make me feel better by making me see that while Nellie had destroyed many of my things, someone had hurt her, so karma had come back around to bite her in the behind. *Justice is justice.*

And yet that only made me feel that karma had taken a sledgehammer to a fly.

Ted texted me back: *Three—two sisters and a brother.*

I texted: *Is Nellie still in the hospital?*

He answered: *No. They let her go home last night, but Manu posted round-the-clock guards at her house.*

Before I had a chance to text him back, he texted: *Whatever it is you're thinking, don't do it. The juggler is with a couple of the undercover officers, and I'll be there in a few minutes.*

I had no answer for that. What did he mean? *Whatever it is you're thinking, don't do it?* How could he possibly know what I was thinking? Not even I knew what I was thinking. Whatever it was lingered in the back of my mind . . . still foggy . . .

lost in the mist. I was trying to retrieve it, but I just couldn't. The only thing I could be sure of was that it had something to do with Katherine and Esme, two fictional characters from a movie made a decade ago. Of course, it had relevance to everything that was going on right here and now! Either that or my stress level was finally sending me over the edge.

By the time Ted got to my booth, he'd already talked with the juggler, and I'd completed the cuffs on the shirt I was embellishing. All that was left was the collar, and that wouldn't take more than a couple hours, barring too many distractions.

I put the shirt aside. "Can you come inside and talk for a few minutes?"

"Sure," he said. "In fact, I told Manu I'd likely take my lunch break while I was here."

When he stepped around the side of the table, I stood and took his hand. I pulled him to the back right side of the booth, where we were least likely to be overheard.

"What's up?" he asked.

"I was going to ask you the same thing," I said. "What did you find out about the juggler?"

"Nothing. He's just a guy. He took off from work in order to come here from Portland and be a part of the Ren Faire," said Ted. "Apparently, he's a street performer up there when he's not working at his day job."

"What's his day job?"

"Busboy."

"No kin to Lacey Palmer?" I asked.

He shook his head. "Sorry to disappoint you."

"So why did he interrupt me that day when I was talking with the Crow?" I asked.

"I questioned him about that. He thought the guy was harassing you. He was trying to help you out."

"Oh." I sighed.

"Again . . . sorry to disappoint," he said.

"I still say find Lacey Palmer's sibling and we find the person responsible for Joe Palmer's death, burning down West's building, and killing Clara . . . and maybe even killing Clara's husband."

Ted grinned. "What about Jimmy Hoffa? Think this sibling can give us a lead on that?"

"Ted, I'm being serious. Think about it," I said. "Everything that was done turned out to be for the good of Lacey Palmer or her children. Joe Palmer dies. He can't hurt his wife anymore, and she gets a sizable insurance payout. West has evidence that could incriminate Lacey in her husband's death. His building is burned down. Clara won't give her stepchildren—Lacey's children— money, and Clara winds up dead."

"But you're forgetting one detail about Clara's husband. He was Lacey Palmer's father," Ted said. "Neither she nor her siblings would kill their own father."

"Erin told me they weren't close," I said.

"Not close and homicidal are miles apart."

"Okay, but will you please look into it?" I asked. "Just find out how Clara's husband died. Please?"

"Fine. But can I go get us some lunch now? I have to get back soon."

"Yes . . . so long as you'll do my bidding later," I said.

He glanced behind him to make sure no one was looking and then pulled me to him for a kiss. "We shall discuss this *bidding* anon, saucy wench."

Chapter Twenty-nine

After lunch, I went back to working on the shirt I'd been embellishing with blackwork. My customer would be here later this afternoon, and I wanted to have the shirt ready for her. Besides, I didn't need to keep obsessing over Nellie's attack and Clara's strangulation and the murder of Joe Palmer—someone I'd never even met.

I worked steadily and finished the shirt sooner than I'd thought I would. I folded it neatly and placed it in a Seven-Year Stitch bag. I was quite productive when I wasn't trying to solve murders.

In anticipation of finishing this shirt, I'd brought another. I was just getting ready to start on it when a text came in from Ted.

Clara's husband died of a heart attack.

I texted back: *Did he have a history of heart disease?*

I felt like Michael Corleone from one of the *Godfather* movies. "Just when I think I'm out, they keep pulling me back in!" Now here I was thinking about the murders again.

Ted answered my text with *No*.

I called him. "Is it a good time for you to talk?"

"I have a minute," he said carefully. "But, Marce, lots of people with no prior history of heart disease suffer heart attacks and die every day."

"But this is all too coincidental, don't you think?" I asked.

"It is, but coincidences *do* happen," he said.

"Did you look at the autopsy report?"

"Yes. The cause of death was myocardial infarction."

I blew out a breath. "Did the coroner check for toxins?"

"Of course. Babe, I think you're looking for something that isn't there to find," he said.

"Maybe I am," I said. "But I can't help feeling all of this is connected somehow. And it all leads back to"—I shifted to a whisper—"you know who. Come to think of it, what if the dad was poisoned but *you know who* had intended to kill Clara? That makes more sense, don't you think?"

"I really do think you're stretching, Inch-High, but I'll call the coroner of record and get his opinion on all of this. Deal?"

"That's all I ask," I said. "I learned from the very best, you know. And you taught me not to leave a single stone unturned."

"Flattery will get you everywhere," he said. "On the off chance you're right about this, I'll never hear the end of it, will I?"

"Eventually." I laughed. "I hope I'm wrong. But I just . . . I've got a feeling . . . you know?"

"Yes . . . I know."

He sounded exasperated, but I also thought he seemed pleased with me at the same time.

After ending the call, I returned to my black-work, content to embroider and wait on customers the rest of the day.

It was nearly closing time—for me, anyway, because I had class to teach at the Stitch. Since I'd canceled yesterday evening's class, I'd scheduled that class and this one together. The joint class would still be smaller than the blackwork class, and most of the stitchers in both classes were experienced enough that they didn't need a great deal of help at this point.

I was tidying up my booth when Amelia arrived. Herodias was perched on her left arm.

"Hi," I said. "I see Miss Herodias is back where she belongs."

"Yes, indeed," said Amelia. "Are you getting ready to leave?"

"In a few minutes," I said. "I have a class to teach tonight at the Seven-Year Stitch, but I don't have to leave yet."

"I've decided I don't want to wait," she said. "How long does it take you to make one of those shirts with the blackwork on the collar and cuffs?"

"Only a few hours."

"Well, put me down for one. Do you think you can have it ready by next Sunday?" she asked. "I want to wear it when I go onstage with Herodias. We're doing a show before the play performance."

"No problem," I said. "I'll put a rush on it and have it for you by *this* Sunday."

"Thanks," she said. "I appreciate that. Herodias, tell Marcy good-bye."

Herodias pierced me with a stare.

"Bye, Herodias! See you tomorrow!"

After Amelia and Herodias had left the merchants' building, Sister Mary Alice popped her head around the side of the booth.

"That little falcon girl is crazy about that bird, isn't she?" she asked.

"She is," I agreed. "I guess we all get kinda silly over our pets. Do you have any?"

She shook her head. "Not currently. The older I get, the more I realize I'm doing well to take care of myself. Have a good evening."

"You, too."

I gave the booth one last look, and then I left. I'd been so excited about this Renaissance Faire. Now every day I dreaded coming to it, and every day I was thrilled to be leaving. I'd be happy when the whole affair was over.

When I got home, I fed Angus and then changed out of my Ren Faire costume into jeans and a red, long-sleeved T-shirt. I was about to call Ted to ask whether he'd be here for dinner when he pulled into the driveway.

I kissed him hello and asked if toast, eggs, and bacon were all right for dinner.

"Sounds terrific to me."

"It's quick, and I need to hurry and get back to the Stitch for tonight's class," I said.

"That's right, you have the double class tonight," he said. "You should've called and had me pick up something."

"This will be even better."

"Then at least let me do the cooking." He took off his suit jacket and tie and hung them on a hook in the foyer. He rolled his sleeves up to his forearms as we went into the kitchen.

"We'll do it together," I said. "I don't want bacon grease popping out onto your good clothes."

"I could take them off."

I laughed. "Even worse! That could be horribly painful!"

"So I talked to the coroner." He got out a nonstick frying pan and the eggs. "How many eggs do you want?"

"Two, please," I said. "Did you find out anything good?"

"He did a routine toxicology screen; but given Clara's husband's advanced age, he only tested for the usual stuff." He cracked five eggs into the pan. "Fried or scrambled?"

"Whichever you prefer. Two slices of toast?"

"Please. I'm going with scrambled because I'm not great at flipping fried eggs," he said.

I kissed his cheek. "You're great at everything." I put the bread into the toaster. "So the coroner tested for what? Stuff like arsenic and . . .?"

"And old lace."

"Ha, ha, Mr. Sarcasm. So you're saying he didn't check for anything . . . I don't know . . . like insulin or something?"

"No, but an insulin spike would've shown up," he said, stirring the eggs with a silicone spatula. "He didn't rule out the fact that Clara's husband could've been poisoned, either on purpose or accidentally. But the cause of death was a heart attack. He didn't feel the attack had been induced, given the evidence he had at hand."

"Well, thanks for looking into it." I got out another frying pan. "When you're finished with the eggs, step aside and I'll fry the bacon."

"Yes, ma'am," he said. "I like it when you're authoritative."

"But not *investigative*, right?"

"I like that, too." He winked. "I just worry that you'll get in over your head."

"I know."

Class went well, but I was really tired when it was over. I wasn't sure if my fatigue was more mental or physical, but either way I was ready to curl up in bed with Angus by my side and watch some goofy sitcom until we fell asleep.

I quickly tidied up the shop and was about to step outside when Sister Mary Alice came through the front door. She'd ditched her habit for black pants and a maroon sweater.

"Hi," I said. "You're too late for the class."

"Oh, that's okay." She looked around the shop. "Your place really is charming."

"Thank you." I frowned. "Is there a specific reason you stopped by?"

"I was in the neighborhood, saw that you were

here, and I thought I'd get a tour of the place since you were in the midst of a party the last time I dropped in." She nodded toward the hallway. "What's back there?"

"Just the storeroom, bathroom, and my office."

"Show me," she said.

"Not tonight," I said. "I'm really beat, and I need to get home. I'll be glad to show you around some other time." I was starting to wish desperately that I'd brought Angus with me.

She smiled, although it was more a thin, malicious line than anything remotely expressing kindness. "You meddle where you shouldn't, you know. Didn't you tell your boyfriend that even the fortune-tellers warned you about sticking your nose into other people's business?"

"I did," I said. "You have excellent hearing. And speaking of my boyfriend, I wonder what's keeping him? He should be here by now."

"Should he? Or are you merely hoping?"

I wanted to spin around and run out the back door, but I was afraid to turn my back on her. What if she had a gun? She'd shoot me before I could take two steps.

"No, he should be here," I said. "My Jeep was making a funny sound when I got here, and he promised to come follow me home."

"Why did you keep pushing for answers about Clara and her husband and Marcus West and things that shouldn't concern you in the least?" she asked. "I tried to frighten you into leaving well enough alone."

"You? You tried to frighten me?" I frowned. "Did you destroy my booth?"

"Yes. And yet you didn't have enough sense to heed the warning," said Mary Alice.

"Why did Nellie confess, then?" I asked.

"Because I told her to. That day that she came by her booth. I saw that the vandalism wasn't going to keep you away from the festival. So I told Nellie that if she didn't want to end up like her sister, she'd confess to trashing your booth." She scoffed. "And then she got that lawyer, and I became concerned about what she'd tell him."

"So you"—I gulped—"you hit her?"

She nodded. "Dressing up like Marcus was a diversionary tactic, although I'm pretty sure she knew it was me."

"Are you Lacey Palmer's sister?" I asked softly.

"Ding, ding, ding! Score one for the meddlesome miss!"

"Your father's death was an accident, wasn't it? Whatever happened to him . . . that was supposed to have been Clara," I said.

"Hon, I'm not confessing *all* my sins to you," she said. "I'm the nun, remember?"

"Why are you here, Mary Alice?" I asked.

"You know."

My eyes widened at the sight of the young rookie Officer Moore on the sidewalk. If only I could get his attention!

"You don't think I'm dumb enough to fall for the old *someone's behind you* ploy, do you?" asked Mary Alice.

Officer Moore walked into the shop.

The jingling bells alerted Mary Alice, and she whirled around. She went to take something from her purse, and Officer Moore drew his gun and ordered her to drop the bag.

She did as she was told.

"You don't know how happy I am to see you!" I exclaimed to him. "What are you doing here?"

"Security detail," he said. "Someone has been watching over you ever since your booth got messed up."

"Well, thank you," I said.

"Glad I could help." He cuffed Mary Alice and began reading her her Miranda rights.

My trembling legs finally gave out and I collapsed onto the sofa.

Epilogue

I didn't gloat to Ted over being right about Lacey Palmer's sibling being behind the murders—at least, I didn't gloat for long. Although she hadn't admitted it to me, Mary Alice told Manu that her father's death had indeed been an accident. She knew from Lacey that Clara was in the habit of taking two aspirin every day for her heart, so during a visit to see her father while Clara was out getting groceries, Mary Alice had emptied the bottle and put two of her pills for hypertension into the aspirin bottle. They looked enough alike that she didn't think Clara would notice the difference. Of course, that *would* have to be the day that her father got a headache and took the "aspirin" himself.

She, Lacey, and their two brothers had suffered a horrible childhood with parents who were alternately abusive and neglectful. The brothers were older, and they both got out of the home as soon as they could. Mary Alice took it upon herself to care for her sister. She'd spent her life trying to pave a smoother way for Lacey.

She'd poisoned Joe Palmer with antifreeze. Then she'd cast suspicion on Marcus West for that crime. She'd accidentally killed their father, who'd tried to reform and be decent to his children in his old age. And she'd killed Clara.

Whether Lacey Palmer was complicit in any of her sister's actions remained to be seen. That would be up to a grand jury to decide.

Officer Moore got his photo in the paper and a glowing write-up by Paul Samms hailing him as a hero.

Nellie stopped by the Seven-Year Stitch the other day to say she was glad I was okay. I nearly fainted. I don't think we'll ever be besties, but maybe we'll be able to act civilly—dare I say kindly?—toward each other from now on. . . .

Yeah . . . I'm not holding my breath.

I reached down and patted the head of my Irish wolfhound, Angus. At only two years old, he still had a lot of puppy in him, but he was mannerly and well-behaved. The patrons of my embroidery shop, the Seven-Year Stitch, loved him.

"Can you believe we've been here in Tallulah Falls for almost a year?" I asked him. I jerked my head in the direction of Jill, the mannequin-slash–Marilyn Monroe lookalike that stood by the cash register. "Jill says she can't." I looked at her as if she'd actually said something. "What's that, Jill? That what you can't believe is how I haven't dressed you in a beautiful new dress befitting the occasion?" I blew out a breath. "All in good time, Jill. All in good time."

Okay, so maybe having a mom who was a Hollywood costume designer led me to do more than my fair share of play-pretend as a child, and maybe . . . just *maybe* . . . that trait had followed me over into adulthood. But I got lonely when I was the only person in the store. And when the only "people" around to talk with were Angus and Jill, I made do. Besides, I was pretty sure that Angus not only understood every word I said but that he communicated with me, too. He had such expressive eyes. And that smile! With Jill, you just had to make it all up as you went and hope she wasn't one of those cursed paranormal items that would come to life and try to kill you one day.

So on *that* creepy thought, I gazed around the store and firmly directed my thoughts back to my upcoming anniversary open house. Since it was October 1, Jill was wearing a witch costume. She wasn't scary—she was more of a Samantha from *Bewitched* type. Before the open house, I planned to change her into either a white or pink dress—more Marilyn than Sam.

Everything else in the store would probably be all right as is, other than tidying up and borrowing a few folding chairs from the library. Since I was good friends with the librarian, Rajani "Reggie" Singh, I didn't think that would be a problem. Under normal circumstances, I had plenty of seating in my sit-and-stitch square—two navy sofas that faced each other across an oval maple coffee table, a red club chair at either end of the table, and ottomans matching the chairs. I wondered briefly whether I should shampoo the red and blue braided rug that lay beneath the table, but I decided a thorough vacuuming would be fine.

I turned to the merchandise part of the store, where I'd been marking down prices and placing specials on the shelf nearest the door. I looked with a critical eye over the embroidery projects that lined the walls. Should I add more? Take a few down? There was the redwork swan, the Celtic cross, the sampler I'd made from Louisa Ralston's original, the bunny done in crewelwork, the Bollywood-inspired elephant, the pirate map tapestry, the cross-stitched bride. . . . With a slight smile, I decided to leave them all. I didn't think it was necessary to add another one—yet—but there weren't any I wanted to take down.

I went over to the sit-and-stitch square, moved aside one of the candlewick pillows, and plopped down on the navy sofa facing the storefront window. I'd come a long way in the past year, professionally and personally. Just before I moved here, I'd adopted Angus, and we were living in an apartment in San Francisco, where I worked in an accounting office. Then Sadie MacKenzie had called and urged me to come to Tallulah Falls and open my own embroidery shop. Sadie had been my best friend and roommate in college. She and her husband, Blake, had a coffee shop called MacKenzies' Mochas right down the street from the Stitch. She hadn't had to twist my arm, and despite my ups and downs in Tallulah Falls, I was happier here than I'd ever been.

I'd barely sat down when Vera Langhorne came through the door.

"Good morning, Marcy," she said.

"Hi," I said as Angus trotted over to greet Vera.

She scratched his head and cooed to him for a minute before joining me on the sofa. Vera had also come a long way in the year I'd known her. She was no longer the mousy brunette in baggy clothes whom I'd met when I had first arrived in Tallulah Falls. Now she wore her hair blond with subtle highlights, and she always dressed with style and class. Today she wore gray slacks, black pumps, and a royal blue short-sleeved sweater twinset.

"You'll never believe what's coming in next door to you," she said.

"Please tell me that whatever it is won't be operated by a relative of Nellie Davis," I said, with a groan.

Nellie Davis owned the aromatherapy shop down the street, and she and I had never been friends. Heck, we'd hardly been civil. I'd tried over the past year to warm up our relationship, but Nellie was convinced that all the mishaps that had befallen Tallulah Falls had coincided with my arrival and that either me or my shop—or both—was cursed. She'd been so antagonistic toward me that she'd recently talked her sister, Clara, into renting the space next to the Seven-Year Stitch—a knitting shop, no less, where she'd also planned to sell embroidery supplies! Unfortunately, Clara had met with a bad end, and the shop was once again for lease. Well, not anymore, it seemed.

"It's gonna be a haunted house!" Vera clapped her hands in excitement. "Won't that be fun? They're only here for the month of October, but from what they told Paul, they plan to do it up right."

Vera was dating Paul Samms, a reporter for the *Tallulah Falls Chronicle*.

"They're going to take the first few days of the month to decorate and move in all their creepy crawly stuff, and the actual haunted house is going to open the following weekend," she continued.

I frowned. "Are they going to be open only during the weekends? If so, how will they make enough to justify renting the building?"

"According to Paul, after that opening weekend, they're going to be open every night," said Vera. "So they believe—and so do I—that they'll make their rent back many times over. They'll have special events throughout the month to draw repeat business, like themed costume contests, local celebrities—news anchors and people like that. Paul might even be one. *And* they're having concessions!"

"They're having concessions at a haunted house? That seems a little odd."

"I'm surprised Sadie hasn't mentioned it to you. She and Blake are in charge of the food."

"Neither of them has said a word to me," I said. "How will that work? I can't imagine where they'll find the time to run a concession stand on top of operating a busy coffee shop."

"Paul says they're going to do fairly simple

stuff—caramel apples, popcorn and kettle corn, cookies, some hot chocolate and a couple of other beverages, maybe—and the patrons have to eat outside the actual haunted house," said Vera. "The haunted house operators don't want to wind up with a colossal mess. And one of the MacKenzies' Mochas waitresses will work the haunted house each night. So it really shouldn't interfere with Sadie and Blake's schedules all that much."

"Cool."

"You don't look like you really feel that it's all that cool," Vera said. "What's wrong?"

"I'm just concerned about how it will affect my evening classes," I told her. "Some of my students are a little older—like Muriel—and I wouldn't want her to be frightened or put it off if she hears a ton of screaming going on next door."

Vera laughed. "Sweetie, you know Muriel can't hear herself think. And I don't know that it'll be *that* disruptive. Maybe you could put on some music or something."

Oh, sure, I thought. That would be great— blaring music to drown out the screaming teenagers next door.

"Besides, you might enjoy going to the haunted house with Ted." Vera winked.

"I'm not saying it won't be fun," I said. "I guess I'm just being selfish. How will this affect me . . . Angus . . . my students . . . my open house?"

"That's right! Your anniversary's coming up!" Vera clasped her hands together. "What are we doing for that?"

"I thought I'd have special sales and mark-downs for the two weeks leading up to the open house. And I want to have gift bags for open house attendees." I leaned forward. "But I'm struggling with what to put in the bags. Any suggestions?"

Vera looked up at the ceiling. "Well . . . you could put something different into every bag—like a cou-pon. Each coupon would be for a different amount off a particular item or the customer's entire pur-chase. And you could have *one* coupon for a free item within a particular price range."

"That's a fantastic idea," I said.

She smiled at me. "Don't sound so surprised, darling."

"I'm not surprised." I laughed. "Honest. I've simply been pondering over what I can give out that will appeal to everyone and not break the bank. The coupons are a wonderful idea."

"Sure," she said. "And you can put candies . . . teeny little sewing kits . . . maybe those braided friendship bracelets the kids like. . . ."

"You have a ton of fantastic ideas, Vera Lang-horne! You should be an event planner."

Vera laughed. "I'll take that under advisement."

Just then, Reggie hurried into the shop. Al-though she was beautifully dressed in an Indian-style coral tunic with matching slacks, Reggie's normally elegantly coifed short gray hair looked as if she'd barely taken time to brush it that morn-ing.

"Have you heard?" she asked us. "Somebody's doing a haunted house next to your shop, Marcy!"

"That's what Vera was telling me," I said, my smile fading. "I'm getting the feeling you're not in favor of haunted houses?"

She dropped onto the sofa across from Vera and me. Angus came and placed his head on the arm of the sofa closest to Reggie. She patted his head absently.

"I'm in favor of the *library's* haunted house," she said. "It's one of our biggest annual fund-raisers. And now this fancy group is going to come in and ruin it for us."

"No, they won't," Vera said. "Their haunted house isn't geared toward small children. It's more for teens and adults. Paul interviewed the event organizers, and they told him all about it. Your haunted house is supposed to be funny and sweet. Theirs is supposed to be scary as heck!"

"You truly don't think their haunted house will have an impact on our fund-raiser?" Reggie asked.

"I know it won't," Vera said. "In fact, I'll insist that Paul give the library equal time. I'll see when he can drop in at the library and do a story on *your* haunted house. I'll make sure he emphasizes the importance of the fund-raiser for the library's annual budget. How does that sound?"

"That sounds terrific, Vera. Thank you." Reggie smoothed her hair. "I'm sorry that I allowed the news of the new haunted house to upset me so badly. It isn't like me at all." She turned toward me. "How do you feel about having a funhouse right next door, Marcy?"

"I'm not terribly happy about it," I said. "I'm afraid it'll drive Angus and my students crazy."

"She was particularly concerned about the effect all the screaming might have on poor Muriel," Vera said. "I told her that Muriel probably wouldn't notice any more than she can hear."

"True, but I see Marcy's point," said Reggie. "At least they won't be disturbing your business during daylight hours."

"That's true," I said. "And it's only for a month. What real harm can it do?"

When would I ever learn to stop asking that question?

ABOUT THE AUTHOR

Amanda Lee lives in southwest Virginia with her husband and two beautiful children, a boy and a girl. She's a full-time writer/editor/mom/wife and chief cook and bottle washer, and she loves every minute of it. Okay, not the bottle washing so much, but the rest of it is great.

Connect Online

gayletrent.com
facebook.com/gayletrentandamandalee
twitter.com/gayletrent